continued . . .

Carpe Demon

Demons Are Forever

Confessions of a Demon-Hunting Soccer Mom

Julie Kenner

JOVE BOOKS, NEW YORK

THE BERKLEY PUBLISHING GROUP
Published by the Penguin Group
Penguin Group (USA) Inc.
375 Hudson Street, New York, New York 10014, USA
Penguin Group (Canada), 90 Eglinton Avenue East, Suite 700, Toronto, Ontario M4P 2Y3, Canada
(a division of Pearson Penguin Canada Inc.)
Penguin Books Ltd., 80 Strand, London WC2R 0RL, England
Penguin Group Ireland, 25 St. Stephen's Green, Dublin 2, Ireland (a division of Penguin Books Ltd.)
Penguin Group (Australia), 250 Camberwell Road, Camberwell, Victoria 3124, Australia
(a division of Pearson Australia Group Pty. Ltd.)
Penguin Books India Pvt. Ltd., 11 Community Centre, Panchsheel Park, New Delhi—110 017, India
Penguin Group (NZ), 67 Apollo Drive, Rosedale, North Shore 0632, New Zealand
(a division of Pearson New Zealand Ltd.)
Penguin Books (South Africa) (Pty.) Ltd., 24 Sturdee Avenue, Rosebank, Johannesburg 2196,
South Africa

Penguin Books Ltd., Registered Offices: 80 Strand, London WC2R 0RL, England

This is a work of fiction. Names, characters, places, and incidents either are the product of the author's imagination or are used fictitiously, and any resemblance to actual persons, living or dead, business establishments, events, or locales is entirely coincidental. The publisher does not have any control over and does not assume any responsibility for author or third-party websites or their content.

DEMONS ARE FOREVER

A Jove Book / published by arrangement with the author

PRINTING HISTORY
Berkley trade paperback edition / July 2007
Jove mass-market edition / July 2008

Copyright © 2007 by Julie Kenner.
Cover art by Mark Gerber.
Cover design by Rich Hasselberger.

ISBN: 978-0-515-14480-2

JOVE®
Jove Books are published by The Berkley Publishing Group,
a division of Penguin Group (USA) Inc.,
375 Hudson Street, New York, New York 10014.
JOVE is a registered trademark of Penguin Group (USA) Inc.
The "J" design is a trademark belonging to Penguin Group (USA) Inc.

PRINTED IN THE UNITED STATES OF AMERICA

10 9 8 7 6 5 4 3 2 1

Demons Are Forever

One

I killed my first demon at the ripe old age of fourteen. Stabbed it through the eye with an ivory-handled stiletto that had been a birthday gift from my caretaker and mentor, Father Lorenzo Corletti.

I had spent two days tracking the demon, living on the filthy backstreets of a poverty-riddled Italian village, eating nothing but the scraps I'd tucked away in a threadbare knapsack. I had one companion—a boy I adored and whom, in fact, I later married. But teenage lust was the furthest thing from my mind during those long days. Demon-hunting is serious business, and I was a serious girl.

Even now, over two decades later, I can still remember the intensity of emotions. The drive of the chase despite bone-numbing exhaustion. And the certain knowledge that this was Important Stuff. From an overall life perspective, after all, very little ranks above thwarting the minions of Hell.

As far as my duties as a Demon Hunter went, my youth was an issue only to the extent that my strength and training gave me a fighting chance to stay alive. By age fourteen, I was physically ready. As for mentally? Well, there was never any question. I knew what had to be done, and I was expected to do it. My age never factored into the equation.

With all that in my personal history, you might think that I would understand better than anyone that fourteen-year-old girls are both strong and resilient.

You might think that, but you would be wrong. Because when it came time to actually have the talk with *my* fourteen-year-old daughter, I was a tongue-tied mess.

And, just so we're on the same page, when I say *the talk*, I'm not talking about the sex one. That one I managed to muddle through. I'm talking about the other conversation: the one where I sat her down and confessed my deep, dark, secret life.

My name is Kate Connor, and I'm a Level Four Demon Hunter with *Forza Scura*, a super-secret arm of the Vatican charged with keeping the forces of darkness at bay. That particular piece of familial history, however, had been withheld from my daughter her entire life despite the fact that her father and I had hunted demons all over the globe until just a few years before Allie was born.

I'd always planned to tell her the truth someday. But somehow "someday" kept getting pushed further and further back. Allie was my baby, after all. For fourteen years, my job had been to nurture and protect her. Skewing her entire worldview with insider information about how evil truly walks among us wasn't something I'd been looking forward to. I knew I had to tell her, though; demon-hunting is part of her family history, even though I often wish it weren't.

It was one thing knowing that I someday had to come clean with my daughter. Having the conversation forced on me was something entirely different. But after a High Demon kidnapped her, I knew without a doubt that the demon-related mother-daughter lines of communication needed to be opened.

And so there we were, sitting on the steps in front of San Diablo's most well-funded museum. Despite the bright sun beating down, we were huddled together under an EMS-issued blanket, waiting to make sure the police and medical folks clustered in the parking lot didn't have any more questions for us, and also waiting for Stuart to come pick us up. My second husband doesn't have a clue about my demon-hunting past. And although this might be the day that Allie learned most of my secrets, Stuart was going to remain blissfully clueless.

"Mom?" she prodded. "So, like, you said you were going to tell me what's going on."

"Right," I said, still not ready, but figuring I never would be. I looked around, ostensibly making sure no one was paying attention to us, but half hoping that some police official was signaling for me to come over and answer questions.

No such luck. I was stuck in this conversation, whether I wanted to be or not. And since there's not really an easy way to ease into the whole demon thing, I decided to just cut to the chase. "What you saw in there," I began, a little hesitantly. "Those creatures, I mean. They're demons, Allie. Honest-to-goodness, from the bowels of hell, evil-incarnate demons."

I wasn't sure what I expected her initial reaction to be, but I balled my hands into fists, readying myself for anything.

"Oh," she said after a moment's pause. "That makes sense. And?"

And? My hands relaxed and I stumbled a bit, because I really wasn't expecting *and.* Not yet, anyway. I figured we had a good half hour of working through the whole demon thing before we got to *and*. Tossing *and* into the mix now threw off my whole equilibrium.

"'And?'" I repeated. "I'm talking demons, kiddo. Isn't that enough?"

As if to prove to me that some things never change, my teenage daughter rolled her eyes. "Mo-*ther*," she said, as if she were talking to an idiot. "I mean, *duh*. Monsters, demons, boogymen from Hell. I was there, you know. I kinda grasp the concept."

Under the circumstances, the kid had a point. After all, there are only so many things that a sulfur-scented creature with paws and claws climbing its way out of a portal to Hell can be. And none of them are good.

"But what about *you*?" she continued, before I could say anything else. "I mean, you were like Wonder Woman in there. It was pretty cool, Mom. But it was also pretty weird, too. And you said you were going to tell me."

That I had. I'd rushed to her rescue, just like any mom would. But by doing that, I'd shown her a side of me I'd carefully kept hidden. So when she'd asked me point-blank if I had a few secrets, I'd had no choice but to admit that I did.

I'd hoped to ease a bit more slowly into my revelation. Allie, though, wanted answers now.

"Let's walk," I said, standing up.

"But what about Stuart?"

I glanced down the road and didn't see any cars coming. Within the cluster of people still in the parking lot, I saw David Long talking with a uniformed officer. He noticed me and turned, a question in his eyes. I indicated Allie and made a walking motion with my fingers. He nodded, and I knew he understood. If Stuart came while we were walking the museum grounds, David would let my husband know.

The irony of the situation didn't escape me. Because I was pretty sure that David *was* my husband, or that he had been at one time. Which sounds a bit weird when you say it that way, but it was true: I was reasonably certain that the soul of my first husband had taken up residence in the body of Coronado High chemistry teacher David Long. I wasn't positive, though, and today wasn't the day to find out for sure. Someday, maybe. But not today.

Allie didn't miss our exchange. "Something's up with Mr. Long, too," she said. "If you were Wonder Woman, then he was totally Superman."

I had to laugh at the image, but the truth is that she was right. Telling my secrets meant giving some of his away, too.

"Come on," I said, taking her hand as I led us down the stairs and over to the gravel walking path that twisted through the museum's landscaped grounds. She didn't try to pull away, which left me feeling both surprised and nostalgic for the long-ago years when I could reach out and expect her little hand to close around mine immediately.

"You know I grew up in Italy," I began, looking sideways at her. "In an orphanage?"

She nodded, because that part of my past had never been a secret. She didn't know how I ended up in an orphanage, or who my parents were, or why an obviously American kid ended up wandering the streets, lost and abandoned, in Rome. But I didn't know those answers either. And for years, I'd told myself that I didn't care. To my mind, my life started the day I met Father Corletti. Everything before that was white noise.

"Well, I wasn't raised in a Church-sponsored orphanage," I said. "I was raised by the Church itself. By a small group within the Church, actually."

"Daddy, too, right?"

"Daddy, too," I said. Allie had more than once heard the story about how I had a crush on my first husband, Eric, when I was barely thirteen. But he—much more wise and mature at almost fifteen—hadn't been the least bit interested in a kid like me. Not at first, anyway.

What Allie didn't know was that Eric had finally come around during our training sessions. He'd been assigned to help me with my pathetic knife-throwing skills, and after a few months of one-on-one time, Eric was just as much in love with me as I was with him. Plus, I could hit the target dead-on every time.

"Okay," she said. "And?"

"You're getting an awful lot of mileage out of that word today," I countered.

To which my drama queen daughter responded by stopping on the path, tapping her foot, and asking me if she was going to have to repeat the word *another* time.

"Once was fine," I said, managing not to laugh. "But remind me when you grew up?"

"About an hour ago," she said, then turned and pointed back toward the museum. "In there."

Point taken.

"*Forza Scura,*" I said. "It's Latin. Translates roughly to the Dark Force. *And,*" I continued, before she could toss the word at me one more time, "it's the name of the organization within the Church that your father and I were trained to work for."

"Trained," she repeated. I nodded, then watched as she processed that new bit of information. "Okay," she finally said. "But trained to do what?"

Now it was my turn to point back toward the museum. "Take a guess."

"*Whoa,*" she said. "No shit?" And then, "Sorry, Mom."

I smiled and gave her hand a squeeze. "No shit," I said.

"*Forza* trained us to hunt demons. And that's what we did for years, and then we retired about a year before you were born."

"Oh, okay." She nodded slowly, as if she was still trying to process our discussion.

"Anything else you want to ask?" There's a lot I could tell her at this point. I could describe traveling Europe with Eric and chasing down the types of creatures she'd met in the museum. I could talk about living in the *Forza* dorms, staying up all night and sharing the kinds of scary stories that all kids tell. Only the stories we told were true. I could tell her about Wilson Endicott, my first *alimentatore*, who helped Eric and me by doing the research even as we went out armed to the teeth.

I could tell her all of that, but I wasn't going to. Not unless she asked. Because this was Big Stuff. And I knew she had to take it in at her own pace.

At least that was what I told myself. And I really think that I was mostly being honest. But even so, I have to admit that a small part of me hoped that she wouldn't be too curious. Because once you truly know about evil, it's hard to be a kid anymore. And I didn't want to be the mother who'd ripped what was left of childhood out from under her daughter.

She took a look around the grounds, taking in the wooden gazebo and the crushed stone paths. Birds-of-paradise and other tropical flowers that thrive in California lined the walkways, marking the way back to the museum in one direction and the San Diablo City Park in the other. Except for us, there was no one to be seen, and after a few moments of silence, I guess Allie decided we had time to hit a few more of the high points.

"So Gramps and Mr. Long," she began. "How come they were with you? Are they with that *Forza* thing?"

"Gramps was," I said, referring to Eddie Lohmann, an

eighty-something retired Demon Hunter who had taken up temporary residence in our guest bedroom and permanent residence in our life. Allie was under the impression that Eddie was her long-lost great-grandfather, and that wasn't an illusion I felt compelled to dissolve. "He's been retired for quite a while."

"And Mr. Long?"

Wasn't *that* a loaded question? But I fielded it the best I could, explaining that David Long was not just a mild-mannered high school teacher, but also a rogue demon hunter. In other words, a hunter not affiliated with *Forza*. He was also, I added, a friend of Allie's father. Which, for all I knew, was the God's honest truth. Because as much as I might suspect that Eric was somehow hiding in David's body, at the same time, I might simply be grasping at straws, desperate to believe that my first love hadn't really perished that foggy night in San Francisco. That somehow the man who'd been my lover and my partner for so many years could still be alive.

It was almost too much to hope for, and at the same time, if David was Eric, what would that mean for me? For my kids? For my marriage?

I didn't know, and every time I tried to think about it, I got lost in a quagmire of emotion so thick that I was certain I could drown in it if I wasn't careful.

Allie started walking again, and I shoved the melancholy aside and moved into step beside her, forcing my thoughts back to my daughter and away from Eric.

"Al?" She was hugging herself, her gaze directed back toward the museum. As I watched, she shivered, her back and shoulders spasming as if the cold finger of Death himself had traced its way up her spine. "Al!" I repeated, this time more urgently, and with my hand on her shoulder. "Are you okay?"

She turned to look at me, her eyes haunted. "You aren't still . . . I mean, that thing could have killed you, Mom."

"But it didn't," I said gently, trying desperately not to cry. My daughter had lost a father only too recently; the idea that she now feared losing her mother about broke my heart.

"You're retired now, right?" she asked with an unfamiliar urgency in her voice. "Like you said. You and Daddy retired before I was born."

I hesitated, knowing that I should tell her the truth. That I'd come out of retirement a few months ago and that lately I'd been neck-deep in demons. My head told me to say the words, but my heart wouldn't cooperate.

So I lied. Or, to be technical, I repeated one truth and neglected to mention another. "Right," I said. "Daddy and I retired."

Her whole body relaxed and I knew that I'd made the right decision. Yes, I needed to tell her the truth. But considering what she'd just been through, the truth could wait a while. It was one thing for Allie to know *the truth* about my past—and to know I survived it. It was another thing altogether to have her worry about me every time I went out at night. Since I already worried about her every second she was out of my sight, I knew what a burden that could be. And it wasn't something I intended to dump on my kid. Not so long as I could help it, anyway.

We walked a bit more in silence before she turned to me again. "So, what I don't get is how come you were there," she said. "In the museum, I mean."

"To rescue you, baby."

She rolled her eyes again. "Yeah, *that* part I got. But if you're not in this *Forza* thing anymore, then how did you know where to find me? And how'd you know that I'd been taken by demons and not just by a bunch of creepy guys?"

"We have David to thank for that," I said, which wasn't entirely true. But the truth would require admitting that I was back on active duty with *Forza*, and I'd already ruled that out.

"So what about Stuart?" she asked. "He doesn't know, right?"

Astute kid. "No," I admitted. "He doesn't."

"Why?"

Another big question, but this one I was prepared to answer. "Because when I met Stuart, my demon-hunting days were long behind me. He fell in love with a single mom with a great kid who happened to be a lousy cook and a mediocre housekeeper."

"Mediocre? Puh-lease."

"Compared to the way you keep your room," I countered with a laugh, "I'm mediocre. And the point is that my past wasn't part of the equation. So I've always thought it would be unfair to spring it on him now."

"Yeah," she said, after pondering that for a bit. "I guess that makes sense."

I'm glad she thought so, because I needed her to help keep my secret. As it was, I expected that I'd soon have to come clean with Stuart anyway. As much as I feared that the truth would drive a wedge into our marriage, I was equally afraid that keeping secrets would do the exact same thing.

"The whole thing's kinda freaky," she said as we headed back toward the parking lot. "But it's pretty cool, too," she added, flashing a wide smile. "My mom, the superhero."

A little trill of satisfaction caught me by surprise. Having your teenager say you're cool is a rare treat, and one that must be savored.

"What about Aunt Laura? Does she know?"

Laura Dupont lives directly behind us and also happens to be my best friend.

"Yes," I admitted. "Laura knows."

"Um." She chewed a bit on her lower lip as she processed that tidbit of information. "So, then, I can tell Mindy?" she finally asked, referring to *her* best friend and, conveniently enough, Laura's daughter.

"I don't know. Let me think about it. And let me talk it over with Laura. It's a big deal knowing demons are out there. That may be more than you want to lay on a friend." It had been more than I'd wanted to share with Laura, but she'd stumbled across my secret and I'd had no choice. Now, I was glad she knew. Everyone needs a confidante, and even though the rules of *Forza* require ultimate secrecy, some rules scream to be broken.

We walked a bit more in silence until Allie stopped abruptly, anxiety coloring her face. "Oh, God, Mom," she said, making me totally fear the worst. "I can still go back to Coronado after the Christmas break, right? I mean, just because there was a demon in the surf club, that doesn't mean I have to switch to a private school or anything. Does it?"

"That's it?" I said, completely unable to keep my amazement—and relief—to myself. I'd just told her that not only had demons infiltrated her school, but that her mother, her father, her (pseudo) great-grandfather, and her chemistry teacher had all been Demon Hunters by trade. And the primary question on her mind was whether or not she was going to stay at the same high school? "That's what you're worried about?"

Call me crazy, but I was expecting . . . I don't know. Fear, yes. But once that was quelled, I thought there would be more. Fireworks. Teenage angst. Huffing and stomping and storming about. Accusations about keeping secrets. Possibly even the silent treatment.

I'd been expecting that, prepared for it, even. And I'd also been expecting that at the end of all the shock, she'd beg to follow in her parents' footsteps. I figured she'd plead for a trip to Rome. Want to meet Father Corletti. At the very least insist on keeping a stiletto and a vial of holy water in her purse.

Honestly, that was one of the reasons I'd held off so long on this talk. Because that's not a life I want for my daughter. I want her safe, secure in her home, tucked into bed at night, and not worrying about monsters in the closet or walking the streets. I agreed to come out of retirement to make San Diablo a safer town, after all. Tossing my daughter into the fray wasn't part of what I was hoping to accomplish.

Apparently, though, I worried for nothing. Because I got none of that. Not then, not during the remainder of our walk back to the museum parking lot, and not during the entire four weeks of Christmas vacation. Instead, I just got . . . well, *Allie*. A slightly more introspective version of Allie, maybe, but nothing to suggest there'd been any life-changing mother-daughter talks in the last few weeks.

"She has a lot to absorb," Laura said on a balmy Thursday in January, just a few days before school was scheduled to start up again. "Give her time. Before you know it, she'll be begging to wield a stiletto and learn how to identify a demon on sight."

At her use of the word *demon,* I turned toward the doorway, the reaction automatic since I knew perfectly well that the house was empty. In a rare moment of domesticity, Stuart had taken Allie and Timmy to the mall for an afternoon of exchanging presents and scouring sales, and Eddie was at the library, more interested in the librarian than the books.

"Thanks," I said as Kabit, our cat, twined between my

legs in the vain hope of snagging some cream. "That makes me feel so much better."

Laura peered at me over the rim of one of my festive holiday mugs, currently brimming with cocoa and whipped cream. "She's a teenager, Kate. Just because she's scared for you doesn't mean that she's scared for her. After all, you're old and creaky. She's young and invincible." She skimmed her finger through her whipped cream and held her finger down to Kabit, who immediately abandoned me and trotted to her. "And she did tell you that the demon-hunting thing was cool, right?"

I nodded. That she had.

"She's processing," Laura said. "Along with boys and cheerleading and school, she's processing the fact that she was kidnapped by a demon and her mother *used to be* a Demon Hunter." She nailed me with a significant look; I'd confessed to Laura my flat-out lie about no longer hunting demons, and my best friend was not exactly supportive of my decision. "Once she's worked it all out in her head, she's going to want to know more. And if you don't tell her that you're still hunting, you're just going to dig yourself in deeper and deeper."

I scowled at my Santa Claus mug. In truth, Laura had a point. A sharp, painful point that I couldn't ignore, even though I wanted to. I'd seen fear in Allie's eyes and so I'd lied about my hunting. I'd been trying to make things better, and by doing that, I'd probably made them ten times worse. "It will be okay," I said firmly, more to convince myself than Laura.

The corner of her mouth twitched.

"What?" I demanded, feeling surly.

She smiled into her cocoa. "Just picturing the battle between you and Allie when the truth comes out."

"And that's funny?"

A tiny shrug. "The odds. Because between you and a demon, my money's on you any day of the week. But between you and Allie? Kate, you don't stand a chance."

I've lived in San Diablo for over fifteen years now. Eric and I moved here from Los Angeles while I was pregnant with Allie. And although I know the town pretty well, it's only been since last summer that I've really gotten a feel for it. For all of it—the good sections and the bad.

For the most part, San Diablo is a nice little town. That's why Eric and I came, after all. We were looking for a demon-free zone in which to live out our retirement and raise our baby. At the time, we thought San Diablo was just the ticket. After all, the historic cathedral that forms the focal point of the town is so infused with the blood and bones of saints that we were certain demons would want no part of the place.

Clearly, we were wrong.

I met my first San Diablo demon right before the school year started. Since then, I'd been spending much of my free time poking around dark alleys, strolling down the boardwalk long after most responsible humans have headed off to bed, and roaming the halls of the hospital and nursing home.

Over the holidays, I'd cut back to about one patrol per week. To be honest, after battling the demon Asmodeus and his minions for the life of my daughter, I was experiencing a little touch of demon-hunter burnout. Moreover, I didn't want Allie to wake up and not find me there. The cops had warned about post-traumatic stress resulting from the kidnapping. I figured they didn't know the half of it. She might seem fine on the outside, but I was worried about her inside, too.

On the Saturday before school started up again, though,

Allie was spending the night at Mindy's, and I was feeling the need to get back in the groove.

I tend to approach patrolling from two directions. On the one hand, I'll occasionally do sweeps through the town, simply keeping an eye out for anything suspicious. As you might expect, that method rarely produces results. I've gotten lucky once in a while, but for the most part the only purpose these broad-based patrols serve is to remind the demons that there's a hunter in town. A subtle suggestion that they should hop on Charon's ferry and sail back into Hades.

I tend to have more luck with my second method. Every morning, I scour that day's *Herald* for articles about recent near-misses—car wrecks that people miraculously survive, near-drownings, heart attack victims brought back to life after an astoundingly long bout of CPR.

Most people celebrate those kinds of miracles. Me, I'm suspicious. Because newly dead bodies are a demon waiting to happen. The human soul moves out, the demon moves in. Trust me. It happens more than you'd think.

I was pretty sure, in fact, that it had happened just the day before. That morning, I'd noticed a short article near the back of the Metro section. A local businessman named Jacob Tomlinson had recently downed a bottleful of sleeping pills, then decided to swim toward Hawaii. A fisherman had pulled his body out and managed to resuscitate the despondent Mr. Tomlinson. The newspaper called the rescue "miraculous." I had a different perspective.

Since it takes a demon a few days to get up to full strength once it's moved into a fresh body, I always follow up on these articles. That's why I decided to go to the beach Saturday night. Demons—like criminals—tend to return to the scene.

San Diablo's northernmost coastline is rocky and unfriendly, and both Saint Mary's Cathedral and the Coastal

Mists Nursing Home are perched high on cliffs overlooking the rough terrain. The jagged rocks and hostile topography, however, gradually fade to the traditional sandy beach as the coastline extends south, finally opening up to wide, inviting beaches that overflow with tourists and locals during the summer months.

That part of the coastline is dotted with parks, public beaches, and private marinas. Since the fisherman had launched his boat from the city beach near the Old Town section of San Diablo, that's where I planned to head once everyone in the house fell asleep.

I assumed I'd be out the door by one.

Naturally, I assumed wrong.

"Less than one week," Stuart said, easing up behind me and hooking his arms around my waist. I was occupied with scrubbing a saucepan, trying to coerce a greasy, gooey mess off the bottom, since I knew our dishwasher was incapable of battling that level of sludge. Considering the press of my husband against me, though, I was fast becoming less concerned about the cleanliness of our dishes.

"Just a few more days," he said, "and then I formally announce. Hard to believe this time next year I could be the San Diablo County Attorney. Or not."

I heard the tinge of insecurity in his voice and shifted my position, grabbing a dishtowel for my wet hands so I didn't soak the man. "Don't even think that way," I said, lifting my damp arms to circle his neck. "You've got more support than anyone."

"Maybe," he said, but I saw the truth of my statement in his eyes.

I batted him with the rag. "Don't give me that. You're going to win this race, and you know it. As far as everyone on the PTA is concerned, it's a done deal. Lose now, and you'll be screwing me out of prime committee picks. And I really don't want to be in charge of the clean-up crew for the Spring Fling."

That worked, and he laughed. "Fair enough. For you, I'll win the race." He leaned in and kissed the tip of my nose. "And I'll do it even though you'd probably rather I lost."

I immediately blurted out a denial. But at the same time, I stiffened a little. Because even though I knew how much winning the county attorney seat would mean to Stuart, at the same time I was selfish enough to want my husband back. Lately, his nights and weekends had been spent campaigning rather than cuddling. And I rather missed the latter.

If I had him back, though, he might be more clued in to the goings-on around the house. Little things like, oh, that his wife hunts demons in her spare time.

All in all, it would probably be for the best if Stuart won the race. If nothing else, his late nights at the office made it easier to keep my secrets.

I turned back to the dishes, just in case he could read my expression. I pretty quickly realized, though, that deep, introspective conversations weren't on the agenda tonight. "Timmy's sound asleep," he said, his lips brushing the back of my ear, the sweet sensation sending a little trill down my spine. "And Allie's over at Mindy's."

"That's very interesting information," I said, unable to keep the smile out of my voice.

"We have an unopened bottle of Merlot."

"Also good to know."

"And if you scoot over, I'll help you with the dishes."

"Now *that's* the way to a woman's heart," I said, shifting to the left to make room for him.

True to his word, he pitched in and the kitchen was quickly

transformed from disaster area to presentable. It wasn't *Better Homes and Gardens*, but it probably never would be.

"It's getting late," I said, hoping he'd take the hint. It was already after ten; if I wanted to go patrolling tonight, I needed him sound asleep soon.

Stuart, however, wasn't cooperating. "It's Saturday," he said. "And it's a brief calm before the storm. We should kick back and enjoy it. The wine. Maybe some cheese. A movie." He pulled me close and traced his forefinger over my bottom lip. "Who knows where it could lead?" he added softly, his tone alone telegraphing at least one rather delightful destination.

I leaned in close, then tilted my head back and batted my eyes at him. "Why, Mr. Connor," I said, in my most breathy voice. "Are you seducing me?"

"I think that might be on the agenda." He kissed me then, and when he pulled back, his smile held the promise of more. "You get the wine," he said. "I'll find a movie."

We ended up snuggled together on the couch watching Sean Connery and Jill St. John do the James Bond thing. Stuart is an Ian Fleming fan, and I'll watch anything with Sean Connery, so while this wasn't exactly seduction material, it wasn't torture either. Even so, the action sequences definitely shifted me from seduction mode into hunter mode. And by the time the credits rolled, I was wired again and ready to go.

So was my husband, actually, but not in the way I had in mind. Still, I have to admit that he won me over pretty quickly. How could he not? This was the man I loved, after all. And this was what I'd been missing.

He pulled me close, his lips brushing mine, and his fingers touching me in a way that was both delicate and possessive. I moaned a little, thinking how lucky I was to have found love twice in my life.

I know it's natural for a widow to think of her first husband. So even though memories of Eric started to sneak in around the edges of my lust, I didn't feel guilty. Stuart knew that I'd loved Eric and that he'd always have a place in my heart.

What Stuart *didn't* know was that Eric might still be alive. Might, in fact, be living in San Diablo.

I pushed the thought away, not ready to deal with that possibility, and tugged Stuart closer. And as I lost myself in my husband's kisses, I tried hard not to think about how complicated my life could become.

A full moon hung in the sky as I made my way down the wooden boardwalk. I had a flashlight tucked in my back pocket but I didn't need it. The night was clear, and the light from the moon was plenty to show me the way.

I'd been patrolling now for about fifteen minutes. I'd parked along Main Street in front of one of San Diablo's numerous artsy stores. I'd walked the short distance to the Pacific Coast Highway, passing pizza places and local coffee shops closed up tight for the night. There's a traffic light at PCH and Main Street, but this late, it was flashing yellow. I'd crossed the highway without seeing any sign that anyone else was awake on this chilly January night, human or demon.

I fervently hoped I hadn't made a mistake in coming. The trip would be worth it if I actually nailed a demon. If not, I was risking family peace should Stuart wake up.

The air hung cold and thick, but I fought the urge to hug myself for warmth. I needed my hands free, ready to defend myself should Tomlinson jump me.

As for that, I kept my senses on alert, my eyes trained to spot anything out of the ordinary, and my ears cued to hear more than just the pounding of the surf.

Even if you don't run across a demon, patrolling is hard work. You have to be at the ready, adrenaline pounding just below the surface. If not—if you relax even a little—that's the moment they'll get you. And that's how Hunters end up dead.

Since dead really wasn't a convenient state of being for me, I was on hyper alert. Even so, I almost didn't hear the faint *pad-thump, pad-thump* of footsteps behind me. The sound was so negligible, I could almost believe I'd imagined it. Or that I'd heard nothing more than a cat crossing the boardwalk in search of a washed-up fish for dinner.

Pad-thump. Pad-thump.

My heart rate increased, multiplying with the tempo of the footsteps. I tried to gauge the distance behind me but couldn't. Whoever was back there, was a master of stealth.

I didn't slow my pace, didn't give any sign that I knew I was being followed. But as I walked, I flicked my left wrist, causing the stiletto concealed inside my jacket sleeve to slide down to a ready position.

Silence.

And not the good kind. I whipped around, my right hand grabbing the handle of the stiletto as I lunged for my stalker. He loomed behind me, at least a head taller, his face hidden by the hood of a dark gray sweat jacket. Without hesitating, I attacked, then faltered when I saw his eyes. He jumped all over my hesitation, parrying expertly and thrusting his cane out to trip me up and hook me sideways off the boardwalk.

"David!" I howled, losing my balance and falling backward into the sand.

He didn't retreat at all. Instead he straddled me, his strong hands pinning me at the wrists, his face only inches from mine.

My breath came faster and faster, but whether from fear, exertion, or something else, I wasn't sure. "Dammit, David!"

"You're out of practice," he said, his face still close to mine. "And that means you're dangerous."

"Only to myself," I muttered. "Now get off me."

He flashed a lopsided grin. "You're lucky it was only me."

"I'm on my ass *because* it was you. You're the one who's lucky. If I hadn't seen your face, you could have a stiletto in your eye right about now."

"Not a chance," he said. "You're too good to make a mistake like that."

I raised an eyebrow. "I thought you just said I was out of practice."

He laughed, then shifted his hips, trying to reach his cane, the pressure more than a little distracting. A second later, he was standing. I was still on the ground, trying to mend my tattered dignity.

He reached a hand down to help me up, and I took it grudgingly. "What the hell are you doing here, anyway?"

"Looking for you," he said.

"Here?"

"I saw the article about Tomlinson. I figured you'd come check it out."

"Monday's the first day back at school," I said, looking up at him as I wiped sand off my jeans. "Your odds would have been better looking for me in the carpool lane."

"Not exactly conducive to what I wanted to say."

"Oh? What's that?"

He leaned in close, his voice low. "That you've been avoiding me."

"I don't know what you're talking about," I said, but I think the fact that I didn't meet his eyes and started walking in the opposite direction suggested otherwise.

He caught up to me in no time, despite the limp and the cane. "Kate, stop."

I turned to him. "David, I'm tired. You jumped out of the dark and tackled me. Forgive me for not being in a chatty mood, okay?"

"Fair enough," he said. "But you still haven't answered me."

"I'm pretty sure I did," I countered. "But if it will make you happy, I'll be more specific. I'm not avoiding you. Not intentionally, anyway."

"You're unintentionally avoiding me?"

"Dammit, David." He was making me laugh, and that wasn't good. "All I'm saying is that I patrolled alone before I met you, and now I'm patrolling alone again. It's not nefarious. It's just logistically easier."

"You only patrolled alone because there wasn't another Hunter in town. You should have someone watching your back." He took a step closer to me. I moved backward, until I was barely balancing on the wooden boardwalk a few inches above the sand. Another step, and I'd fall on my rear again. *Not* the way to appear in control of the conversation.

I opened my mouth to say something, realized I didn't know what to say, and pushed past him. I was here to patrol, and I told myself that's what I was going to do. Not stand around arguing.

David and I had hunted together while we were trying to stop Asmodeus. But before that, I'd never hunted with anyone other than Eric. He'd been my partner in so many ways— my lover, my friend, my husband. He'd known me better than any person ever had or, I'd believed, ever would.

There's an intimacy to hunting, a bonding and a trust that has to be there if you're going to step out together against the bad things in the world. I'd opened myself to that trust with David, and through that crack had swarmed a desperate melancholy. I'd done *this* with Eric, I'd thought. And this, and this.

The memories and sadness had blindsided me, as fresh as that cold night when I'd first heard of Eric's death.

Those raw emotions had been painful enough. But when I'd started to suspect that David was more than Eric's friend—that he was Eric himself—well, my emotions had whirled into a tailspin.

I'd loved my life with Eric, but I also loved the life I now had. My fabulous daughter. My precious little boy. My wonderful husband who adores me despite the fact that I can't cook worth a damn and have yet to figure out a method for ensuring that we all have clean laundry on any given day.

The thought of hurting Stuart paralyzed me, and yet I couldn't help but fear that I was on that very path—that merely by contemplating this David/Eric mystery, I was hurting him. If not in fact, then in my heart.

For weeks now, I'd been balancing on a knife edge, desperately hoping that Eric had returned even while fearing that very same thing. Because if Eric really had escaped his body on that dark day in San Francisco, then he'd been a disembodied soul until the day several months ago when David Long wrecked his car. And that meant that when the "real" David died and his soul had departed, Eric had squeezed into his body using the exact same method that the demons use.

Black magic, Eddie called it. And he was certain that no good soul could play with dark forces and come out unscathed.

That wasn't something I wanted to think about, much less believe, but I had to concede that the argument had merit. Still, David had helped me save Allie. He'd never done a thing to harm me. So maybe Eddie was wrong? Or maybe David wasn't Eric at all, but simply the man he purported to be—a chemistry teacher who'd survived a nasty car wreck. A rogue Demon Hunter who used to be Eric's friend, all those years ago.

Or maybe the blackness in him was growing, and one day—when I'd need him most—David would turn on me.

I shivered slightly, pushing away the thought. I had three things going for me in this life—my family, my strength, and my faith. Whether he was Eric or not, I believed that the man I knew as David was good. That he would never willingly harm me. I believed that with every breath in my body. And I held fast to that belief. Because without that faith—without that hope—I knew that I would be truly lost.

But while I might trust David and long for Eric, that didn't mean I was ready to learn the truth. I wasn't. If David truly was Eric, I wasn't ready for the ramifications—to Eric's soul or to my family. And if he was simply David? Well, I wasn't ready to give up the hope that somewhere—somehow—my Eric was still alive.

So I'd done the only thing I could do—I'd avoided the problem by avoiding David.

I should have known better. When you grow up in *Forza Scura*, you grow up knowing that the things you try hardest to avoid are the things that jump out at you in the dark.

His footsteps quickened behind me, the padding sound of his shoes underscored by the tap of his cane. "Kate," he called. "Katie, wait."

I kept walking.

"Katie! Damm——" The curse died on his lips, but I heard him speed his pace. I considered taking off in a jog, decided that would be taking the coward's way out, and turned to face him.

"I don't need help," I said. "I'm fine patrolling on my own."

"Why do it on your own when I can help you?"

"You're not a Demon Hunter."

"The hell I'm not," he answered.

I stared him down. "You told me yourself you're not with *Forza*. You're rogue. And that's a complication I just don't need."

"That's a bullshit excuse and you know it," he said, taking a step closer. "It's not that I'm rogue that's complicating matters."

"No?" I countered, my voice breathier than I wanted. "Then what is?"

I watched his eyes, saw him hesitate, and decided to go for the jugular. "How far are you willing to go, *David*?" I pressed, stressing his name. "How complicated do you want things to be?"

I watched his face, frustration coupled with anger. It was the pity, however, that surprised me. "Katie, I'm sorry. I swear, I never meant to hurt you like this."

I reeled, his unexpected words like blows. "David," I stammered. "You don't have to—"

"I should have told you the truth at the museum. I should have just gotten it over then."

I couldn't move. My feet weren't accepting signals from my brain. Either that, or my body had been transformed into ice. I didn't know. All I knew was that no matter how loudly I was screaming inside my head to run, my feet were staying firmly planted on the boardwalk.

"I know what you think, Kate, but it's not true." He cupped my chin in his hand and looked me straight in the eyes, his never blinking. "I'm not him, Kate. I'm sorry, but I'm not the man you loved."

His words seemed to come at me from under water, and as I moved, I was certain I was slogging through Jell-O. I'd moved from the real world to some surreal place, where nothing quite made sense. Not even the words David spoke to me.

"What?" I finally managed. "But . . . but you—"

"I knew him," David said. "That's all. I knew the man, and pretty well, too. I'm sorry, Kate. Truly sorry."

I wanted to say something, but words wouldn't come. The tears, though, had no such qualms. They trickled quietly down my face in silent mourning to a fantasy that was finally dying.

"I realized that day at the museum that you'd gotten the idea fixed in your head. I should have told you then but I couldn't. I thought maybe you needed to believe that Eric had come back to help you save Allie. After a week or so, I figured you'd realize the truth. But when you started avoiding me, I knew I had to tell you the truth once and for all."

"Oh," I said, since that was about all I could manage. "Right. I understand."

I took a tentative step, decided that I was relatively stable again, and started to walk slowly down the boardwalk. I needed to move. Needed to feel the solid earth under my feet and find my grounding again.

He fell in step beside me. "Are you okay?"

I drew in a breath and considered the question. "No," I said. "But I will be." His words had killed something inside me. And yet maybe he'd freed me, too. Because as much as I hated to admit it, the specter of Eric had been haunting my marriage.

"You're sure?" he said.

"Yes." And then, because it was true, I added a simple, "Thank you."

He didn't answer me, and I took his silence as both an acknowledgment and closure. And as he quickened his pace and pulled ahead of me, I used the pad of my thumb to wipe away the last of my tears.

We patrolled the next half hour or so in silence, each alone in our thoughts, our attention focused not on each other, but on our surroundings, and the ultimate question of just what was out there with us.

By the time we'd circled back, I was ready to pack it in. "No demons," I said, as much to break the silence as because I believed it. "Maybe they've moved on."

I was only mouthing my discouragement, but he seemed to seriously consider the possibility. "Maybe they did. You were here for, what, fourteen years before you caught whiff of a demon?"

"Literally," I said, remembering the first demon I'd sniffed out in the pet food aisle of Wal-Mart.

"Then two in quick succession."

"And both times the demons wanted something that was located in San Diablo," I added.

"Wanted it badly enough to put up with the fact that the cathedral makes this town less than appealing to the general demon population."

I lifted a shoulder. "That was our theory, anyway. Mine and Eric's."

"I say it was a good one," David said. We'd reached the children's playscape, and he leaned casually against the monkey bars. "So, Sheriff, now that you've run all the bad guys off, what will you do with your time?"

I laughed and started counting out on my fingers. "Dishes, laundry, dust-bunny wrangling. Candy Land with the kiddo. Mediating boyfriend disputes, overseeing makeup purchases, and surviving the dangerous rite of passage known as the Teenager with a Learner's Permit."

His mouth curved into a smile. "And here I thought you'd be bored."

"Never," I said. I started to take a step away. I needed to get back to my car and head home. Patrolling, I can justify. Casual chitchat? Not so much.

I never made it that far. I'd barely reached the boardwalk when something dark and fast tackled David, sending him sprawling into the sand. "Are you the one?" it demanded, then sniffed deep, like a bloodhound searching for a scent, even as I raced toward them. "If you are he," it hissed, "release Andramelech. Release him from his shackles and know that when you do, your end will come."

The words still hung on his lips by the time I reached the demon. He had David by the collar of his shirt, but one swift kick to the gut knocked him off.

The demon teetered, and I pounced. Then, without hesitation, I thrust my stiletto through his cold, gray eye.

The body went limp as the demon departed, the familiar shimmer in the air the only sign of its passage.

"Mr. Tomlinson, I presume?" David asked, climbing to his feet.

"I think so," I said. "But why did he attack you? He didn't have a weapon, and I was standing right there. It was a no-win situation."

"He was newly made," David said. "Maybe he was just stupid? Had me confused with someone else?"

"If you are he," I repeated. "But who?"

David looked at me, his eyes serious. "I don't know. But my guess is he's looking for whoever captured Andramelech."

"Looking for the captor so they can kill him," I said, shuddering. "But who's Andramelech?"

"No idea," he said, looking completely baffled. "But I do know one thing for certain."

"There are still demons in San Diablo?"

"Exactly," he said. "And they're up to something."

Two

"Oh, Kate," Laura said, after I told her about David's revelation. "Are you okay?"

I shook off her sympathy and took another sip of my morning coffee. "I'm fine. Really." I even think I was telling the truth. After all, I'd had a few hours to get used to the idea.

I'd called Laura first thing Sunday morning, and she'd come right over. Now we were drinking coffee and eating the coffee cake Laura had made that morning in a fit of unbridled domesticity. Eddie kept wandering into the kitchen to cut himself "just a tad more," but Allie and Stuart were still upstairs getting dressed for Mass. A good thing, since I didn't want them overhearing this particular conversation.

Timmy was in the living room, pushing the Thomas the Tank Engine train set he got for Christmas around the room while *Frosty the Snowman* played in the background. He'd already watched the show at least twelve dozen times over the last few weeks, but so far, he showed no sign of losing interest. I could only hope that he could maintain this level of interest throughout his academic career. If so, I had a Harvard valedictorian on my hands.

"Honestly," I said in response to Laura's querying look. "I'm truly okay. It's for the best," I added, forcing a cheery note into my tone. "I can get back to my regularly scheduled life."

The truth is, I believed what I was saying. But knowing what was best in my head didn't necessarily mean that the truth was easy on my heart.

"It might not be true," Laura said.

I looked at her curiously. "You think he's lying to me?"

She shrugged. "There are so many little things, you know? All that stuff you've told me about why you thought he was Eric."

She was right. The way he called me "Katie," and the way he moved when he fought. So many little hints that had finally built up until I suspected my first husband had come back to me.

Even so, though, I had never been sure. Not until last night, anyway. "He wouldn't have lied to me," I said. "It's one thing to keep quiet. To say nothing and leave me unsure and guessing. But to flat out lie?" I swallowed, realizing I'd done that very thing to Allie. Then I shook my head, banishing the thought. "No. I know Eric, and there's no way he would do that to me."

Laura, I could see, disagreed. But she was kind enough to let the subject go, shifting the conversation instead to the demon-related part of the story. "So who is this Andramelech that the demon wants freed?" she asked, as Eddie came in to get yet another serving.

I shook my head. "I wish I knew."

From his perspective above the coffee cake, Eddie harrumphed. I looked sideways at him. "Do you know who Andramelech is?"

He replied with a sad little shake of his head. "I don't know what the hell *Forza* was thinking when your generation of Hunters came along," he muttered. "Not know who Andramelech is. That's damn pathetic, Kate."

I started to retort that I'd been primarily concerned with killing the beasts, not making sure I had their proper names for engraved invitations to formal functions, but bit my tongue. Better to just get the information from Eddie and forgo the *Forza* bashing. Considering Eddie had been betrayed—and then spent several decades as a rogue demon hunter since he no longer trusted his *Forza* contacts—I understood where he was coming from. But that didn't mean I wanted to hear about it again today.

"Just tell me what you know," I said.

"He's a bad one," Eddie said.

"I figured as much. I haven't met a good one yet."

His bushy eyebrows rose and he chuckled. "You got a point. *My* point is that he's badder than most. One of the high chancellors of Hell. A Throne Demon."

I grimaced, because that *was* bad. Apparently your average run-of-the-mill demon had no use for San Diablo. All the demons I'd met so far were either High Demons, or had come to San Diablo to do a High Demon's bidding.

"Hold on a second," Laura said. "What's a Throne Demon?"

"There's a demon hierarchy," I explained. "Just like with the angels."

"Like archangels," she said.

"Right. So the High Demons are the baddest of the bad,

and the chancellors of Hell are pretty much Satan's right-hand guys."

"In other words, incredibly, horribly bad," Laura said. "That's all I needed to know."

"So what else do *you* know?" I asked Eddie as I got up to refill my coffee.

"Not much that would be of use to you," he said. "Apparently some of the ancient Assyrians sacrificed children to him. But what that has to do with the fellow who jumped David . . . well, damned if I know."

I shivered, then took a step back so that I could see Timmy. I couldn't find him at first, and a pulse of terror pounded through my body. I opened my mouth to call for him when a little wooden train came barreling down the entrance hall into the living room, stopping with a *thud* when it hit the leg of our coffee table, leaving a scrape mark I could see from fifteen feet away.

The train's path had originated near the front door, and I could only assume my little boy was down there, too.

"Timmy?"

Nothing.

"Timmy!"

Soft footsteps, and then the boy himself, his little face peering around the corner, his eyes wide and innocent. "What, Mommy?"

"Are you supposed to be knocking your trains into the furniture, young man?"

His eyes managed to widen even more, and his mouth formed into a little pout. One tiny shake of his head. "I didn't do it, Mommy."

"Timmy . . ."

"I didn't!" he protested, little hands clenched in fists.

I shot him a frown, then crossed the short distance to the

coffee table and picked up the runaway train. "Then how did this end up all the way over here?"

His face scrunched up with concentration. "Rolled there, Mommy," he finally said, which, technically, was the absolute truth. "I was over there." He pointed very firmly toward the front door.

I sighed and considered pulling him into my lap and having the short-form discussion on responsibility, along with a toddler-level lecture on physics. More particularly, cause and effect.

At the moment, though, I was more concerned with the local demon population than whether my son battered the furniture with his newly acquired train set. A dishrag around the table legs would save the furniture. Saving the world from the forces of darkness required a bit more finesse.

"Just be more careful," I said.

"Okay, Mommy," he said, giving me two thumbs-up.

I shook my head, amused, and headed back to Eddie, but not before calling up to Stuart and Allie. It was already almost ten, and we needed to get out the door soon if we were going to make the eleven o'clock service.

"Are you going to the library after Mass?" I asked Eddie. He'd met the librarian of our local branch library right before the holidays, and although he'd never come right out and said so, I could tell he was smitten. She worked the Sunday afternoon shift, so Eddie had a tendency to drift over there after church on a weekly basis.

"I might do that," he said, a false casualness in his voice.

"Well, *if* you do," I said, "maybe you could do a little research, too? Get on the Internet. Check encyclopedias?"

"That's what you got Ben for," he said, referring to Father Ben, my still relatively green *alimentatore*. "This one, too," he added, hooking his thumb toward Laura. "Me, I'm done with hunting. We already had this talk." He squinted at me. "Or is your memory going?"

"My memory is just fine," I said. "And I talked to Ben about it last night when David and I went to the cathedral to hide the body." A sad fact of my new demon hunting life is that *Forza* no longer sends out disposal teams. And since demons don't just conveniently disappear into a puff of smoke with every kill, I'm left to clean up the mess. Not one of the better perks of the job, I assure you, but Father Ben had come up with the brilliant solution of hiding the bodies in the cathedral's catacombs. It wasn't perfect, but it was better than digging holes in my vegetable garden. Especially since I was too domestically challenged to have a vegetable garden.

"So Ben's on the case then," Eddie said. He turned to Laura. "You got your fingers dancing over the keyboard there, girlie?"

"If you mean am I up for doing Internet research," she answered, "the answer is yes."

He made a satisfied snort. "There you go," he said to me. "You're all set."

"I was kind of hoping for a little more input. Father Ben and Laura are both new at this. You're a veteran."

"I was never much good at research," he said. "And I'm out of this business. If I told you once, I told you a thousand times."

"Oh, really? I seem to remember you rushing into the middle of a demonic ceremony just a few weeks ago." I crossed my arms over my chest and stared him down. "Or had *you* forgotten?"

"That wasn't about hunting," he said. "That was about Allie."

"So is this," I argued. "If demons are infesting San Diablo—"

He cut me off with a wave of his hand and a snort. "Bah. This isn't for Allie. It's for David." He looked at me over the rims of his reading glasses. "Or maybe it's for your sweet patootie."

"My sweet pa— *what?*"

"You heard me. You're getting all your girl parts in a tizzy, wondering *is he* or *isn't he?* Like some damned farmer's daughter picking daisies in a field. Humph. Woulda thought you'd been trained better, but with *Forza* in such a mess these days, I guess I shouldn't be surprised."

"David *isn't* Eric," I said, giving both him and Laura a hard look. "I already told you."

Eddie gave a sad little shake of his head. "Damn women are just too damn gullible," he muttered under his breath.

I cursed under mine, reining in my temper, which was about to explode. "You know what?" I finally said. "It doesn't even matter. All that matters right now is that we've got demons again. It's like the whole town's been infested and we haven't managed to find the nest to wipe them out. Whether or not David is Eric is completely moot."

He aimed a hard stare at me. "I hope so, girlie. Because I may not know everything, but I know one thing for sure."

"All right," I said, still battling my temper back down after the gullible comment. "What?"

"Bad news," Eddie said. "That boy is bad, bad news."

I didn't get to grill Eddie about the bad news statement, because Stuart chose that particular moment to rush down the stairs into the living room. Not that I needed to interrogate Eddie; he'd been certain that David was Eric from early on, and even David's denial wasn't going to change his mind.

As Stuart came into the kitchen, a tie in each hand, Laura

took the opportunity to head home. "Mindy left at the crack of dawn to go paint set pieces for the school musical," she said. "And since I have the house to myself for a few more hours, I might as well get started on that . . . um . . . little project."

Her coyness was lost on Stuart, however, who was too absorbed in his fashion dilemma to pay attention to our good-byes. "Which one?" he said, laying them out on the table in front of me, and forcing my mind to shift from contemplating the mysteries of the universe to the more mundane mystery of men's fashion.

I took the blue one with little gray stripes out of his hand and held it under his chin. Then I switched it out for a gray one with little blue stripes. "This one," I said, handing him the gray one. "Definitely this one."

"Thanks, babe," he said, then proceeded to slip the blue one around his neck. He caught my exasperated expression and grinned. "What can I say? After so many years of marriage, I've learned."

"Just for that," I said, "you get to handle all potty-training emergencies this week."

"You're brutal, sweetheart."

I blew him a kiss as I headed out of the kitchen and aimed myself for the stairs. If he only knew . . .

My retreat was for more than just getting the last word. I was also intending to light a fire under my daughter. We needed to be out the door in fifteen minutes, or else we'd be skulking into the back of the bishop's hall ten minutes into Mass. That's awkward enough at any church. When the priest is your *alimentatore*, those little faux pas become all the more embarrassing.

Allie's door is at the top of the stairs, and—as usual since she's hit the wondrous teenage years—it was shut. I tapped lightly, got no answer, then tapped a bit harder.

Still nothing.

I briefly debated whether or not I should go in. She's almost fifteen (although how that happened, I'll never know) and privacy is a Big Issue. Our rule is that after one knock, I can go in. But even with that tacit permission, I still like to wait for her to give me the okay.

Today, though, she was giving me nothing.

I frowned. The odds were good that she hadn't even heard my knock. She'd downloaded a whole slew of new songs to her iPod over the holiday, so she was probably plugged in and completely oblivious to the fact that in about ten minutes, we were going to be officially running late.

I turned the doorknob and gave the door a push. One inch, then, "Allie? Are you about ready?"

Another inch, another question, another deafening silence.

Screw it. I pushed the door all the way open, then froze right there on the threshold. The fact that she was still in her pajamas was enough to get my temper flaring. But what stopped my heart was the rest of the picture—my pajama-clad teenager poised in front of her full-length mirror, her feet in a near-perfect fighting stance, her iPod blasting who knows what into her head, and Stuart's Civil War–replica sword tight in her hands.

Before I could say anything, she lunged at her reflection, the movement changing her perspective and apparently giving her a full view of me. She yelped, then twirled around, managing to shield the sword behind her back as she did so.

"I already saw it, Al," I said, as soon as she'd yanked the earphones out of her ears. "You want to tell me why you have it?"

"I . . . well . . . you know . . ."

I was desperately afraid I *did* know. "Do you want to talk about it?"

She shook her head. "It's no big. Honest."

On the contrary, I thought it was totally big. The question, though, was how to handle it. For that, I didn't have a ready answer.

"Does Stuart know you have his sword?" I asked, mostly because it was the first thing I thought of. "Isn't that the one he keeps hanging in his office?"

"Um, maybe?"

"Well, put it back before he notices it's gone. And get dressed," I added, fixing her with my stern mother look. "We need to get going."

"Okay. Sure thing. No problem." She started scrambling for her closet, clearly happy to have escaped a full grilling.

As for me, I slipped outside the room and pulled her door closed again. I leaned against the door frame and closed my eyes, certain I'd completely mishandled the situation but too raw emotionally to go back in her room and start over.

Once upon a time, I'd thought demon-hunting was hard. But that was before I'd become a mom.

Trust me. In comparison to parenting, stalking and killing demons is a piece of cake.

"Higher, Mommy! Higher!" Timmy squealed, his little legs dangling over the pea gravel as he flew through the air in the bucket-style swing.

"Hey, squirt," Allie said, swinging high next to him. "Just kick your legs like me. Then you won't even need Mom."

"Thanks a lot," I said, feeling a little pang in my heart. Because it was true. Allie was almost to an age where she didn't need me. And even though Timmy wasn't yet three, one of these days, he'd get there, too. That's the bittersweet part of being a mom. You slather on all that love and attention so that your kids will grow up strong, confident, and self-sufficient. And if you've done your job right, you've raised grown-ups who can go off and manage just fine without you.

We were in the cathedral's play yard, having retrieved Timmy from the infant-to-three nursery (a lifesaver, in my opinion, and an unfortunate rarity among Catholic churches). Now we were surrounded by children of all ages. They were swinging, climbing on monkey bars, teetering on see-saws, and basically burning off all that pent-up energy that comes from sitting (mostly) still through more than an hour of Mass.

We'd come in two cars, and Stuart had already headed on to the office. Technically, today was the last day of his vacation, but I should have known the lure of the job would be too strong to resist. Now, I was waiting for Father Ben to finish the post-Mass meet-and-greet so that we could spend a few minutes discussing this Andramelech thing.

"He's in a Pull-Ups," I told Allie. "But if you need to change him, there are some more in the van. And some wipes and a change of clothes, too."

"Mo-*om*." She dragged her heels, skidding to a stop, then twisting around in the swing to look at me. "How come I have to watch him?"

"I already told you. I need to chat with Father Ben for a few minutes."

From the depth of her sigh, you would have thought I'd told her she had to repeat junior high.

"It's just for a few minutes, Allie. Have you got anything better to do?"

One shoulder lifted, and she scuffed her toe in the gravel. "Dunno. Why can't I go with you?"

My heart did that pitter-patter number as I wondered just how much of my secret life Allie suspected. After all, wasn't it pretty much genetically encoded for teenagers to completely discount everything their parents tell them? If she thought I was still in the demon-hunting biz, then it would make sense that I'd have a priest as a contact.

And even though I was experiencing a certain amount of guilt over the lie I'd told her, I still didn't come clean with my daughter. I wasn't ready, and I suppose I was still clinging to the hope that she was simply being your average whiny teenager, desperately seeking an excuse to avoid babysitting her toddler brother.

"I'm only talking to him about the archives," I said. "Nothing interesting at all. And Timmy would be bored out of his mind," I added, giving him another push on the swing in response to his ear-splitting scream for attention.

"Just archives?"

"That's it," I said. "And I seriously doubt you want to give up cheerleader practice to help me sort through and inventory bug-infested boxes of records. But if you do . . ."

I let the offer hang out there, reasonably sure she would run far and fast. If I was wrong, of course, I'd have to amend my agenda for today's discussion with Ben. The upside, though, would be that I'd have a helper for my deathly dull committee duty.

I'd signed on before the summer, and even though the project was supposed to have been finished by autumn, it was still dragging on—the universal nature of volunteer work. You would have thought that after years in the PTA I would have expected it.

She held on to the chains that supported the swing, then bent backwards, letting out a low, suffering groan as she did. Her long hair brushed the gravel, and I saw her chest rise and fall as she sighed. Honestly, I couldn't tell if she was frustrated or practicing to join a contortionist group. I also couldn't tell what she was thinking. As hard as it was for me to admit, I could no longer look at her face and see what was going on in her head. As life skills go, I suppose she'd learned from the best. I am, after all, a master at lying to my family.

"Allie?"

She lifted herself back up into a sitting position, then hopped off the swing. "Okay. Fine. I'll stay here with Timmy." She held out her hands. "Keys?"

I hesitated, and she noticed.

"In case I need to change Timmy," she said. "I mean, come on. You think I'm going to take the van and go joyriding or something?"

I didn't, but I also had never expected her to sneak out of the house after I'd told her in no uncertain terms that she couldn't go out. But she had. And the consequences had been bad, bad, bad.

She rolled her eyes, apparently able to read my thoughts. "I got it, Mom. Lesson learned."

"Good kid. And since I know it's a huge pain to watch your brother, why don't we swing by the mall before we go home?"

"Are you buying?" she asked, perking up. "Cuz I've totally blown my allowance."

"I was thinking we'd stay in the parking lot," I admitted. "You can apply for your learner's permit soon. If you want to practice a little, I'll sit quietly in the passenger seat and try not to freak out."

"Yeah?" she asked, eyes bright.

"Why not?"

"Thanks, Mom," she said, rewarding me with a rare hug. "And it's not that much of a pain to watch him," she admitted, scooting over to swing-pushing position. "As brother's go, he's pretty okay."

As kids go, both of mine are more than okay, and I felt a nice little tug of mommy pride as I left them in the play yard and headed to find Father Ben. Thankfully, my timing was perfect, and we retreated into his office in the rectory.

"Anything?" I demanded, as soon as he shut the door.

"Possibly," Ben said. "I called Father Corletti last night, and he was able to get back to me this morning."

"What did he say?"

"About seven years ago, cults sprang up throughout Europe and Asia. Cults that worshipped Andramelech. And made sacrifices to him."

I winced, remembering what Eddie had said about the Assyrians. "Children?" I asked, barely able to voice the question.

"I'm afraid so."

"What happened?"

"The police in the various regions investigated the deaths and disappearances, as you would expect. And, naturally, the cult activities were secret, so the local authorities didn't make the connection at first."

"But *Forza* did."

"Exactly," he said, with a slight nod of his head. "I'm still rather overwhelmed by the organization's resources."

"If the resources are that good, then how come we're hiding bodies in the catacombs?"

He grinned at me. "Ah, Kate. You're becoming old and jaded."

"Am I? Or are you just new and naïve?" Father Ben was relatively new to the whole *Forza* thing, having been informed of the organization at the same time that he was recruited to be my *alimentatore*. So far, he's got a grand total of almost three months under his belt. On the whole, I thought he was adjusting remarkably well. Even if he was a bit naïve.

"I may be new, but I'm the one with the information you need," he said, holding on to a sheaf of papers.

I immediately turned contrite. "I take it all back," I said. "You might be new to the job, but you bring a freshness and exuberance that more than makes up for your lack of on-the-job experience." We were teasing each other now, but I actually meant every word of that.

"Such flattery." He motioned toward one of the guest chairs even as he settled in behind his desk. "The rest of the story is quite interesting, though I have nothing that I'd call concrete."

"What do you have?"

"A name," he said. "Nadia Aiken."

"Should that mean something to me?"

"Not necessarily. She's a Hunter, and she was assigned to investigate these cults. To see if in fact the members were doing Andramelech's bidding."

"And?"

"According to her reports, the demon was indeed active. He was seeking to raise an army comprised of both demons and human followers. She encountered several of his minions—demons in human form—and disposed of them."

All of this was news to me, but that made sense. Seven years ago Allie was a precocious second grader, and the only battle on my mind was the one to get my daughter to clean her room and do her homework. A demon running around fomenting cult activity wasn't tops on my priority list back then. For that matter, demons weren't even *on* my list.

"And then what happened?"

"Apparently the cult continued to spread, gaining toeholds in other areas, including the United States. She traveled here, while other Hunters remained behind in Europe.

She found cults in San Francisco, New Orleans, New York, and Florida."

"Dear God," I said. "Was she able to do anything?"

"Her last report was quite cryptic. She said that she'd contacted an *alimentatore* who might be able to offer assistance. She didn't say who, though, nor did she report this communication to her assigned *alimentatore*."

"So what happened?"

"We don't know," he admitted, closing the file folder.

I fell back in my seat, frustrated. "That's it?"

"No, Kate. That's not it. We don't know what she did, but we do know that the cults began to break apart. Some of the members were interviewed by *Forza* investigators later, and they spoke of feeling a snap, almost as if one minute they were bound by Andramelech, and the next minute they had been freed. Many of the cult members turned to the Church. Some, though, attempted to summon the demon again."

"But they weren't successful."

"No," he confirmed. "They weren't."

"Andramelech's shackles," I murmured. "That's what the demon on the beach said." I looked up at Father Ben. "So seven years ago, he was free—probably even in human form—and running around gathering followers and doing his demon thing. But someone managed to imprison him, and the spell over his cult members was broken. Is that right?"

"As far as we know."

"So who imprisoned him? Nadia?"

"We assume so, but there is no way to be certain."

"She died?" I felt a twinge of loss for this Hunter I'd never met.

"We don't know. According to Father Corletti, she ceased all communications about five years ago. He believes her efforts to entrap Andramelech killed her."

"What do you believe?" I asked.

He smiled thinly and shook his head. "Perhaps it's because I am so naïve—or perhaps it's because I can't bear the thought of anything happening to you—but I choose to believe that Ms. Aiken is still alive."

"If she's alive, though, why is she hiding?"

Father Ben met my eyes. "We're talking about one of the chancellors of Hell, and she'd made it her mission to bring down the army he was raising. If I had to guess, I'd say that she's terrified."

Three

"But terrified of what?" Laura asked, after I relayed the conversation to her. "If this Andre demon is locked up now, what's Nadia still got to be terrified of?"

"That's what I don't get either," I admitted, as I teetered on the ladder in front of the house and tried to disentangle the Christmas lights Stuart had so carefully hung a few weeks ago. "And I didn't have the chance to ask Ben what he meant because Delores came in to talk about the committee stuff with me." I made a face. "Apparently Allie saw her outside and told her Father and I were talking about the archives, so . . ."

Laura's laughter trickled up from the foot of my ladder. "You are so busted."

"I know," I admitted. As much as I wanted to believe that Allie was simply trying to be helpful, I couldn't help but think that sending Delores our way had been her passive-aggressive teenage way of letting me know that she knew I'd pulled one over on her.

"You need to tell her. It's one thing to have kept quiet

about something in your past. Kids inherently understand that. I mean, I still to this day won't admit to Mindy that I wore one of those goofy sweatbands in my hair during high school. But lie about something happening now . . ."

She trailed off, looking wistfully toward the inside of my house, where our girls were currently sitting on the couch, enthralled by the latest fashion mags to have hit the newsstand. "Trust me," she said. "For that, it's much tougher to earn forgiveness."

I immediately shifted to best friend mode. "How's she doing? Any better?"

Laura's husband, Paul, had recently dropped the divorce bomb. They'd decided to keep quiet about it until after the holiday, but that plan hadn't gone over particularly well. In addition to crying and sulking because of the actual divorce, Mindy had been supremely pissed off that they'd "treated her like a baby and played pretend family" over Christmas. Considering Laura and Paul were trying to ensure that Mindy at least had a decent Christmas, their daughter's reaction had been a bit disappointing, to say the least.

"She's speaking to me again," Laura said. "But not to Paul." She grinned, wickedly. "About that, though, I'm not terribly upset."

"It'll keep getting better," I said, because despite the wry comments about Paul, I could still hear the pain in her voice.

"I know it will. Because we had a good reason for not telling her the truth right away. She might not agree with the reason, but it's legitimate."

"I had a reason for waiting," I said, latching on to the subtext.

"Maybe," she acknowledged. "But you can't keep putting off telling her the truth."

"I know, I know. You're right." I unhooked the last of the

lights and let them drop down to Laura. "I just don't want her to get the hunting bug, you know? And that little display with the sword this morning didn't exactly leave me with a warm fuzzy feeling."

"You're the mom, Kate. If she wants to hunt, you're going to have to resort to that time-honored tradition of just saying no."

"Thanks. You're a big help."

She laughed, holding tight to the ladder as I carefully descended. "Happy to be of service." She checked her watch. "Although . . ."

"I know. You guys need to run."

"Trust me," she said. "I'd rather stay here. But the refrigerator is empty."

I almost asked if she wanted to leave Mindy while she ran to the grocery store, but I already knew the answer. As much as Mindy practically lived at our house, these days Laura was keeping her kid close to her, repairing the frayed threads of their relationship. I needed to be doing the same. Because as much as I didn't want to believe it, I knew that the secret I was keeping was going to cause more than a few ragged edges between Allie and me, too.

While I gathered up the lights, Laura gathered up her daughter. By the time I made it back inside, they were heading out the back door, and Allie was fighting with Timmy over the remote control.

"Want to watch *Dora*," he said, then plopped the remote down on the floor and sat on it. Over the last few weeks, he'd had a growth spurt, and not only had his little body grown several inches, but his vocabulary and level of articulation had increased, too. Unfortunately, he mostly used his newfound chattiness for arguing.

"Timmy . . ." She stared him down, her expression one

I'd seen a hundred times on my own face. Like mother, like daughter. "Give me the remote."

"*Dora,*" he said, stubbornly crossing his arms over his chest.

She made a frustrated little noise that only increased in pitch when she looked up and saw me. "Mother," she howled in a full-blown whine. "*Do* something."

"Timmy," I said, in my sternest Mommy voice. "Give me the remote. *Nobody's* watching television."

"But Mom!" Allie wailed.

"*DORAAAAA!*" Timmy screamed.

I took a deep breath and wondered if it was too late to turn around and go back outside. Surely there were still one or two decorations that needed to be taken down. A bush that needed trimming. A flower bed begging to be weeded. A demon that needed slaying.

But, alas, there's never a demon around when you need one.

"You," I said, pointing to Allie, "go get his craft box. And you," I added, pointing to Timmy, "I've got a nice surprise waiting for you in the kitchen."

That wasn't entirely true, but it piqued his interest. And in less than ten minutes, Allie and I had him settled at the kitchen table, a pile of leftover wrapping paper, a glue stick, and a collection of construction paper fragments scattered in front of him.

"Make a star, Mommy," he demanded.

"Go for it," Allie said. "I'm going to go claim the remote."

"No TV," I said as she headed into the living room. She stopped, gave me *the* look, and waited for me to explain this travesty. "We need to finish taking down the tree," I said. "Go get the boxes out of the attic and meet me in the living room."

Her eyebrows rose. "You're leaving him alone with a glue stick? Wow. And I thought you were brave in that museum."

"Very funny," I said, trying hard not to show how absolutely thrilled I was that she could joke about it. I pointed a finger. "Now go."

She went, and for the next five or so minutes, I drew a star on construction paper, used Timmy's safety scissors to carefully cut it out, then helped my budding artistic genius glue little bits of tissue paper all over it.

"Fabulous!" I said, holding it up.

"No, Mommy. Not done yet." He snatched it out of my hand, and proceeded to pile on more tissue paper. "Glitter? Please, glitter? Red and blue and silver and green and—"

"Whoa, whoa," I said, laughing. The glitter would make a huge mess in the kitchen, but good manners were worth a lot, so I caved. Besides, I'd be vacuuming up pine needles in an hour. How much more trouble could a little glitter be?

By the time Allie came down from the attic with all the ornament boxes, I realized my mistake. The floor beneath the table was covered in a thin layer of glitter, as if a colorful snow had fallen. There was glitter in every crack and crevice, glitter clinging to the table and chair feet, and glitter hiding under the baker's rack tucked in the corner near the picture window. I had faith in my vacuum cleaner, but this was above and beyond.

Even Eddie noticed the mess, his bushy eyebrows rising in silent amusement as he padded through the room, grinning like the cat who ate the canary. Or, more likely, the old man who'd just had a hot date.

"You getting any sparkles on that star, boy? Or are you just decorating the floor?"

A wide grin split Timmy's face, and he scrambled out of

his chair and sat in the middle of the floor, a glue stick in hand. Then he rubbed the stick on his palm and pressed it down hard. When he held it up, his palm was silver, gold, and green. And my little boy just laughed and laughed.

I looked at Eddie. "You are *so* going to pay for suggesting that."

He waved the threat away. "So the boy gets his hands messy. It could be worse."

That was true enough, and I had a sudden image of glitter in the furniture, Timmy's hair, the air-conditioning ducts . . .

"Fair enough," I said. Then I smiled sweetly. "But since I'm going to have to wash glue off the floor, you do owe me a little bit, don't you think?"

"Depends. What do you want?"

"Watch him while Allie and I finish taking down the tree."

He cupped his chin with his palm, in full bargaining mode. "What do I get out of it?"

"You *don't* have to help with the tree. And you get my love and devotion." He snorted. *"Plus,"* I added, "you can have one of the apple fritters I bought on our way home from Mass."

"Now you're talking." He nodded at Timmy. "Okay, kid. Let's see what kind of mess we can make."

"Mess!" Timmy repeated, then tossed a handful of glitter into the air.

I left the room, figuring that was a better option than having a nervous breakdown right then and there.

While Eddie and Timmy wreaked havoc in my kitchen, Allie and I undressed the tree and carefully packed away all the ornaments, tinsel, and little holiday knickknacks we've collected over the years. We gathered up the boxes and rubber tubs and headed upstairs to the attic. As for the now-naked tree, I'd get Stuart to drag it to the curb later. After that, I'd vacuum the living room and kitchen. Both, I knew, would sorely need it.

Our house boasts a fabulous attic, the kind that you access through a regular door that opens on to regular stairs leading up to a large room. The room is more or less finished (though not painted) and Allie swears she's going to convince me to let it be her room once she turns sixteen. I haven't yet committed, as I know the value of holding out in exchange for increased bargaining power in other arenas. Forget lawyers; moms are the best negotiators out there.

We tottered up the stairs, barely able to see over the piles in our arms. Allie dropped hers on the floor, earning a frown from me since more than a few ornaments were not only glass, but sentimental.

"Sorry!" she said, immediately contrite.

"They survived Timmy," I said. "Let's see if we can't make sure they last another year."

"I know, I know. I said I was sorry." To her credit, I didn't have to tell her what to do next. She took her boxes and loaded them up on the set of shelves we have on the far side of the room to hold various holiday accoutrements. And then, as if to prove she deserved a Good Kid award, she finished loading my boxes as well.

"Thanks," I said. "Now in only eleven short months we can pull everything out again."

We started back for the stairs, but I soon realized that Allie'd stopped following me. I turned around and found her kneeling in front of my Hunting trunk. I keep it under a pile of old linens, but that didn't stop her. She'd already pulled them off, and now she was looking at the brass latch, and the polished leather and oiled wood that formed the trunk itself.

"So what do you really keep in here?" she asked. In the

past, I'd casually mentioned that there were various keep-sakes in the trunk. Nothing important. Only a sentimental thing or two.

Considering what she'd recently learned, though, her question was legitimate. Still, I didn't hear natural curios-ity. I heard accusations: *Is this your Hunting stuff? You're still using it, aren't you? And if you are, why did you lie to me?*

I sternly told the voices in my head to shut up, then crossed to her side. "I keep my old *Forza* tools in there," I said. And then, because I knew I had to, I added, "Do you want to see?"

Her eyes sparkled, and she nodded.

"Okay, then." I keep the trunk locked for obvious rea-sons, and I have the key hidden on a small nail on one of the rafters. I snagged it, then crossed back to Allie, handing her the key so that she could do the honors.

She put the key in the lock almost reverentially, then tugged the heavy brass lock open. She looked at me then, and I nodded. With that silent encouragement, she took hold of the lid and pushed it up.

"Oh, come *on*, Mom," she said, her voice full of irritation and accusation. "Are you jerking me around or what?" She reached inside and came out with a recipe card. "Like you're ever going to make a mango-strawberry soufflé."

I laughed, because I'd forgotten that she wouldn't see my tools right away. The trunk is the kind that has a fitted, shal-low tray on top, and in a clever attempt at camouflaging, I'd filled the trunk with recipes, decorating tips, and other household hints that I'd ripped from magazines.

"I'm not conning you, Al," I said, leaning over her to pull the entire tray out, revealing the black velvet cloth I keep over my tools. I grabbed a corner and tugged it aside, too. From inside the trunk, my well-polished tools gleamed in the dim attic light.

"Whoa," she said, her tone full of astonishment and awe. "Now *that's* cool."

"I know," I said, kneeling down next to her. Maybe I should have discouraged her enthusiasm, but it *is* cool. And I could hardly lie to my own daughter.

"So what is all this stuff?"

"Well, let's see." I shifted position, then reached in and grabbed up my trusty crossbow. "This little guy saved my life on more than one occasion."

"Awesome." She reached out tentatively, then drew her fingers back.

"It's okay," I said, passing it to her. "You can hold it." I almost didn't let her, fearing that by holding it she'd catch the demon-hunting bug, as if it were a virus spread by contact. But the truth is, I knew better. It wasn't a virus, it was a gene. And now that her fear was fading, my battle was all about timing.

Surprisingly, she didn't inspect the crossbow for as long as I expected. She gave it a good look-over, stroked the wood that had been oiled until it gleamed, then set it aside to peer once again into the trunk.

"All of this stuff," she said, her voice filled with awe. "It's like you're fighting in a medieval war or something."

"In a way we are," I said. "The war between good and evil has been going on for a long time."

I expected a patented Alison Crowe eye roll for that, but instead she just nodded sagely, as if she'd been contemplating the character of good and evil her whole life.

"How do you know?" she asked after a moment. "I mean, unless they look like those monsters we saw, how do you know who's a demon and who isn't?"

I'd been wondering when she was going to ask that. Wondering if she'd been seeing demons around every corner, in the faces of her friends and the people she passed on the street. Honestly, that's not all that far from the truth. Demons *are* around us. All the time.

Fortunately, they're mostly incorporeal, which means they're just floating around in the ether, wishing they had a human body.

"But sometimes they do," Allie said, after I explained all of that. "Have a body, I mean."

"Right," I acknowledged. "They can do that a couple of ways. They can go the old-fashioned possession route, but that's no fun because the whole head-spinning *Exorcist* schtick doesn't really blend in with the general population."

Allie managed a smile. "No, I guess it wouldn't."

"Possessions are a priest's problem. But your dad and I were Hunters. We went after the demons who managed to blend in."

"How?"

"By taking over the shell of a newly vacated body. The soul goes out, the demon goes in."

A combination of fear and disgust filled her eyes. "Wait, wait, wait. Are you saying that after I die, my body could be—"

"No, no," I assured her. "A demon can't inhabit the body of the faithful. Our souls *fight*. There's only a tiny window of opportunity for the demon to slip in. Miss it, and the body is just a body. Nothing more."

That, actually, was why demon infestations tended to concentrate on places where their odds increase. Hospitals are number one. And in San Diablo, the demons have laid a serious stake to the nursing home.

"But if they do slip into a body," I continued, "then they can walk around like you and me, and nobody's the wiser. Or, at least, nobody except a Demon Hunter."

"Which is exactly what I asked in the first place," she said. "How come you can tell but nobody else can?"

I gave her the CliffsNotes version of Demon Spotting 101, running through the various tests on which a Hunter relies, with breath being first on the list.

A demon's breath is beyond putrid. But in this day of Listerine strips and Trident White gum, even the nastiest breath can be masked.

A better test is holy water, but it can be awkward trying to douse a potential demon to see if the water burns. And, of course, a demon can't walk on holy ground. But like the saying goes, you can lead a demon to church, but you can't make him walk inside.

Or something like that.

"So once you're sure," Allie asked, "then what? You get 'em with the crossbow?"

"That's one way," I said. "But to kill a demon you have to get him right in the eye."

"Ewwww." She scrunched up her face, appropriately grossed out. "And then they're dead?"

I shook my head. "No. But then they don't have a body anymore." The only way to *truly* kill a demon was to cut it down while in its true form. But once encased in a human shell, demons very rarely revealed their true nature. Allie, in fact, was one of the few who had seen a true demon and lived to tell about it.

She turned her attention back to my trunk. "So to kill the demon, you have to get close enough to jam that through its eye?" she asked, pointing to my stiletto.

"Or learn how to throw it accurately."

She looked at me with respect. "You can do that?"

"Yeah," I said with a small laugh. "I can't make a chocolate cake from scratch, but I can nail a demon from twenty paces."

"Pretty cool," she said.

Indeed.

I was grinning when I took the knife from the trunk, explaining how Eric had given it to me for our third anniversary. He'd had it custom made, and it boasted a double-action release system. What I didn't tell her was how much of a workout the blade had gotten lately. I can't traipse around San Diablo with a crossbow, but the stiletto fits nicely in the sleeve of my favorite leather jacket.

She took a bit more interest in the knife than she had in the crossbow, even going so far as to slash it through the air one or two times. "Pretty cool," she repeated. "And romantic," she added, her voice dripping with sarcasm.

"Well, it was romantic," I said, laughing at her expression. "Thoughtful and useful. What more could a woman ask for?"

"Stuart usually gives you flowers and jewelry."

"Which I also love," I said.

"They're not useful."

"But they're thoughtful," I retorted. "And considering I don't have nearly enough jewelry to wear to all these various parties he and I go to, the pieces come in handy as well."

"I guess," she said, but she was looking at the knife, and I couldn't help but think that she was mentally comparing her father to Stuart. I couldn't blame her; at the moment, so was I.

My love life, though, wasn't nearly enough to hold her attention, and she started pawing through the trunk again. She carefully lifted various items out—glass bottles for holding holy water, crucifixes, dangerous knives with ornate handles. She examined each, then inevitably moved on to something else.

At one point, she pulled out a tiny velvet bag. She looked

at it curiously, then started to untie the strings that firmly sealed it at the top. I gently tugged it out of her hand with a quick shake of my head. "Careful with that."

"What is it?"

I hesitated.

"Oh, come *on*, Mom. Either you're telling me the truth or you're not. I mean you can't just—"

I held up a hand to ward off her diatribe—not to mention my guilt. "Fine. You win. Take a peek, but open it carefully."

She did, moving slowly and reverentially. As she peered into the bag, I saw her forehead crinkle, and when she looked up at me there was no mistaking the confusion on her face. "It's dust," she said.

"Powerful dust," I countered, a small sampling of the relic that Goramesh had come to San Diablo this past summer to find. I'd managed to foil him, but it hadn't been easy.

I'm not entirely sure why I kept the dust. Superstition, maybe. A memento from my defeat of a High Demon even when I was out of shape and out of practice. And, more, a reminder of why I was willing to come out of retirement in the first place. To keep my kids—my family—safe.

"So what's the big deal about the dust?" she asked. "It's not like you couldn't find twenty bags' worth under the living room sofa."

"Very funny, Miss I'm-About-to-Get-More-Chores."

"Seriously," she said, closing the bag and holding it up. "What's it do?"

"Nothing much," I said. "Nothing except bring the dead back to life."

Her eyes widened. "Whoa. No sh— No kidding?"

"No kidding," I said. At least, that was my understanding.

I never actually got to see the dust in action, and now the bulk of it was safely tucked away in the Vatican.

"Where'd you get it?" she asked, staring in wonderment at the little bag.

I took it gently from her hands and placed it back in the trunk. "Long story," I said. "One of these days, I'll tell you."

I expected her to press me on the point, but I guess the lure of the trunk was too strong because she was off and running again.

"What's this?" she asked.

"What?" I leaned forward, trying to see what she'd found under a pile of old *Forza* reports that had spilled out of a leather folio near the bottom of the trunk. She shifted, and I saw the brown paper bag in her hand. My heart gave a little stutter, and I think I made a soft sound, because Allie looked at me, a question in her eyes. "That's your daddy's stuff," I said, my voice thick. "The things that were with him when he died."

"Oh." Just one small word, but it hung between us. She looked at me, and I saw the storm start in her eyes.

I scooted over and pulled her close to me. We sat that way for a while, both of us thinking about Eric. Finally, I looked at her, my hand on the bag. "Do you want to open it?"

She gave only a tiny nod in reply.

"Go ahead, then."

She carefully opened the sack and peered inside. I knew the contents by heart. His wallet. A blank postcard showing the Golden Gate Bridge emerging triumphant from the fog. A man's gold ring with a ruby surrounded by tiny diamonds, one of the many rings Eric collected and wore, although this one was a bit bigger and gaudier than his usual style.

When the police had sent me the bag, I'd stared at the contents daily, my heart aching for the man who'd been going about his business, oblivious to his killer until it was too late. At the time, I'd cried myself to sleep wondering if we were his last thoughts, and pitying the man who wouldn't see his daughter grow up.

Lately, though, I'd cried for a different reason. Because Allie and I had recently learned that Eric's death hadn't been the random mugging we'd once believed. It had been deliberate. It had been murder.

And, undoubtedly, it had been the result of his demon-hunting past.

She slipped on the ring then held her hand up, the stones glimmering in the attic's dim light. "I remember this," she said.

"You do?" I frowned, surprised by that. After all, *I* barely remembered the thing. Eric had always had a thing for rings, something I found amusing since I rarely wore jewelry. He'd owned at least three dozen rings, collected at various places across the globe, and he would wear a different one each day.

"I was looking for my birthday present and I found it in his sock drawer. I thought it was cool."

There were so many things wrong with that statement, I didn't even know where to begin. "You were looking in your father's drawers for presents?"

"Come on, Mom. It wasn't like I was snooping around yesterday."

Good point. "Yes, but how can I ever trust your judgment again. I mean, you've just admitted to thinking *that* is cool."

"Yeah, well, like I said. I was a little kid." She took the ring off and put it back in the bag, then pulled out Eric's wallet. I knew what she'd see when she opened it—his driver's license was still in the little plastic envelope, although his money had been taken.

I watched as my little girl swallowed, then pressed her fingertips over her father's photo. A single tear snaked down her face, hung tenaciously to the end of her nose, and then finally landed with a plop on the wallet. Only then did she look up at me.

"Do you think he's still watching me?"

"Oh, baby. I know he is."

"I can't even think up his face anymore. When I close my eyes, all I can see is that picture of us in my room. It's not a memory of the past, you know? It's just the memory of a picture, and that's not the same."

"You remember *him*, sweetheart. Who he was and how much he loved you. If you can keep that in your heart, it doesn't really matter what he looks like." I tapped her nose. "All this is just a shell anyway, right? It was the man inside you loved."

My voice cracked a little as I spoke, and it hit me again how much I'd lost with David's announcement last night. For weeks, I'd been entertaining the fantasy that while Eric's form had changed, the man himself was still around. Still watching over Allie.

Now, I knew there was only me.

My chest seemed to fill with lead, the weight of loss and the unknown pulling me down. I hugged Allie close, and we sat that way for a long time, just the two of us, lost in memories.

After a while, she shifted a little, then lifted the bag and toyed with it. "So how come you kept it all up here? Daddy was retired when he was killed, right? So why keep his stuff with your demon-hunting things?"

I started to answer, but she got there first, her head cocking to one side. "He *wasn't* retired," she announced triumphantly. "Daddy was still hunting demons, right up to the day he was killed."

"I think he might have been," I admitted, though that wasn't why I kept his stuff in the trunk. That was simply because it seemed to belong there, with the things from my past that were special to me.

"You think?"

"Because of the notes we found," I explained. "My best guess is that your dad was hunting again." Right before Christmas, Allie and I had found two cryptic notes from Eric. To both of us, it had been clear that Eric had been purposefully killed. From the subtext, though, I'd gleaned that he'd stuck his toe back in the *Forza* waters. Whether he'd gone so far as to hunt again, though . . .

That I wasn't sure about, and that one simple question had weighed on me for weeks. I'd lived for years with the belief that I knew Eric inside and out, just like he knew me. And then, with one cryptic note, everything changed. Suddenly, I'd learned that Eric had secrets. Big secrets.

Reality had slapped me hard across the face and I was still reeling.

"When we moved to San Diablo," I began, in response to Allie's querying look, "it was because we'd retired. We were done with hunting. It's not exactly a career you want long term. There's a pretty high mortality rate, and we were starting a family."

She scooted around until her back was against the chest and her knees were tucked up under her chin. Then she nodded, my signal to continue.

"I gave up hunting completely, and I thought your dad had, too. I stayed at home with you. He got a job in the rare books room at the library. We invited the neighbors over for dinner, went to birthday parties for your friends, spent weekends at the beach. It was normal."

"Except Daddy wasn't really . . ."

"Apparently not," I said. "But let me tell it my way."

She nodded, and I kept on.

"I didn't know it at the time, but apparently your dad had been training to be an *alimentatore*."

"A what?"

"It's like a coach for a Hunter. Does research. Tells you where to go and who to fight. That kind of thing."

"And you didn't know?"

I shook my head. "I only just learned, actually. I called Father Corletti a few weeks ago. He told me. And he told me that your dad had wanted to keep it a secret."

"Oh." The sound was small and insecure, essentially a mirror to the way I felt. The knowledge of Eric's secret pursuit had stung, the pain all the more intense because I couldn't help but wonder if the life we had together wasn't enough for him. That *I* wasn't enough for him.

I took a deep breath, determined to stay in control for Allie's sake. "So when he went on that business trip to San Francisco," I continued, "I had no reason to think it was anything other than what he'd told me. Now, though . . ."

I broke off, my voice cracking. Allie leaned forward and took my hand. "It's okay, Mom. It's okay to be mad at him."

I blinked, startled. Because she was absolutely right. I *was* mad. I'd had no idea he was in danger; no idea that he'd reentered the world of *Forza*. When we'd hunted together I'd been prepared. But ten years later, when we were supposedly retired? His death just about laid me flat. And to know now what I should have known then . . . well, yeah. *Mad* is pretty much an understatement.

Her hand was still in mine, and I tugged her close and hugged her fiercely. "I love you, Allie. Don't you ever forget that."

"I know, Mom," she whispered, and hugged me back just as tight. "Daddy loved you, too," she said, after a long pause.

"Oh, baby, I know that. I'm a little mad, but mostly I'm confused. And maybe my feelings are hurt. But I've never doubted for a second that your dad loved me. You can keep a secret from someone and still love that person. That's just the way the world works."

She considered that only for a moment before turning to me, her eyes cool and deliberate. "I want to know, Mom," she said. "I want to know why Daddy was killed."

"I do, too. But we tried. It's been five years. There's not a lot we can do now." Eric had left us a series of clues, but we'd hit only dead ends. "I've tried, baby. But I haven't learned a thing."

"There's got to be something," she said, her voice choked with unshed tears. "I mean, we can at least keep looking. Can't we, Mom? For a little bit longer."

The pain and loss in her voice just about ripped me to pieces. And I pressed a soft kiss to her forehead as tears pooled in my eyes.

"Of course," I whispered. "We'll do everything we can."

Four

Everything we can.

My words echoed in my head for the rest of the afternoon, a dark cloud that seemed to weigh me down as I moved through the rest of the day, putting away laundry, sweeping the back porch, making dinner. Now I moved through the breakfast room to the archway that divided the room from the living area. Allie was in there with Timmy and Eddie, and the three of them were playing Hi Ho Cherry-O. Allie had Timmy on her lap, and Eddie was muttering something about the bird taking his darn cherries. The scene was domestic and sweet, and I never wanted it to change. Never wanted it painted red with fear or gray with distrust.

More, I didn't want Allie to long for the day she turned eighteen so that she could break ties with me and walk away. For two years after Eric's death, we'd been each other's strength, and even now that we had Stuart and Timmy, there was still an inescapable bond between us. Mother and daughter, yes, but something more, too.

The revelation about Eric had left seeds of distrust in my soul, and even though I didn't want to, now I was questioning our entire relationship. To know that Allie might soon feel the same about me—to know that the thread of trust might start to unravel—both terrified me and broke my heart.

I had to tell her the truth. I had to tell her that I was still hunting demons. And I had to tell her soon.

The weight of that obligation stayed with me, counterbalanced a bit by the relief that I'd made a decision. Having decided but not yet acted, though, made me a jittery wreck. And I spent the rest of the afternoon doing domestic chores simply because I knew that no one else in the household would likely volunteer to help me. I needed alone time, and scrubbing toilets was the best way I knew to get it.

By five, the bathrooms were no longer functional science projects, I'd gotten a decent cardiovascular workout by lugging two boxes of neglected toys to the backyard storage shed, and I'd vacuumed the entire upstairs, evicting at least a dozen families of dust bunnies in the process.

By the time I returned to the living room, my family had moved on to other activities. Timmy was outside, playing in his sandbox. Allie was reading on the porch, and Eddie was parked in his recliner, glasses perched on his nose as he muttered vague obscenities at today's crossword.

I busied myself cutting up broccoli to go with the simple chicken casserole I'd cobbled together an hour before. I'd learned long ago to stick with the basics for our meals. Meat loaf, pancakes, pasta, Hamburger Helper. Those I could handle. Braised salmon in a mango-chutney sauce? Not so much.

I was just putting the broccoli in the steamer when the phone rang, and I grabbed it up, tucking it between my ear and my shoulder as I filled the steamer with water.

"Kate," David said. "Can you talk?"

I heard the urgency in his voice and abandoned my broccoli. "What's wrong? Are you okay?"

"I'm fine now," he said. "But this morning . . ."

"What? What happened?"

"Attacked. In my own goddamned apartment."

"By a demon?" Which was an idiotic thing to ask, but the first thing that came to my mind.

"Considering I'm only a rogue," he said, "it hardly seems like I should have to put up with that crap."

There was humor in his voice and I clung to it because it meant that he really was okay.

"Is he—"

"Dead," David said, which was the shorthand way of saying that the body was out of commission and the demon was back in the ether, technically still in existence, but no longer a nuisance.

"Do you need me to come help you?"

This time, he laughed for real. "He's already dead, Kate."

I scowled at the phone. "I was offering to help get rid of the body," I said. "But I think I'll retract the offer now."

"It's been taken care of," he said. "I decided to use the opportunity to try out a new disposal method. The cathedral doesn't have endless vault space, you know."

"I had hoped that San Diablo didn't have endless demons," I said dryly, trying not to think about the body-disposal methods that a chemistry teacher could concoct.

"I think that hope's been shot to hell," he said.

True enough. "Any idea why he attacked you? Did he want something?"

"From what I could tell," David said, "he wanted *me*. And alive, too. He caught me off guard, Kate, but he never went for the kill shot. If he'd wanted to kill me, he could have."

I hugged myself, suddenly chilled. "David, you need—"

"To be more careful. Yeah. I got that. I want you to be careful, too."

I was immediately on alert. "Did he say something?"

"No, but the more I think about it, the more I worry. You're the Hunter here, and if it's a Hunter they want . . ." His voice washed over me, low and gruff and very sincere. "Promise me, Katie. Promise me you won't let down your guard."

I shivered, more than a little undone by his tone. "I promise," I whispered. "And David?"

"What?"

"I'm glad you're okay." The words seemed flat somehow, but I meant them sincerely. I'd lost Eric twice—in San Francisco, and again last night. I didn't think I could stand to lose David, too. He might not be the man I'd once loved, but I had to admit that I cared for him, possibly more than I should. Perhaps my feelings for him were colored by all the weeks that I thought he was Eric, but that didn't change the fact that the man had become important to me. And, yes, little by little he was sliding into the role of hunting partner, too.

As I hung up, I felt a little numb. I could hear our garage door begin its laborious climb to the top, and I splashed some water on my face, trying to wash the worry and fear for David off my face.

Minutes later, Stuart trundled in, a bag of marshmallows in one hand and a plastic grocery bag with graham crackers and Hershey bars in the other.

"Sweet tooth?"

He just grinned. "And I've got firewood in the trunk."

"It's seventy-six degrees out," I said, mimicking what he always says to me during the winter months when I beg for a fire despite our California climate.

He nodded, all serious. "Good point. I'll go crank up the air conditioner." He started out of the room but I tugged him back, then planted a kiss on his lips.

"Thanks," I said. "You know how to cheer a girl up." More than that, Stuart was my rock—a demon-free zone in a life that had once again become filled with uncertainty. I hugged him tight, soaking up that deep sense of normalcy. I'd craved a normal, safe life with Eric, and I'd believed that I'd gotten it. Only recently had I learned it was only an illusion.

I sighed, pressing my face against Stuart's shoulder. In truth, my safe little life with Stuart was an illusion, too. Only this time, I was the one who'd brought the danger to our doorstep.

He gave me a final squeeze, then pulled back far enough to get a good look at my face. His eyes moved as he looked me over. "Want to share what's been on your mind?"

I gave my head a little shake. "Just melancholy. It's nothing. Probably PMS."

He put the groceries on the counter and took my hands. "Is it Eric?"

I balked, because that was really not a question I was expecting. "I—no," I stammered. "I mean, why would you think it's Eric?" Had I been putting out an "Eric" vibe? Had Allie said something?

"It's that time of year," he said. "You always get a little moody."

"Do I? Yeah, I guess I do." Eric had been killed in early January, right after the holidays. This year, I'd been so caught up with all of my other Eric issues—not to mention the issue of almost losing my daughter to a hell-bound demon—that I'd glossed right over my annual depression.

I leaned forward and gave Stuart a kiss. "Thanks for being so understanding."

He stroked my cheek. "That's part of the job description, remember?"

I raised an eyebrow. "So this is the 'for worse' part?"

His eyes danced with mischief. "No, sweetheart, *that's* your cooking."

I swatted him with the marshmallow bag, trying hard not to laugh. "Go, husband," I said. "Go forth and make fire."

"Ugh," he said, with appropriate caveman inflections.

I rolled my eyes as he left, but at the same time, I realized I was grinning. Stuart might not know my past, but he did know me. More important, he knew how to make me smile.

I watched, satisfied, as Timmy raced around like a wild thing while Stuart tried to light the fire. I had a good life, after all, with a family who loved me.

And I couldn't help but wonder if, by pursuing a mystery from the past, I'd be risking everything I had in front of me.

Mornings around our house are never calm, and the first day back to school and work after a vacation are always the worst. And if I happen to have carpool duty, you can pretty much triple the insanity quotient.

I awakened to a rousing chorus of "Elmo's World," performed a capella by my budding Pavarotti. The *duh-duh-duh-duh*s blasted through the baby monitor, and despite pulling the covers up over my ears, I knew that morning had inevitably arrived.

Stuart elbowed me. "Jstgoengitdeboy," he muttered.

"You go get him," I retorted. "My alarm hasn't gone off yet." Stuart's had, though, and he'd already hit the snooze button twice. I figured I had bed equity, and I was hanging on for all it was worth.

He groaned, then propped himself up on his elbow and blinked a few times. My husband has never been one to come awake easily. "What time is it?"

"Seven minutes since the last time you hit the snooze button," I said as his alarm started blaring again.

"Shit," he said, suddenly wide awake. "I'm running late. Can you get Timmy? The kid sounds wide awake."

And so the day began.

I decided to save the battle with my clueless husband for later. Instead, I rolled out of bed, grabbed my robe, then padded down the hall to Timmy's room. He'd started climbing out of his crib not too long ago, and we'd moved him to a toddler bed. I found him on top of it now, apparently convinced it was a trampoline.

"I flying, Mommy!" he squealed. "I'm Super Timmy!"

I caught him midleap. "Hey there, Super Dude. Even superheroes need breakfast. Are you hungry?"

"Toast with butter cheese," he demanded as I pulled off his pajama bottoms and helped him into a dry Pull-Ups.

"Fine and dandy," I said. For reasons I don't actually remember, Timmy started calling margarine "butter cheese" about the time he learned to talk. Since it's so damn cute, we haven't bothered to correct him. So long as he gets it right before college, I figure we're okay.

I got him dressed, then led him to Allie's room. I tapped once, heard nothing, then tapped again. Vague sounds of life drifted to me through the closed door. I considered that a good sign and pounded once again.

"What?"

"Time to get up. First day back to school. Pencils. Teachers. Books."

No response.

"Cheerleading. *Boys.*"

That did it. "I'm up, already."

"Twenty minutes, Allie," I said. "I want you downstairs in twenty."

"I said okay!"

My motherly harassment duty accomplished, I led Timmy to the top of the stairs, opened the baby gate, and let him scamper down.

I found Eddie asleep in the recliner, in exactly the same position I'd left him last night. I tucked a blanket around his shoulders and decided not to bother him. I'd been considering asking him to watch Tim for a few hours—the day care follows the elementary school schedule, and it's closed until tomorrow—but seeing him made me change my mind. It's easy to forget he's past eighty when he bursts onto the scene fighting demons with the same gusto with which he pursues his librarian lady friend.

By the time Timmy's toast was ready, Stuart was in the kitchen, pouring himself coffee. By the time Allie finally barreled into the kitchen, Stuart was gone, a travel mug in his hand and my kiss on his cheek.

Over the next ten minutes, I got Timmy cleaned up, let Mindy in the back door, helped Allie find her student ID, argued with her about makeup (mascara yes, eyeshadow no), raced upstairs to throw on sweats and a T-shirt, and finally managed to usher the family out the door and into the van.

"Two minutes to spare," I said, backing onto our street. "And to think I could have squeezed in a shower."

The other girls in the carpool, Susan and Emily, were ready to go when I honked, which was a minor miracle, and as the girls got settled, the noise level increased.

Mindy is the editor of the school paper, and Susan is on her staff. They immediately dived into a discussion of a human interest story for the upcoming issue. "The history of San Diablo," Mindy said. "That's cool, don't you think?"

"I guess," said Allie. "But it's not like this town's all that interesting."

"Are you kidding?" Mindy retorted. "It's totally cool, isn't it, Mrs. Connor?"

"Hold on there, kid," I said with a laugh. "How did I get designated community liaison?"

I didn't even need the rearview mirror to know that Mindy was rolling her eyes. "Trust me," she said. "This is a totally happening part of California. We've got the whole Hollywood heyday thing, from back when the stars used to come up from L.A. to hang on our beaches. And all those fabulous houses they built over Emerald Point. I mean, how cool is that?"

I agreed that it was very cool.

"And we've got even older history, too," Mindy continued. "There are at least three Chumash cave paintings nearby. And the stone table, right? I mean that's like our own Stonehenge. Some experts even think it was used for human sacrifices thousands of years ago."

I was doubtful as to whether a flat piece of stone topping two perpendicular pieces of stone qualified as Stonehenge, but I knew where she was going.

"You're right," I said. "San Diablo is a fascinating topic for a human interest story."

"And the modern stuff is cool, too," she assured me, although by that time we'd reached the school, and even had a few minutes to spare. I gave myself a silent cheer. I'd conquered the wild world of carpools. Hopefully I'd have the same success with the Andramelech and Eric mysteries.

As the girls got out—Mindy promising to fill us in on more local history during my next turn to drive the carpool—I half considered parking the car and going into the school. I wanted to know if David had figured anything else out. Or, for that matter, if he'd been attacked by any more demons. But this wasn't the time or the place, and I knew that if he learned something, he'd call me. And if another demon had come to finish what the one in his apartment had started . . . well, I'm sure Allie would tell me if David wasn't at school.

This new surge of demon activity, however, had reinforced exactly how much I couldn't afford to let my training slide. I hadn't been to Cutter's studio for over two weeks, but somehow I'd manage to squeeze a trip into today's busy schedule.

"Okay, buddy," I said to Timmy as I pulled back out onto the street. "You ready for the day?"

"Rock and roll, Mommy!" he yelled, shoving a little fist high into the air.

And that, I thought, pretty much summed it up.

I keep a giant family-event calendar in the kitchen, but other than that, I'm not disciplined enough to keep an organizer. Instead, I keep a list scribbled on one of those little spiral-bound pads you find in the checkout line at Wal-Mart. Many of the essentials of my life, in fact, were acquired while waiting in the checkout line.

Today's list was pretty basic. A quick run to the grocery store for milk, an ever-dwindling staple in our house. Home for a shower. Review what I knew about Eric's death and try to decide where to start tackling the mystery at this late date. Run the vacuum once through the house in anticipation of the play date scheduled at our house for one-thirty. Shop the post-holiday sales with Timmy for new shoes since the kid was growing at an astounding rate. Wait patiently—ha!—for Ben to call me with more info about Andramelech and the mysterious hunter. Visit Cutter for a quick workout. Cook dinner. Eat dinner.

Normal life stuff (well, except for the murder and demon parts), and we whipped through them pretty quickly. I still had a good hour before we had guests and—remarkably enough—the living room and play room were both clean enough for company. Truly, miracles do happen, and I ended up on the floor with Timmy, playing with Duplo blocks while we waited for play date time to arrive.

That quiet interval lasted all of fifteen minutes before Timmy started begging for a snack. I obliged, putting a few grapes and apple slices in a bowl and then sending him back to the living room and Eddie. While he munched, I parked myself by the sink and started to cut up some more fruit and arrange it decoratively on a plate. Laura had promised to bring by some of her famous chocolate chip cookies later, but I wanted at least the illusion of good nutrition gracing my play date table.

I was leaning against the sink, sneaking a few grapes, when I heard the scraping outside, a faint noise, like the rustling of branches against the house. Immediately, I was on alert. The noise was coming from the breakfast area, and I was quite aware that the picture window that dominates that wall is not a sufficient barrier to prevent a determined demon.

I'd stocked up on ice picks during a recent sale, and now I grabbed one out of the childproofed utility drawer. I eased toward the window, keeping my back to the wall so that I was mostly out of view of anyone who might be looking in.

Scrape, scrape.

I froze, the sound coming again, this time less muffled. I peeked out the window, my entire body primed to expect an explosion of glass as a demon came crashing through.

Nothing.

Shit.

I stood there, debating what to do, David's warning fresh on my mind. In the end, there really was no debate, though. If there was a demon out there, I needed to nip that little problem in the bud right now. Because if I didn't—and if Mr. Hellbound himself decided to barge in during Timmy's play date—well, that would put quite a damper on the kid-does' fun.

The window in the breakfast room looks out over the side of the house rather than the backyard, at an angle that also offers a view of our neighbor's backyard and fence. Since there's no access to that side of the house from the backyard, I slipped into the living room and headed for the front door.

"Keep Timmy in here with you," I said. *"Right beside you."* I added the last with extra force and a significant look. To his credit, Eddie understood right away.

"You rolling the trash can up from the curb, girlie?"

"Something like that," I said.

"Need any help?"

I lifted a brow. "You can stay with him," I said, pointing to Timmy. "After all, taking care of the trash isn't your job anymore, is it?"

He leaned back in the recliner. "Right you are," he said,

grabbing the remote and clicking on the television. "Go get 'em, Tiger."

I rolled my eyes and continued to the front door. I slipped out quietly, then made my way around the side of the house to the window and the shrubs growing just below the glass. From the corner of the house by the garage door, I could tell that he was still there. The shrubs were moving, and not with the wind. Which meant we either had a demon problem or a nest of feisty raccoons.

I was betting on demon.

Slowly, slowly, I moved down the length of the house until I was just inches from the shrubs. I couldn't see who was back there—the foliage was too thick—but the leaves had quit moving. The demon knew I was out there, and he'd gone still as death.

The world seemed just as stagnant, and I barely breathed as I waited for some sign—some hint of where to attack. Dive in now, and I couldn't be certain. And if I was off by even a centimeter, I'd lose the advantage of height and leverage.

No, the best plan was to wait him out. A movement, a sound, and I could target my attack.

And I *was* going to attack. No way was a demon stalking my house going to come out of this fray alive.

There!

Just the slightest of movements, but it was enough. I launched myself in, reaching through the brush to pull the demon out. The limbs and leaves scraped against my bare arms, but the fingers of my left hand closed around flesh. The branches slapped back against the demon as I tugged, and his wail rang in my ears.

I had the ice pick ready in my right hand, and as soon as the demon emerged, I slammed it forward.

"Aaaaaiaiiiggghhhh!"

I froze, the pick only inches from his face, and my fingers released the grip on his arm even as I jumped back. "Brian? Brian Dufresne? *What the devil are you doing hiding in my shrubs?*"

In front of me, nine-year-old Brian stared google-eyed at the ice pick that had just about done him in. "I—I—"

I cursed, then slipped the thing into my back pocket. "For heaven's sake, Brian! I thought you were a— I could have killed you!"

"You thought I was a what?" he whispered, still looking at the hand that earlier held the pick.

"A coyote," I said, which was the best I could come up with. "A coyote's been terrorizing Kabit. I thought you . . ." I stopped, put my hands on my hips, and tried to remember who was supposed to be in charge here. "This isn't about what *I* thought, young man. It's about what you were doing." I pointed to the shrubs and raised my eyebrows in question. "Why didn't you come out? You were deliberately hiding from me."

His face turned bright red. "You're not going to tell my mom, are you?"

"Brian . . ."

He sighed and shoved his hands into his pockets. "I hit my baseball over our fence. And I'm not supposed to go into the neighbors' yards, so I didn't want to say anything. I'm really sorry. I didn't mean—"

"I know you didn't." I sighed, feeling extremely relieved I hadn't impaled the kid, and more than a little foolish. I gestured back at the shrubs. "Is the ball in there?"

One quick nod.

"Well, go get it."

He started to, then stopped, looking up at me with puppydog eyes.

"I won't tell your mom," I said. "But Brian, she's right." I looked him straight in the eye. "You need to stay in your own yard, okay? Venture out, and you might get hurt."

After all, there were scary things out there. Bad drivers, muggers, thieves, demons. And, yes, there were also crazy women with ice picks.

And those, I thought, should be avoided at all costs.

My heartbeat hadn't yet returned to normal when Fran arrived with her three-year-old daughter Elena, who is a little angel. Fran and I have gotten in the habit of getting to each other's play dates ten or so minutes early, just so we can chat before the other moms show up and shift the conversation around to nail salons and new high-end boutiques.

While Timmy and Elena played in the inflatable ball corral that had been a present from Santa, Fran and I loitered in the kitchen. Kabit snaked through my legs, and I bent down to scratch him on the head.

"So how is Allie doing?" Fran asked, her expression appropriately sympathetic. "That nightmare at the museum. So horrible."

"She's doing pretty good," I said. "She's a resilient girl. I'm worried, of course, but honestly, she seems to be okay." Certainly more so than I'd expected, I thought wryly.

"I'm glad. I can't believe we had that kind of gang and drug activity going on right here in San Diablo," she went on, warming to the subject. "I mean, who would have thought?"

"I know exactly what you mean," I said. And then, because I couldn't think of a graceful way to shift conversational gears, I simply picked an entirely different topic. "Remember the last time we were here? How much Elena loved that pink rocking pony?"

"I looked everywhere for one for Christmas," Fran admitted. "Where on earth did you find it?"

"It used to be Allie's," I said. "But Timmy's growing so fast he's already too big for it. Besides, he told me that pink was for girls."

Fran laughed. "Well, he has a point."

"I told him it was a girl pony, but that boys could ride her. I'm not sure if he bought it or not, but it doesn't matter, because he's over ponies. He's moved on to jets and rockets. So we bought him a new one for Christmas. A plane, that rocks and has wings that go up and down."

"Aww," she said. "It sounds precious."

I assured her that it was. "But I was wondering if Elena wants the old one? She's got time to get some good use out of it, and it's just going to go to waste in our storage shed."

"Seriously?" Her eyes were bright, and I knew why. Fran's a single mom who works from home doing medical transcription. She's never come right out and said it, but I'm sure money is tight. And while I doubted she'd take direct charity, a hand-me-down toy seemed more than reasonable.

"Absolutely. I'll just end up dragging it to Goodwill in a year or two."

"Oh, well, if that's the case. Sure."

"Great." And, since I didn't want the conversation turning back to the museum and the inevitable question of why I happened to be there, I took a step toward the living room. "I'll go get it now before the others get here." Because once they did, there was no way Fran would mention the museum. Not in front of Marissa—whose oldest daughter had also been caught in the demonic crossfire. Thankfully JoAnn didn't remember a thing. A small blessing when compared to the rest of the overall horror, but a blessing nonetheless.

I trotted off before Fran could argue, leaving her to arrange our afternoon snack.

Our yard is half gravel and half grass, which gives us both a nice play area and a nice lawn. The storage shed is in the back of the gravel area, and as soon as I was out on the back porch—having been entirely ignored by both Elena and Timmy as I walked by—I realized I'd forgotten the key. Fortunately, Stuart is both lazy and a creative thinker. After coming out to get lawn equipment and forgetting the key on three separate occasions over the Christmas holidays, he finally got the bright idea to hide a spare in one of those fake rocks.

I circled the shed, ending up on the back side where we keep the ramshackle gardener's bench. There's a collection of clay and plastic pots off to one side, a five-month-old pile of topsoil covered with a tarp, and a little flower bed graveyard tucked up in the corner formed by the shed and the privacy fence. In the spring, I had the best intentions of trying to breathe some life into that garden.

Really.

In the meantime, Timmy's been using the area to plant his "things." As in, he uses his plastic shovel and rake to dig holes, then he fills them with a wide variety of toys. I'm not sure what the point is—maybe he thinks he'll grow a toy tree—but it keeps him occupied on the weekends.

Stuart had hidden his hollowed-out stone under the corner of the storage shed nearest the fence, shoved back behind one of the cinderblocks that forms the shed's foundation. I picked my way over all the debris—Timmy's toys, bags of potting soil, chipped clay pots, a coiled garden hose, a rusty watering can—then bent for the key. Above me, a nice wind from the ocean rustled the leaves in the tree, and I thought what a nice day it would be for an outdoor play date. Maybe I'd suggest to Fran that we bring the kids out on the patio.

I was debating whether it was warm enough to fill up Timmy's sand-and-water play table (and debating how much the other moms would hate me for getting their kids wet and dirty), when I heard gravel crunch behind me.

"Sorry I'm so slow," I said. "I forgot the—"

But the words died in my throat. Because that wasn't Fran barreling down on me.

This time, it really was a demon.

Five

The demon launched himself at me, and from my precarious bent-over position, I barely managed to defend myself. An offensive maneuver was out of the question.

Pots clattered as I fell backwards against the potting table, one clay pot cracking and slicing hard against my exposed upper arm. I tried to get my footing, but the ground was damp, and my feet slid in the muck.

The demon took advantage of my poor balance and lunged forward, pressing me backwards so that the edge of the table was digging into my back, just above the waistband of my jeans. A few minutes ago, I'd had an ice pick tucked in my back pocket. But I'd foolishly tossed it into the sink when Fran and Elena had arrived.

Not one of my brighter moves.

With one hand, the demon held my neck, and with the other, he wielded a knife, the tip of it pressed right against the corner of my eye. I stayed perfectly still, my heart pounding against my ribs, and my body screaming in pain from the splintery edge cutting into the exposed skin of my back.

He'd shoved my whole body upward, too, so now my feet barely touched the muck. I wanted to kick, but knew it wasn't any use. I had no leverage. And he had a large steel point just millimeters from my eye.

"Where?" the demon growled, his voice low and breathy. His dark hair matched the near-black eyes that were now locked on mine. All in all, he looked to be about thirty years old—or the shell of his body did, anyway. And that shell had been in damn good shape when it had died. Considering the grip he had on me, I think it was safe to say the body's former owner had worked out quite regularly. "Where is the stone? What have you done with the stone?"

I stayed silent, both because I was mentally calculating my odds, and also because I had no idea what stone he was talking about.

"Speak!" he demanded, his sour breath bathing me with the stench of rotting eggs and bile.

I fought a gag, then managed to cough out a response. "What stone?" I asked, completely perplexed.

I kept my eyes on him, watching for his reaction even as much as I was trying to trap him with my attention. Because if he was watching me, then maybe he wasn't watching my hand. The one that was currently stretching slowly—so slowly—toward the little silver potting trowel.

"*Bitch.* Do you think you cannot die, Hunter? Do you think we can only find it if you live?"

"Actually," I said, my fingers finally closing around the handle of the trowel, "it's you who isn't going to live."

As I made my declaration, I kicked up, taking advantage of what little leverage I had. I didn't need much, just enough to distract. At the same time, I thrust the trowel toward his face, aiming for his eye. I was hyperaware of the knife next to *my* eye, and I turned my head sharply away at the same time that I thrust, risking choking if he tightened his grip on my neck, but deciding I'd rather gamble with my breath than with my eye.

His scream of pain echoed my own, and I felt the fiery burn as the point of his knife grazed the soft tissue from the corner of my eye to my hairline.

I could see, though. Better, I could breathe.

Unfortunately, the point of my trowel had missed its mark, smashing against the occular bone rather than the eye itself. The demon wasn't dead, but he did release his death grip on my throat as he howled in pain.

I scrambled to keep the advantage, throwing myself on top of him, and upsetting the potting bench once again so that it finally collapsed in a clatter. I barely noticed. Instead, I was too busy aiming the silver point of the trowel once again at the demon's eye.

"Kate!"

Fran's voice. For a split second, I froze—and that was all it took. The demon twisted sideways, wrested the trowel from me, and put his extra hundred pounds of muscle to good use, shoving me down hard and holding the trowel against my throat.

"Kate?" she tried again. "What was that noise? Are you okay?"

I watched the demon, who nodded and let up on the pressure on the trowel.

"I'm okay," I yelled back. "I just knocked some stuff over."

"You need help?"

"No, no," I said, probably too quickly. "I'm fine."

In truth, I desperately needed help. I couldn't believe I'd let myself be distracted like that, but the fact is that I still haven't gotten used to hunting around civilians. But there was no way I was letting Fran come into the fray. My own life, I'd take responsibility for. The rest of my son's play group? No way.

"Well, okay," she said, dubiously.

"The others should be here any minute," I said. "Grab the door for me, okay? I'll only be a few more minutes." I kept my voice cheery as my eyes stayed on the demon.

He didn't waste any time. The instant Fran shut the door, he was back in my face. "The stone," he rasped. "You will release the stone."

"I don't know what you're talking about," I said, which happened to be the God's honest truth. Considering the trowel he had pressed against my neck, I was hardly in any position to bargain. Still, though, I couldn't resist. "And even if I did, I wouldn't give it to you."

I held my breath—not hard to do since he'd mostly cut off my air supply—and wondered if I'd gone one step too far. He obviously thought I had something he needed. I was banking on him wanting it badly enough that he kept me alive.

"Foolish Hunter," he hissed, the stench of his breath almost enough to kill me without the trowel. "His followers gather. We will free him from the shackles of his prison. We will make him whole."

Free him? My heart stuttered a bit as I remembered Tomlinson's words. "Free who? Andramelech?"

He bared his teeth in acknowledgment, his eyes burning red with fury.

"Where is he?" I insisted. "Where is he imprisoned?" As I spoke, I twisted, trying to upset his balance or get free enough to grab Timmy's green plastic rake, laying in the muck mere inches from my fingertips. But there are only so many things you can do with a sharp metal point pressed hard against your neck, and at the moment, escaping wasn't one of them.

"Give it to us," he insisted. "Or vengeance will be ours."

He shifted the trowel then, so that the handle rather than the metal point pressed against my neck. He was still sitting on me, my hands and hips crushed under his weight. I struggled to breathe, the world turning a hazy red and then sharply gray, as if someone had flipped it inside out.

I was losing consciousness, and no matter how hard I tried, I couldn't hang on. I had no strength. No energy. No . . .

"*Aaaaaaghhhh!*"

Suddenly, the trowel was off my neck, and as I gasped for breath, chocolate chip cookies rained down upon me.

I didn't waste any time pondering that oddity. Instead, I clambered to my feet, coughing and choking even as I reached for Timmy's rake. Laura stood frozen behind the demon, her expression absolutely terrified. Apparently she'd clobbered him with a Pampered Chef stoneware cookie sheet, and he didn't appear to be too happy about it.

As he lunged at my best friend, I launched myself back into the fray, my son's plastic rake my only weapon.

The demon had reached her, sending her scurrying backward behind the storage shed. "Laura, watch out!" I called, but it was too late. She stepped onto a curve of broken pot, fell backwards, and landed heavily on her arm.

I heard the snap of bone even from a few yards away. So did the demon, and he was on her in a nanosecond. I was just as fast, though, and I tackled him before he could get her. We rolled over and over, my anger fueling my actions. Anger at myself for foolishly being unprepared for an attack in my own backyard. And anger at the demon for going after my best friend.

He reached out, clawing for my neck, but this time, I kept my balance and footing. And I was pissed.

I knocked his arm away, then twirled the rake around like a baton until the handle was facing him. One solid punch to the face with my free hand—just because I felt like it—and then bam, I drove the rake home.

This time, I didn't miss his eye. The dense plastic sank in, and the demon was sucked out.

I allowed myself one sigh of satisfaction, then crawled through the muck to Laura.

"Damn, this hurts," she said, her face a little green.

"You could have gotten yourself killed," I countered.

She hugged her arm close to her chest. "Yeah," she said through gritted teeth. "Well in comparison, maybe this isn't so bad after all."

I put an arm gingerly around her and squeezed her tight. "Thank you," I said. "You scared me to death, and if you ever do anything like that again, I'll kill you myself. But thank you."

"Any time," she said. "And sorry about the cookies. I know Timmy loves chocolate chip."

"That's okay," I said, climbing to my feet so that I could help her up. "I think this play date is over."

I haven't been in a cast since I was eleven," Laura said, looking mournfully at the chunk of white plaster that now encased her forearm.

The doctor chuckled. "This only proves how young at heart you are."

"It proves how much of a klutz I am," she countered, bolstering our story about how she'd tripped in my backyard. We'd wanted to come up with something a bit more original, but Fran and the rest were in my house, and they'd witnessed Laura's ignominious entrance. Of course by that time I'd hidden the demon's body under the tarp that Stuart had used to cover the pile of topsoil. And at the first opportunity, I'd called Father Ben and begged him to deal with the body before Stuart got home.

I'd driven Laura to the emergency room, and Fran had taken Timmy and Elena back to her house. I wasn't happy that Laura had been injured, but I also knew that it could have been a lot worse. And for that, I said a silent prayer of thanks.

For that matter, I'd been mostly silent for the last twenty or so minutes. Because my soon-to-be-single friend—now happily hyped up on Vicodin—was chattering on with the doctor about anything and everything.

"Well," he said. "I think you're good to go."

"What now?" she asked, lifting her arm.

"I'm going to have the nurse come in with a referral slip and a prescription for painkillers. I want you to see Dr. Kline in a few days to follow up." He turned to me. "What about you?" he said, tapping his temple.

My hand automatically went to my own injury. "It's nothing."

"You trip and fall, too?"

Laura giggled, the reaction presumably the result of the Vicodin. "More or less," she said.

"Hmm." Finally, the doc nodded. "Keep some antibiotic ointment on it," he said. "And you might consider a tetanus booster."

"Right. Absolutely. No problem."

He nodded at me, then turned to go. He paused in the doorway and flashed Laura a smile as white as his lab coat. "Keep me posted," he said. And then he was gone.

Laura released a very long sigh.

I laughed. "Careful, Laura. You're not single yet."

"I'm pretty damn close," she said dryly. "We've filed the paperwork, and as soon as our sixty days are up, it will be final."

I frowned, and rolled a stool over so I could sit in front of her. "Laura, are you sure? All these years. Maybe you can work it out."

She shook her head. "No. I've been thinking about this for a long time now." She lifted a shoulder. "It's over. He had an affair. End of story. There's no going back from that for me. I can forgive a lot, but not cheating. Never that."

"I know," I said. "I couldn't either."

She leaned forward, propping her forehead in the palm of her uninjured hand. "God, Kate. How did I get here? How the hell did I get to the point where I'm flirting with doctors?" She held a hand up before I could comment. "No, don't answer that. I don't even want to go there."

"All right," I said, unable to keep the smile out of my voice. "What shall we talk about? Maybe we could take bets on whether Dr. Kline is more or less cute than your jailbait ER friend."

"He's at least thirty," Laura said.

"Uh-huh."

She pointed a finger at me. "Be nice to me," she said. "I know your secrets."

"Damn. You're right. I'm stuck with you as a friend forever."

That earned a genuine laugh. "I'd say we're stuck with each other. Who else would put up with us?"

I glanced at the door. "Doc Cutie Pie looked interesting . . ."

She smacked me with her free hand, and I shut up.

"Changing the subject to something less dangerous," she said. "Why the hell did I bean a demon with my best stoneware?"

"Because you love me and didn't want me to die at the hand of someone whose breath smelled worse than day-old broccoli?"

"Well, yes. Obviously. But why was Broccoli Breath in your yard?"

"I'm not sure," I said. "But it was pretty ballsy. The middle of the day. Other people around. That's not the usual modus operandi for the general demon population."

"He must have wanted to get you pretty bad," Laura said.

"I think he was more interested in some stone than in me," I said, then gave her the rundown of the demon's demands.

"But what stone?" she asked. "And isn't it bizarre that David was attacked out of the blue, too? Although I guess you guys *are* the only Hunters in town. If they're looking for something all demon-spookylike, you two would be the ones to harass."

"Mmm," I said, not particularly thrilled about being on that particular hot seat. But I'd gone in with eyes wide open, so I could hardly complain now. Still . . .

"Eddie's a Hunter, too," I said. "And considering the way David just popped up out of the blue, who knows? Maybe San Diablo is flooded with rogue Hunters that I don't know anything about." Suddenly I was feeling a bit less special. If San Diablo was well-protected, maybe my return to the workforce wasn't necessary after all. I could quit, return to my old way of life, and just be Kate Connor, toddler-wrangling soccer mom.

Honestly, I wasn't sure how I felt about that possibility.

* * *

I dropped Laura back at her house, then called Fran to check on Timmy. After she informed me that both he and Elena were napping on Fran's living room floor, I decided to head for Cutter's studio. Brian, the demon, and Laura's arm had foiled my plan to get in a workout. But there were a few things I wanted to talk with him about, and I figured now was a good time to do it. After all, I knew better than to interrupt Timmy's nap. Trust me, a demon has no fury like a little boy deprived of sleep.

Cutter's place—the Victor Leung Martial Arts Academy— is in a strip shopping center right at the entrance to our subdivision. I'd originally picked the place because of its proximity to my house and the 7-Eleven next door, which meant I could work out and stock up on milk all in the same trip.

The name had been a draw, too, but I'd quickly learned that Victor didn't exist. Sean Tyler, aka Cutter, had made it up, rightly figuring that it would more effectively draw in the customers.

In fact, Cutter shouldn't have had to resort to such blatant advertising ploys. He's one of the best martial arts experts I've ever met, and his resume is as long as my arm. He's a black belt several times over and he put his skills to practical use in the military.

His best qualification, though? He's patient. He's known since the first day I laid him out that I had a secret or two— call it stereotyping if you want to, but there aren't that many near-forty moms who could take down a former Special Ops commando—and yet he's never pushed me to reveal anything about my past. The strong, silent type—that's Cutter. And although I've known him for less than a year, I already knew I could trust him with my life. I could probably trust him with my secret, too. But I wasn't quite ready to go there yet.

He was finishing up a kickboxing class as I came in,

and nodded for me to wait for him. Usually I work out a minimum of three times each week, but over the holidays, I'd cut back, and I have to admit it was nice to see him again.

I sat in one of the chairs along the side of the dojo and watched the class work. Most of them were women, and most I recognized—moms who lived in the neighborhood, taking advantage of the time when their kids were in school to get a good workout.

For the most part, their form was decent. But this was all about toning and building self-confidence. Maybe the guttural yell would scare off an attacker, but maybe it wouldn't. And I'd hate to think what would happen if a demon passed one of these women in a dark alley and decided to cause a little mischief. One dead housewife might make a nice home for a waiting demon, after all.

I shivered a little, not liking the direction of my thoughts. There was a reason I'd agreed to come out of retirement, and those women were part of it. Even if San Diablo overflowed with rogue Demon Hunters turned high school chemistry teachers, I knew I'd stay on. My work might be secret, but it was important. And even though they didn't know it, those women were depending on me.

I spent the next five minutes watching Cutter finish the class. As they kicked and shifted and bounced, I watched and coached and silently urged them to chamber a little bit tighter, keep their arms a little bit stiffer, plant their feet a little bit harder.

Finally, Cutter dismissed the class and headed in my direction. "What do you think?"

"They look good," I said.

"Not as good as you," he said with a grin.

"If they did, you'd be out of work."

"True enough." He headed toward his desk and I followed. "Just give me a few minutes and we can work out."

"Not today." I wasn't dressed for a workout, but it wasn't unusual for Cutter to assume that's why I was there. I'd long ago convinced him that I had no intention of wearing a gi to work out. Why should I? I'd never once met a demon who would let me run home and change.

"No?" he said, stopping short of his desk, so that he was right in front of me, with no barrier between us. "In that case, to what do I owe the pleasure? Or is this the day I finally learn your secrets, Kate Connor, woman of mystery?"

He said the last in such a deep, melodramatic voice, that I had to laugh. "What do you think?"

"I think I'm out of luck again. Tossed aside. Kicked to the curb. No, no. Don't try to make me feel better. I know I'm just a black belt to you."

"But a charming black belt."

He grinned. "Well, yeah. That part goes without saying."

"Actually, you're not too far off the mark. I'm not here to reveal all, but I was hoping to get a little help from you."

He immediately turned serious—another reason I liked Cutter so much. "Whatever you need."

I hesitated a little bit. Other than Allie and Laura, I hadn't shared the details of the Eric mystery with anybody. But the truth was, I wanted help. More, I needed it.

And, yes, I trusted Cutter. So maybe this was my way of testing him. Get his help with a smaller secret, and work my way up to the bigger one.

"Do you remember that time you bumped into me in the bank?"

"You'd found a safe-deposit box key and you were trying to figure out which bank to go to."

"Right," I said. "And I did."

He waited patiently, and for that I gave him even more credit.

"I found the box, and it had a single slip of paper in it. A note from my first husband."

"I'm guessing it wasn't good news?"

"He was murdered, Sean."

Pity and sadness filled his face. "Oh, Kate," he said, and the pain in his voice so reflected my own deep hurt that I couldn't hold the tears back. They flowed down my cheeks, my shoulders shaking with the effort to pull them back in, to make it so that this had never happened.

Cutter said nothing, just pulled me close so that my face was pressed against his shoulder and let me cry it out.

I let him hold me as I tried to control my breathing, my body trembling with the effort of fighting to regain control. After a moment, I finally had it together enough to pull back and wipe my eyes and nose with the tissue he silently handed me.

"I'm sorry," I said.

"Don't be." Then he grinned and wiped at his now-damp shoulder. "Although I will say that you do always seem to be dousing me with water."

I rolled my eyes at his feeble attempt at humor. During our first meeting, I'd splashed him with holy water. Just to be on the safe side.

"Feel better?"

"Yes," I admitted. "And no." The no was for the embarrassment factor. And I was tempted to go out on the mat with him, just to prove that I could beat him up despite crying on his shoulder.

"Don't worry about it," he said, apparently understanding. "If your husband was murdered, I think you have cause to be a little shook up. Are you sure?"

"Pretty sure." I explained that the note led to another one, and between the two, insinuated that Eric had gotten in over his head with something, but I didn't know what. That much, of course, was true. I conveniently neglected to mention that I knew the general subject of Eric's involvement—demons.

"Eric's note said I should go talk to an old friend in Los Angeles," I continued. "But he'd passed away not long before I got there."

"So you're at a dead end."

"Literally."

He hooked a leg over his desk. "Fair enough, but what can I do?"

"Think like a guy," I said. "What would you do?"

"You mean if I'd gotten involved in something that might get me killed? But I didn't want my wife to know about it?"

I scowled, but he'd pretty much nailed it. "Didn't want your wife to know about it unless something went wrong."

"I'd tell a confidante," he said. "Although it sounds like Eric did that. The dead guy in L.A., right?"

"You're not helping me here, Cutter."

"I'm just getting warmed up," he said. "If it were me, I'd have a backup plan. In case my confidante died. After all, if it's the kind of thing that can kill me . . ."

He had a point. "And?" I prompted.

"Hide in plain sight," he said. "Who paid the bills?"

"I did."

"Did he have a desk? A pile where he kept scraps of paper? A box of stuff that was sent home from his old job after he died?"

"I've been through all of that," I said. "I looked at every single thing after he died."

"But you weren't looking for clues then."

"No," I said, agreeing with him. "I wasn't. I just wanted to keep as much of him around me as possible."

"Do you still have the stuff?"

I nodded. I hadn't been able to bear to part with it. "It's in the storage shed. A pile of banker's boxes."

"I'd take another look," he said. "This time, you might see something you missed."

I thought about that, and hoped he was right.

"What about the safe-deposit box?" he asked.

"What about it? There was only the one piece of paper in it."

"Are you sure Eric didn't have another one?"

"Honestly, I hadn't thought about it. The fact that he had one at all was enough of a shock."

"You were named on it, right?"

"Right. I don't remember signing for it, but I must have."

"So maybe he also had one all by his little lonesome."

I closed my eyes and took a deep breath. That Eric had a secret bank box that we both could access was one thing. That he'd had one entirely separate from me—a box that existed essentially outside our marriage, meant to hold his secrets—well, that was another thing altogether.

I thought about what Laura had said about cheating, about how she could never forgive Paul. Eric hadn't done that, at least not that I knew. But I hated this feeling—as if I'd lost a level of intimacy with my husband.

Even more, I hated the fact that a year ago I would have vehemently defended Eric against any claim that he was cheating on me. Now, my protests would still come but without quite the same amount of vigor.

"Why don't I poke around for you?" Cutter said.

I realized I was looking at my hands, and now I looked up, grateful for the support. I didn't relish the idea of traipsing around town looking for a mysterious secret box that might or might not exist. If Cutter was willing to inquire for me, I was more than happy to let him.

"Thanks," I said, expecting him to tease me that payment for services rendered would be the revelation of my secrets. He didn't, though, and I appreciated that. All in all, the man was a good friend. "Thanks," I repeated, this time going up on my toes to kiss him on the cheek.

"Oh, no you don't," he said. "I can stand your tears once because your husband was killed. Tears because I did a nice thing? No way. You'll completely burn me out on good deeds."

I laughed, then sniffed. "No tears," I said. "Totally dry here."

"Glad to hear it," he said. I started walking to the door, and he followed. "How's Allie doing?"

"She's good," I said. "I mean, after what happened . . ."

I trailed off. Everyone in town knew what had happened at the museum. Cutter had called me the day the story hit the papers, then called Allie and sent her flowers and a stuffed bear dressed in a karate outfit.

"I was only—" He cut himself off with a wave of his hand.

"What?" I demanded, hearing more than just curiosity in his tone. "What's going on?"

"Nothing. Never mind."

"Cutter . . ."

He sighed. "Dammit, Kate. I'm probably breaking a confidence here."

"She's my daughter and she's fourteen. Screw confidence."

"It's just that she was already so ramped up about learning to defend herself. Before what happened, I mean. Private lessons. Extra sessions. The works."

"And?" I prompted. That much, at least, was old news.

"So Christmas Eve, she calls me. Tells me that this semester she wants to step it up even more. Get in more practice, really kick it up a notch."

I nodded, trying to look unconcerned, but with a bad feeling growing in the pit of my stomach. "Did she say why?"

"Not specifically," he said.

I tried to shrug it off. "Well, it makes sense that she wants to be more prepared. After what happened, I mean."

"True, but this seemed to be more than that."

"What do you mean?" I asked warily.

He shook his head. "Almost like she had an agenda. I don't know. I'm not really sure. Honestly, that's why I wasn't even sure I should mention it to you."

I sighed. It didn't matter if Cutter was sure or not. I was.

My daughter was training to kick demon butt. And she was doing it without me.

Six

"Stone," David said, leaning against his desk and tapping a finger against his lower lip. "I don't have a clue."

"Damn," I said, leaning back against a giant periodic table of elements that had been affixed to an entire wall of David's classroom. "I'd hoped—"

"That since the demons attacked me first that maybe the mention of a stone would jog my memory? Make me suddenly recall that I'd tangled with a badass demon named Andramelech?"

"Something like that," I admitted sheepishly.

He laughed. "Sorry, Katie. I don't think this one's going to be that easy."

"No," I said dryly, "I'm beginning to get that impression."

"I don't like that a demon came to your house," he said, taking a step closer to me. He looked down at Timmy, who'd made himself comfortable on the floor. "The kids."

I nodded, touched by his concern. "I know. I called the alarm company from the car. I'm going to have them come in and add a few more motion detectors and some of those automatic lights for the front and back yards. And I called the cops, too."

"Really?"

I lifted one shoulder in a shrug. "I'm hoping regular patrols by the cops will keep the demon population on edge." After the museum incident, the police knew us, and were happy to help keep my already traumatized daughter safe. Plus it didn't hurt that my husband was running for county attorney, and happened to have garnered the law-enforcement vote.

"Katie . . ." His voice was soft, his eyes piercing, as if he could read every thought in my head.

There was an intimacy in the way he looked at me, in the way he called me Katie. And while I knew that I should run from it, I couldn't. "What? What is it?"

He shook his head, and the expression faded, leaving me to wonder if I'd seen it in the first place.

On the floor in front of us, Timmy banged on the floor, then laughed wildly. He was using one of David's red pencils to scribble a masterpiece on a sheet of lined notebook paper. "Look, Mommy!"

I bent down, happy for the distraction, then seriously contemplated his project. "Looks good, buddy," I said. "Is it a horsie?"

"Mom-*my*," he wailed. "It's Thomas!"

"Thomas?" David repeated.

"His train," I explained. Then I looked at the paper again, shifting a little so that I was coming at it from a different angle. "*Oh,*" I said enthusiastically. "Off to the side I couldn't see it clearly. But now I can totally tell it's a train. A really excellent train."

He grinned, then held the paper out to me. "For you, Mommy."

"Aww, thanks, sweetie. I love it." I gave him a quick kiss on the cheek. "And I love you, too. You're being such a good boy."

He was, too. I'd retrieved him from Fran's apartment after leaving Cutter's studio, and we'd come straight to the school. I'd come early on purpose, knowing that Allie would still be on the field for cheerleader practice. I felt a bit guilty, but I wanted to talk to David about this sudden flurry of demon activity. And I wanted to do it when Allie wasn't around.

"Three demons," I said, getting back to business. "And no clear idea what they want. A stone, but *what* stone? And where is Andramelech being held? And why did the demon in your apartment let you live? For that matter, why go after me at all? I don't have any stone."

"True," he said. "Maybe Andramelech is trapped in a cathedral cornerstone or something."

"Maybe even our cathedral," I added, liking the fact that we were at least exploring a few ideas. "Or maybe the stone is part of a ritual."

"Like a rune, you mean? A bloodstone that has to be placed perfectly when the moon is high."

"And then the demons dance naked around it and sacrifice a virgin?" I added.

"Something like that," he said. "It's a good theory."

"But it's only a theory. And unless we know what kind of stone we're talking about, it's a useless theory."

"A relic of some sort?"

"Possibly," I said. There was certainly precedent for that. Relics—like the bones of saints—are often desecrated by demons as part of some malevolent ritual.

"Father Ben's probably thought of it, but you should mention it again, just in case."

"I will," I said. "And as much as I hate the idea, I'll take a look through the donation inventory the committee's been putting together. I should put in a few hours this week anyway." The donation boxes were musty and smelly and I'd run across more than one determined bug, so this wasn't a project I was looking forward to.

I pressed my fingers to my temples and closed my eyes, wishing there were an easy answer. "The problem is that we have too many possibilities and no way to know which one is right," I said. "What we really need is Nadia Aiken."

"Who?"

"A Hunter Father Ben told me about," I said.

"And her name was Aiken?"

"Right. Why?" His forehead was lined with concentration. "David? What is it?"

"There's something familiar about that name," he said. "But I can't place it. *Damn.*" He shook his head, like a dog shaking off fleas. "Go on. What about her?"

"Is it related?" I asked, latching onto the Aiken thing. "Something to do with a stone? With Andramelech?"

"I told you I don't remember," he said. "But I can't imagine that it would be. I've never heard of Andramelech, and I can't recall any mission I've worked on that involved a stone."

"The Hunter herself? Father Ben said she was hunting Andramelech, then disappeared about five years ago. Have you met her?"

He shook his head slowly. "I suppose I could have, but . . . No," he finally decided. "That doesn't feel right."

"Damn."

"It'll come to me."

"Maybe she went rogue, too, and your paths crossed?"

"Dammit, Kate, I already told you I don't remember."

"Fine," I said, holding my hands up in surrender. I knew I'd been pushing, but David's vague memory was the only lead we had. Which, considering it wasn't a lead at all, was pretty pathetic.

Near my feet, Timmy started banging his red pencil on the ground, gleefully shouting, "Dammit, Kate! Dammit, Mommy!"

David sighed. "I'm sorry."

I shot him a frown, then bent down to distract Timmy. That was the key in these situations. Telling him no would only burn the forbidden words into his brain.

"Okay," I said, sitting cross-legged by my son, who immediately started rolling the red pencil over the floor. "So the Aiken connection isn't going anywhere . . ."

"That's because there *is* no Aiken connection."

"—so that leaves Father Ben," I finished. Beside me, Timmy had climbed to his feet and was chasing the pencil, then kicking it when he got close. The game was proving most entertaining, and he was belly laughing as he scrambled after his exciting new toy.

"And patrols," David added. "As determined as these demons are, I wouldn't be surprised if there were a few more of the freshly made critters running around San Diablo."

"Tonight," I said, agreeing. "We'll watch the news and go tonight."

"Allie, Mommy!" Tim hollered. I turned to find him halfway in the hallway, the red pencil at his feet.

"Come on back in the room, sweetie," I said, looking at my watch. "And I haven't forgotten about your sister. She's not due for another twenty minutes."

"She's early," my daughter said, sidling in to the doorway. She aimed a hard look at both me and David, then leaned against the frame, her arms crossed over her chest. "So, like, you wanna tell me what's going on?"

My heart skipped a beat, and I glanced over at David.

He held his hands up. "I think that's my cue to exit," he said.

"Chicken," I countered.

His smile reached all the way to his eyes. "You're the parent here."

That I was.

"Come on, Tim," David said. "We can play race in the hallway."

That got my little boy's attention, and he toddled after David, giving his sister a happy wave, which she completely ignored.

"Well?" she demanded, her tone an exact duplicate of the one I use when trying to cajole my daughter into explaining some particular bit of misbehavior.

"Shut the door," I said. "We should talk."

From her expression, I expected a snarky response. But apparently my fourteen-year-old was growing up, because she reined it in, then gently shut the door. It was the *gently* part that really impressed me.

"So, what's the deal?" she asked. "You told me the thing at the museum was a onetime thing, and that—"

"David was attacked at the beach Saturday night and then again at his apartment. And I was attacked this morning. In our backyard."

"Holy shit!" She clapped her hand over her mouth. "I mean, no kidding?"

"No kidding," I said.

"So, like, you guys are going to go out tonight and try to find who did it? Is that the deal?"

I almost said yes. It would be so easy. I could simply say that this was another unusual, off-the-cuff, never-gonna-be-repeated incident.

But while the words might come easily, the lie itself wouldn't. Not anymore.

It was time to tell Allie the truth, consequences be damned.

"That's the deal," I said. "But it's not the entire deal."

Her brow furrowed, and I could see the wheels turning. "You never really stopped, did you? You and Daddy had a whole secret thing going, and I never even knew! *God*, Mom!"

"No!" I said, wanting to stop her tirade before it got started. "No."

She stood there sullenly, waiting for me to go on.

"We did retire. And I was happily retired for years. I loved my life with your dad. No demons. Just us. The three of us. And no monsters sneaking in around the edges to shake things up. Even after Daddy died," I added. "Even then, we were just living our life, you and me. Remember?"

"I remember. But?" She still sounded surly, but the curiosity was winning.

"But then something happened last summer. And, yeah, I kind of came out of retirement."

"Last summer?" she repeated. And I knew she was thinking back to what had happened one summer day. Danger to her and her brother, and my own terrifying fear.

That day had to make more sense to her now. If demons ever really made sense, that is.

"So, like, you've been doing this demon-hunting thing for four months?"

"About that," I said.

"You lied to me." Her voice was small, the hurt unmistakable.

"Parents have to make decisions every day, Allie. I'm not sure if I made the right one, keeping it from you back then. And I'm not sure if I'm doing the right thing now by telling you. All I can do is stumble through, and hope you know that no matter what, I love you more than anything."

She didn't say anything. Instead, she slid into one of the student chairs and put her head down on the little desk.

"Al?"

Nothing.

"Al?"

"What?" came the muffled reply.

"Do you understand?"

She looked up at me. "I asked you point-blank, and you *lied*."

I moved closer and put my hand on her shoulder. She immediately jerked away. I grimaced and tried again. "You're absolutely right," I said. "One hundred percent, on the nose right."

That worked. Or, at least, it worked a little, because she lifted her head and peered at me suspiciously. "Go on."

"You were so scared that day," I said, stumbling over my words. "I wanted to keep you safe, your body and your heart. I wanted you to feel safe, to forget about what happened and not be haunted by it."

"So you lied."

I drew in a breath. "Yes, Allie, I did. And I'd probably do it again, too. I truly believed I was doing the right thing."

She cocked her head. "But . . ."

"But I knew I couldn't keep the truth from you forever. For one thing, you have a right to know. And for another . . ." I trailed off, tilting my head back to look at the ceiling, as if drawing strength from above. "When I learned that your dad had rejoined *Forza* without telling me, it hurt. It hurt a lot, actually. And I realized how much it would hurt you to learn that I'd been keeping secrets, too."

She shoved her tongue into the corner of her cheek, but didn't say anything.

"That's why I wanted to tell you, Al."

"You *didn't* tell me," she countered. "I walked in on you. Or had you forgotten?"

"Watch the tone, Allie," I said. "This may be an argument, but I'm still your mother."

A beat, then she slumped down again. "Whatever."

I almost called her on it, but the snide tone had disappeared. And, honestly, I could understand her irritation.

"I was going to tell you," I promised. "I'll admit I wasn't entirely sure when or how. But I really did have the intention. You just forced the issue."

Another sullen stare.

"Cross my heart and hope to die," I said.

The blood seemed to drain from her face, and I realized too late that was the absolute worst thing I could have said.

"I'm *not* going to die," I said. "I promise." Which was a ridiculous pledge, but one I fully intended to keep. Thankfully, my daughter didn't call me on it.

"So, like, what? You and Mr. Long are going to walk around town looking for creepy guys?"

"Something like that," I admitted. "Although simply being creepy won't cut it. There are a lot of creepy folks who aren't demons."

She slid out of the chair and walked to the window, then stood there, staring out at the side of the building where the school buses were pulling in to pick up the kids from extracurricular activities. I watched her in silence, not wanting to press, knowing that I was doing the parental version of walking on glass.

I wanted her to say it was okay, and that she loved me. At the same time, I also knew that was a fantasy. Allie was deep in puberty, and that translated to hormonal hell. I wasn't going to be getting hugs and kisses out of this deal. I'd be lucky to avoid the cold shoulder and months of locked-in-her-room, plugged-into-her-iPod sulking.

Finally, she turned back to me, her expression determined. "I want to help."

So much for my fantasies of household peace.

"No," I said, bracing for a bout of teenage fury.

"*Mother!* I can totally help. I *want* to help."

"Fine," I said. "You can help. You can go by the cathedral every day and fill bottles with holy water for me and David. You can read the newspaper and listen to gossip and if you hear anything suspicious, you can let me know. You can even help me keep the weapons clean and oiled. But you're not going out on the street with me. You're not patrolling."

"Why not?" she demanded.

"Because I say so."

"That is *so* unfair!"

"Yes, it is. It's incredibly unfair that I would want to keep you safe."

She lifted her chin. "I can fight. I can take care of myself."

I nodded slowly. "Right," I said. "Because you've been working out. You've been practicing. Eating right. Getting in shape."

"Yeah," she said, but her head tilted sideways, the way it always does when she hasn't quite figured out which direction I'm coming from.

"Keeping a few secrets from your mom, kiddo?"

She pressed her lips together, opened her mouth, then closed it again and looked at her shoes. Didn't matter. I knew what she was thinking: I had secrets. She did, too.

I gave her credit though, for not throwing that back in my face.

"What did you tell Cutter about why you wanted to work out more?" I asked gently.

"It's no big, Mom. I'm just trying to, you know, punch it up a bit."

I waited an appropriate beat, and then, "Allie, sweetheart. Don't bullshit a bullshitter."

I could tell from her eyes that she knew she'd been busted. Self-defense was the last thing on my daughter's mind.

Again, to her credit, she didn't deny the accusation. "Then let me help," she pleaded. "Cutter says I'm good."

"You're not good enough."

"I could be."

"You're fourteen."

"So were you," she shot back.

"And now I'm almost forty, and I'm your mom, and I say no."

"You're being completely unreasonable!"

"You're right. I'm a horrible, horrible person."

"I hate you!" she screamed, the words ripping through me like a hot wire. "You totally lied to me and now you're not even trying to make it better."

Tears streamed down her face and she wiped them away angrily, then stomped toward the door.

"Allie!" I called, but it was too late. The door was open and she was in the hallway. I was right behind her, but she was already gone. "Allie! Come back here right now."

"I'll get a ride from one of the girls," she shouted back, not even turning around. And then she disappeared around a corner, and I leaned against the door frame, banging the back of my head against the hard metal.

In the hall, David and Timmy were still playing with the pencil. David sent me a questioning look, but I waved it away, really not in the mood to rehash the scene.

Timmy didn't catch onto the nuance of my expression. He looked up at me, the pencil clutched tight in both hands.

"Allie mad, Mommy?"

"Yeah, baby," I said. "Allie's mad."

Dinner that night crackled. And not because I'd burned the food. No, this time all the heat was coming from my daughter, who had reluctantly emerged from her bedroom, tromped down the stairs, and plunked herself in her seat at the table.

"Al, can you pass me the butter?" Stuart asked.

"Sure," she said, her voice bland.

"And the rolls this way, please," I said.

Allie ignored me.

"Allie," I said sharply. "The rolls."

She kept her mouth closed, but ran her tongue over her teeth. Then she handed the basket to Eddie. "Could you pass that to my mother, please?"

Eddie snorted, then looked at me. "Hoo-boy. You're in the doghouse, eh?"

I scowled at him, but took the rolls.

Stuart looked from me to Allie to Eddie. "What?" he asked.

"It's nothing," I said.

"Yeah, right," Allie said. "If it were so much nothing, then—"

"*Allie.*"

She sank down in her seat and took a bite from her roll.

"Is anyone going to tell me what the trouble is?" Stuart asked.

"No," Allie and I said in unison, causing Eddie to snort and choke on his iced tea.

Stuart looked at me, but I pretended not to notice, instead patting Eddie gently on the back.

"Allie's mad, Daddy!" Timmy said, apparently wanting to join in the fun.

I held my breath, wondering how much of the earlier conversation my little human sponge had heard.

"I got that, Sport," Stuart said. "How about you? Are you mad?"

"Nuh-uh. Want a joke?"

"Sure," Stuart said.

"Knock, knock."

"Who's there?"

"Banana!"

"Banana who?" Stuart asked.

"Banana poop!" he exclaimed, then cackled as if that was the cleverest joke ever. To him, it probably was, and I decided to forgo the usual lecture on appropriate dinner-table conversation. Because as much as I prayed that we'd pass swiftly through the toddler potty fascination phase, I also had Timmy to thank for very definitively changing the direction of the conversation.

Stuart apparently decided that it was best not to get in the middle of an estrogen-drenched argument. "Here's one for you, Tim. What's a ghost's favorite berry?"

"I dunno."

"A *boo* berry."

Timmy, as expected, laughed and laughed. Then he shoved his fist into the air. "Me! Me!"

"Go on, kid. It's your turn."

"What's a ghost's favorite dinner?"

"I don't know," Stuart said.

"Peanut butter!" Timmy announced, so tickled with his own brilliance that he almost fell off his booster seat.

Which pretty much set the tone for the rest of dinner. The men telling each other bad jokes with no punch lines, and the women not talking to each other at all.

Welcome to suburbia.

After dinner, Allie cleared her plate without being asked. "I'm going over to Mindy's to do homework," she told Stuart, who looked at me for confirmation.

I nodded, he relayed it, and Allie ran upstairs to get her backpack.

"What's this all about?" Stuart asked me.

"You really don't want to know," I said.

"Mmm." He watched me with curious eyes, then traced a finger along the scrape on my face. The one I'd already forgotten. "And this?"

"Long story," I said, feeling suddenly lost and alone. I shook my head, trying to get my emotions back on track. "It's nothing. Really."

He caressed my face, then gently cradled my chin. "Kate, sweetheart, have you thought that maybe I *do* want to know?"

I forced a laugh. "Stuart, don't be silly. There's nothing to tell. It's just a scratch."

His forehead creased. "And this spat with Allie? Is that a scratch, too?"

"She's fine. Everything is fine." I turned away from him, deliberately cutting off the conversation. I could feel his eyes on me, then heard him exhale loudly before getting up to make himself a scotch and soda. I turned, saw the hurt in his eyes, and cursed myself for keeping secrets.

"Well, we've got dinner out tomorrow," he said, referring to the celebratory dinner we'd planned for the night before he officially announced his candidacy. "Tell me everything will be back to normal by Wednesday," he added.

"Totally."

"And by everything, I mean Allie, too."

"Right," I said. "I got that. No worries. Teenage angst. It'll blow over by the morning."

Not an entirely accurate statement, but since my nose didn't start growing, I figured I was safe. For now. How much longer I could keep spinning a web of lies, though, *that* I didn't know.

I spent the next half hour or so puttering around the kitchen, cleaning up, avoiding Eddie's amused glances, and trying to ward off another spate of completely un-funny jokes from my son.

What I didn't intend to do was run after Allie and make her talk to me. She needed time to calm down. Needed space from her mom. For that matter, it would probably be best if she just spent the night with Mindy and calmed down.

Theoretically best, that is. But I couldn't quite get my head around that.

The fact is, this was the first real knock-down, drag-out

fight I'd had with Allie. And I really didn't like the feeling it left in the pit of my stomach.

I sighed and tossed a dishrag into the sink. "Dammit," I muttered.

Stuart had long since retreated to his study, but Eddie was at the table, working a crossword puzzle. "Go on," he said. "You know you want to."

"That obvious?"

"Like a goddamn bonfire."

I stood undecided in the kitchen for a few more minutes, trying to decide how much stock I would lose with my daughter if I headed over there and made her talk this out. Lots, I figured, but I didn't much care. Who was it who said you should never go to bed mad? Whoever it was, they probably had a teenager.

Our backyard butts up to Laura's, our yards separated only by our two fences and a narrow utility easement. I slipped on a pair of Keds, grabbed a light jacket and one of the ice picks—just in case—and took off across the yard.

I tapped on Laura's kitchen door, then let myself in. "Laura?"

"In here," came the reply from the living room. I found her on the couch, surrounded by boxes of photographs and photo albums.

"Revisionist history," she said, in response to my querying look. "I can't burn the bastard's picture since Mindy still has some allegiance to the scum-sucking pig. But at the same time, I don't want his pictures in our living room."

"So, you're . . . what?"

"Reframing the photos for around the house, making her an album for her room, and then tossing the rest of the damn things into a box in the storage shed." She aimed a sweet smile at me, then held up her cast. "And when this is better, I may even ceremoniously cut him out of a few of our wedding photos."

I'm not entirely sure her enthusiasm for erasing Paul was healthy, but considering I wasn't exactly the picture of perfect family life at the moment, I was hardly in a position to comment.

"Did you talk to Allie?" I asked, taking a seat on the couch next to her.

"Allie didn't appear to be in a talking mood," Laura said. She aimed a curious glance my direction. "What happened? Another fight about eyeliner? Did you ban her from cheerleading?"

"Worse," I said. "I banned her from demon-hunting."

"Whoa." She put down the picture she was holding. "Tell me."

So I did. The whole bloody, gut-wrenching thing.

"Oh, sweetie," she said, leaning over to give me a quick hug. "She's a teenager. She doesn't really hate you. And this is going to blow over."

"But?"

"But I did warn you."

"Yeah," I said, "you did." I pushed up off the couch and started toward the stairs. "Is she in Mindy's room?"

Laura shook her head and gestured toward her back door. "They went across the street to the park. I told them to be back by eight."

Our neighborhood has several small parks scattered throughout, and one large community center with a rec room and a pool in the middle of the subdivision. Laura's house is right across the street from one of the nicer playscapes, and lately the girls have been going over there in the evening to sit on the swings and ponder the great mysteries of life. Either that or talk about boys.

Laura suddenly gave me a sharp look. "Oh, God. Was that okay? Should I have kept them here?"

"Of course not. There's no reason to think the girls are in danger. And it's not like they haven't been to the park a million times before." All of which was true, but I still couldn't help the quick twinge of fear in my chest. I took a breath, suppressing it as paranoia. Even for a Demon Hunter, there's a fine line between being protective and being ridiculous, and I couldn't keep Allie in my sight every second of every day. And the park really was safe, brightly lit as it was, and surrounded on three sides by charming houses that vaguely resembled Laura's home.

I snagged two Snickers from Laura's stash, then headed across the street, my peace offering in my jacket pocket. Sure enough, I found the girls on the swings, their backs to me, their heads close together.

I tromped across the gravel, and Mindy twisted around, saw me, then whispered something to Allie. My daughter, I noticed, didn't bother to turn around.

I jerked my thumb back toward Laura's house. "Why don't you give me and Allie a few minutes?"

"Sure, Mrs. Connor," Mindy said. And then she was up and out of there, clearly wanting to get far away before the blood started to fly.

I took her seat on the swing next to Allie, then offered my kid a Snickers. She took it with a mumbled, "Thanks," and we sat there quietly for a few moments, using our toes to push ourselves back and forth in the swings.

"I'm sorry I said I hate you," Allie said, and I'm pretty sure my heart swelled nine sizes. "But you're being totally unfair."

"Whoever told you the world was fair?"

She sighed, letting her head drop back as if she were

contemplating the length and breadth of the universe. "*Puh-lease*, Mom! That's such a lame comeback."

I laughed. "Maybe," I said. "But it's true. The fact is, I worry about you, Al. You're always going to be my baby, and I'm always going to want to protect you."

"You can't protect me forever, Mom."

She jumped off the swing and started to pace in front of me, kicking gravel up with the toes of her sneakers and making a clatter that echoed through the night. Loud enough, in fact, to muffle the sound of approaching demons.

Which explains why I didn't hear the one who sprinted from behind a cluster of cypress trees, his knife glinting in the moonlight as he raced straight for my daughter.

Seven

"Allie!" I leaped off the swing even as the spry, elderly demon leaped toward my daughter, his wrinkled face split wide with a devilish grin. He got there a second before I did, his grimy hands going for her throat and knocking her to the ground.

Allie screamed, and I landed a roundhouse kick right in his gut, sending him tumbling off her and into the gravel. He barely even looked at me, but lumbered back up, then tried once again to grab Allie as I pulled the pick out of my back pocket.

As the demon scrambled again for Allie, she kicked and screamed, trying to climb to her feet and get away from his grasping hands. His back was to me, and I needed an eye, so I leaped on him piggy-back style. He howled, then slammed me backward hard against the tiny stones. He was on top of me and I could barely move. My arm, however, was free, and even though I couldn't see his face, I knew where to aim the pick.

With a burst of energy, I thrust it toward the demon's

face, at the same time saying a quick prayer that the weapon would hit home.

I missed, though, and instead of gliding through his sclera and opening a portal to suck out the demon, all I did was land a nasty stab wound in the fleshy part under his eye.

He howled in pain, the sound echoing through the neighborhood. I held my breath, wondering if the neighbors would come out and half hoping they would. I'd rather kill the beast, but if Neighborhood Watch wanted to arrest the cretin, I could live with that, too.

Nothing, though, and I hardly had time to worry about it since the odious creature was scrabbling for Allie's throat again.

Enough.

I launched myself at him, knocked him to the ground, then trapped his neck with my shoe. "I am not the only," he growled, even as I raised my pick.

"But you're the one who's dead," I countered.

I started to slam the pick down, but the lights on the houses on either side of the park flipped on, startling me. Damned if the demon didn't use that to his advantage. He thrashed, getting out from under me, then disappearing into the dark night with a swiftness that was hard to reconcile with his ancient appearance.

I took my pick and slid it back into my pocket, then dropped down beside Allie and pulled her close.

She cried and trembled in my arms, her face pressed against my shoulder as I battled down my own anger that a demon had not only attacked my kid, but that he'd survived.

"I'm such an idiot," she said. "If you hadn't been here—"

"*No,*" I said, hugging her even tighter. "Don't even say that."

"I thought I was all that, you know?" she said, her face

still pressed against my chest. "Working out with Cutter. But I'm not. I totally suck, and I—"

"You can train," I whispered, tilting her chin up so that she was looking at me. "I'll train you myself."

"Really?" she asked with a sniff.

I saw the scrape marks from the demon's fingernails on her neck and down into her collar. I traced my finger there, my heart just about to break. "Yeah," I said, my fingers closing on the long chain she wore. "Really."

A ring hung on the end of the chain, and I tugged it out. Eric's ring.

Her hand closed over mine, and a small frown trembled at her mouth. "I'm sorry," she said. "I missed Daddy. I guess I thought of it like a good luck charm. So I went back up into the attic and got it out of your trunk. Some luck though, huh?"

"We're alive, baby. And it was lucky I came for you." I kissed her forehead. "Never discount good fortune," I said, dropping the ring back down into her shirt. "Even if it's wrapped up in bad."

"I can really train with you?"

"Yeah," I said. "You can. But that doesn't mean you're ready to help me. Not yet. Maybe not ever. But I want you ready to defend yourself."

I paused, expecting her to argue. She didn't, and I knew that I'd won this round. The cost, though? That, I still didn't know.

I offered Allie a moviefest in my bed, the way she used to when she was a little girl, but she turned me down in favor of a long, hot bubble bath. Considering how appealing that sounded, I couldn't say I blamed her. What was that old commercial? "Calgon, take me away"? That's how I felt at the moment. I'd gone from a demon-free holiday (well, after the whole kidnap-my-daughter incident) to suddenly having multiple mysteries on my plate. And to make matters worse, I wasn't making progress on any of them.

I still had no clue as to where Andramelech was imprisoned, or what the demons wanted with David. Worse, I had no idea why his minions were jumping me (and now, apparently, Allie). I didn't know the location or identity of the mysterious stone. And I had no idea what my husband had been up to that had ended up getting him killed.

All in all, it sounded like a damn fine night for a bubble bath.

Instead, I decided to conquer the storage shed.

When Eric died, his assistant had given me three large boxes filled with files and papers. I'd glanced through them at the time, but just seeing his handwriting had been enough to bring me to tears.

The stuff was mostly junk, but I couldn't bear to part with a single Post-it note. I'd sealed up the boxes with packing tape and shoved them in the hall closet.

After Stuart and I married and bought our house, the boxes had been moved to the storage shed, where they remained, buried under the dribs and drabs of our new life.

It was after eight by the time I added the shed to the evening agenda, and the yard was pitch black. Not that a little night ever slowed me down. I grabbed a flashlight, popped my head into the playroom to tell Stuart and Tim that I'd be in the backyard, and then I set off to tackle the boxes.

After fifteen minute of pulling out boxes and furniture and bug-covered lawn equipment, I was beginning to wish I'd waited until the morning. There was no stopping me now, though. I'd already cleared a path to the back of the shed, and I'd be damned if I was going to put it all back without even reaching my goal.

I hauled out an ancient exercise bike and box of Stuart's old eight-tracks (*why* do we keep this stuff?), and then *finally* found the first of four boxes underneath a sewing machine cabinet I'd bought on a lark at a yard sale about two years ago. As foolish purchases go, that one was particularly off the wall, since I neither own a sewing machine nor know how to sew. In my defense, at the time, I'd been meaning to learn. I just never seemed to get around to it.

The boxes were in two piles, and I pulled the top two down, sat on one, and peeled the lid off the other. Papers, knickknacks, and a few bound notebooks. That looked promising, and so I hefted it up, then hauled it onto the back porch so that I could peruse my first husband's secrets under the light of the porchlight.

The papers smelled musty, but thankfully I found no bugs as I dug through the box, trying to find that one gem that would explain everything to me. Unfortunately, mining for gems in file boxes is about as futile as doing it in a backyard, and I was coming across precisely nothing except dust and the promise of a killer allergy attack.

I was about to give up and go get another box when I noticed a small leather-bound book at the very bottom of the box. It was about one-quarter of an inch thick and bound in heavy-grained leather with Addresses printed across it in faded gold stenciled letters.

Not that there's anything inherently odd about an address book, but in this case, something didn't seem right. During our marriage, we'd kept a family address book by the phone in the kitchen in which we collected the names and numbers of our friends and Allie's school friends. General life numbers.

After our retirement from *Forza*, I'd made a big production out of buying Eric the trappings of a traditional office, a luxury we'd never experienced. I'd spent more money than I should buying a leather organizer complete with tabbed sections and enough organizational tools to run a small country. It even had a matching pocket-sized address book in which the busy executive who had everything could transfer information so that he was never without his contacts.

Eric had sworn to me that he loved it, and I'd seen him use it often enough, both the large organizer and the tiny address book.

So why did he have this battered black book?

Feeling more than a little trepidation, I grabbed it, wiped the dust from the cover, and flipped the book open. There, neatly printed in familiar handwriting, was the name *Eric Crowe*, and his old office number.

I started to flip through the pages, driven by an odd mixture of curiosity and foreboding, but I didn't get very far. The back door burst open, and Stuart stuck his head out. I immediately dropped the book back into the box.

"What on earth are you up to?"

"Oh. Um. Nothing?"

He looked at the open box at my feet. "Then you're looking in the wrong place. That box is completely full."

"Ha-ha," I countered. "I just had the urge to start cleaning out the storage shed."

"And why not?" he said. "That's what every reasonable person does after dark on a Monday."

"Fine," I said, hefting the box to carry it back to the storage shed. "You can help me this weekend."

He chuckled. "Me and my big mouth."

I put the box on the ground in front of the shed, then

reached in and grabbed the book. I tucked it into my back pocket and hoped Stuart wouldn't notice. Not that I was doing anything that odd. Technically, it was my address book now. I could look at it if I wanted to.

Fortunately, it was a nonissue, and instead of calling me on my strange behavior, he helped me reload the storage shed. "You really want to tackle this mess over the weekend?"

I shrugged. "Maybe not. Now that we're putting everything back, the urge is dimming."

"Mmmm."

"So were you looking for me?" I asked.

"Timmy's conking out. Is it a bath night? Because Allie's still in there. I can bathe him in our tub if you want . . ."

He trailed off, and I could tell from his tone that he dearly hoped I didn't want.

"He can skip tonight," I said. "It's already way past his bedtime. But get him in his jammies, would you? I want to go check on Allie." I would have preferred saying nothing to Stuart, but he'd seen us come in the back door, and he'd immediately honed in on Allie's pale appearance and fear-filled eyes. I'd told Stuart we'd seen a strange man in the park, and he'd been creepy enough to scare Allie. I figured if any of the neighbors bordering the park reported a man climbing their fence, the stories would jibe.

"Will do," he said, then pulled me in for a kiss. "I love you girls, you know."

"I know," I said.

"After that fiasco before Christmas . . ." He trailed off with a shake of his head.

"What?"

He pulled me in close for a hard, deep kiss. "I just worry about you, Kate. About you and the kids. It's a crazy world we live in."

"I know," I said, meaning it more than he could know. "I worry about us, too."

By the time I got upstairs, Allie had finished her bath and retreated to her room. I decided that reinforcements were necessary, so I detoured to the kitchen, got milk and Oreos, then returned to her room with our treats carefully balanced on a tray. Obviously neither one of us was sticking to a diet today.

I found my daughter sitting up in bed, her knees pulled up to her chest, and her well-loved stuffed tiger clutched in her arms. She wasn't wearing her iPod and the stereo wasn't blaring. She was just sitting there hugging TigTig. My daughter, who hadn't stopped moving since the first time she'd kicked me in utero.

It just about broke my heart.

"Allie, honey. How are you doing?"

She shrugged, and I slid the tray carefully onto the foot of the bed, then crawled up and got next to her.

"I brought Oreos," I said. "If the commercials are right, Oreos can pretty much make anything better."

The corner of her mouth curved up, and she tilted her head to the side and looked at me. "Even the fact that I'm an idiot?"

"You're not an idiot," I said. "You're young and you're eager, but you're not an idiot."

"I guess."

I pulled her close and hugged her hard. "No idiot talk," I said. "That's my best girl you're talking about."

"Mo-*om*," she said, in her most exasperated tone, giving me a peek at the Allie I knew hiding under the shell of the scared teenage girl.

"Don't 'Mom' me," I countered. "I love you. Even if you are an idiot."

That earned me a thwap on the head with TigTig, but it also earned me a smile.

The smile, however, quickly faded. "You were lying to me, weren't you? Earlier, I mean."

I frowned, because I wasn't sure where she was going with this. We'd already hashed and rehashed my nondisclosure, so this had to be something new. What about, though, I didn't know.

"The promise, I mean," she said. "What you said about promising not to die."

A thousand little knives stabbed my heart as tears brimmed in my eyes.

"I can quit, Allie," I said, taking her hands in mine. "If you're scared, I can walk away right now." That was a promise I would absolutely keep. I didn't want to—in the short time I'd been back on active status, I'd come to realize how much hunting was part of me—but I would. For my kids, I would absolutely give it up.

She shifted on her bed, stretching her legs out in front of her and turning to face me more directly. Her expression was bland, but there was a spark in her eyes as she worked through my offer.

"They'd still be there, though, right?"

"The demons? Yeah, they're pretty much not going to go away."

"And they might not know that you've quit. I mean, they might think you're still out to get them."

"I suppose that's true."

"I've been thinking that you're sort of like a cop. Or like Angie's dad."

"That's fair," I said, thinking of Angie, her friend whose

father was in the military. "But there is a risk, Allie. There aren't any guarantees in life, and I shouldn't have promised not to die. I can't make that promise. Nobody can."

She gave a shaky nod and pulled TigTig closer.

"What about that stuff? Do you take it with you? When you go out to fight the demons, I mean?"

"Stuff?" I repeated, trying to think what she could be referring to.

"The dust," she clarified. "Up in the attic."

"*Oh.* No," I said, vehemently shaking my head. "No, I don't take it."

"Why not? If you got hurt . . . I mean, someone could, you know . . ." She squirmed a bit. Apparently *you know* wasn't easy to speak.

I took her hands in mine and very gently shook my head. "The world doesn't work that way, Allie. We can't play God, sweetheart." I pressed our hands over her heart. "You know that, right?"

She nodded.

"But I *do* promise to be careful. Okay?"

"Okay, Mom." She gnawed on her bottom lip, clearly wanting to add something else.

"What is it, Al? What's still on your mind?"

"Mr. Long helps you, right? I mean, so that you're not alone? He'll help keep you safe?"

I thought about David. About patrolling with him night after night, the way he watched me so protectively, and the concern he showed for my kids.

"Mom?"

"Sure, baby. David will help keep me safe."

"And Eddie?"

I managed to withhold a smile. Eddie had flat out told me that he was out of the game. He wouldn't refuse his only pseudo-great-granddaughter, though. "You ask him to, okay? You ask, and I know he'll watch my back."

"And me? I want to help, too."

"Allie . . ." I fought to keep the sharpness out of my voice. "Didn't we just have this—"

"No, no. I get that. I mean like what you said before. Reading the newspapers and, I don't know, keeping an eye out for creepy guys."

"My priority right now is to get you to be able to defend yourself. You have enough to do with school and working out to keep you busy."

"But if I get the work done? Then you'll let me? Please?"

I looked in her eyes and knew that I had to say yes. Demon Hunting was part of her life, too, and she wouldn't be satisfied unless she was helping. I knew, because I could remember feeling the exact same way.

"Your schoolwork comes first."

"Totally," she said, crossing her heart with her forefinger. "So give me the lowdown," she said, and she looked so eager that I had to laugh.

"Later," I promised.

"But Mo-*om*. You know I'll just keep bugging you. Please? Please, please, please?"

"Fine," I said. "But this is the short version." I told her about Andramelech and Nadia, promising to fill in the details later. "Until then, if you have any time to do research, maybe you can learn what you can about the demon. Or see if you can find any reference to Nadia on the Internet. It's a long shot, but . . ."

"Sure. I can totally do that."

"Good," I said, then got up. "Now get some sleep."

"But what about Daddy?"

"What about him?" I asked.

"You're still going to let me look, right? Try to figure out what happened?"

"Yeah, sweetheart, I am. Same rules, though. School—"

"Comes first. Yeah. I got that."

"Good," I said, hiding a smile.

"Mom?"

"What, baby?"

"You still love Daddy, right?" It was a question she'd asked earlier, and my heart twisted with the realization that she could doubt that, even for a moment.

"Allie, sweetheart, I will *always* love your dad."

"No matter what we find out?"

"No matter what," I said.

She nodded, considering that. "Mom?"

I reached over and stroked her hair. "What, baby?"

"I love you."

My heart swelled. "I love you, too. More than all the stars in the sky," I added, in the familiar bedtime ritual from when she was a little girl.

"And all the angels in Heaven," she answered, and I swear I saw a little girl in footie pajamas curled up on the bed where my fourteen-year-old should be.

I'd spent the last fourteen years trying to keep her safe, and still she'd ended up in harm's way simply by being my daughter. Now, I could only pray that I was doing the right thing by continuing to hunt—and by letting her train.

I knew God would watch over my baby, but if she was good with throwing a knife . . . well, it never hurt to give the Lord a little bit of help with the job.

Eight

"I want answers," I said, unable to keep the anger and fear out of my voice. "The bastard attacked my daughter. If anything . . ." My voice hitched, and I tried again. "If anything happens to her, I . . ."

I shut my eyes, unable to even go there. Beside me, David took my hand, then gave it a gentle squeeze. I squeezed back, gratefully soaking in his strength. "We're going to figure this out," he said. "And we're going to keep her safe."

I closed my eyes and nodded. It was a hollow promise; I knew that better than anyone. But at the same time, I knew he meant it with all his heart and soul.

"All the good intentions in the world aren't going to help us," I said, looking at Father Ben, who was sitting behind his desk. I'd dropped Timmy at KidSpace that morning, then hooked up with David and Father Ben at the cathedral during David's lunch hour. The wait hadn't done my patience any good, and I was a bundle of nervous energy. I wanted answers, yes, but I also wanted to hit something.

"They've attacked David, me, and now Allie. And we still don't have any idea what the hell they want. Some damn stone that doesn't mean a thing to anybody." I gave Father Ben a significant look. "Or does it?"

"We might be getting close," he said. "I talked with Father Corletti a few hours ago. I know a bit more," he said. "But still not enough."

"Every little bit helps," David said, settling into a chair. "Shoot."

"Did you find Nadia?" I asked, taking the chair next to him.

"No luck there," he admitted, "although investigators are back on it. There's still low confidence within *Forza* that she's alive, but with this new activity related to Andramelech, the investigators have decided to renew their efforts."

"Good," I said. "But if it's not about Nadia, then what news did Father Corletti have for you?"

"Apparently he found a reference in an ancient text from within the Vatican library. An obscure reference to Andramelech. An interview with one of his followers."

I frowned. "I thought there were a lot of interviews with his followers."

Father Ben nodded. "Recent ones, yes. The cult members who suddenly snapped out of his spell, presumably because the demon's powers were cut off when he was bound. This interview is much older."

"What did it say?"

"Unfortunately, not enough," Father admitted. "The text was from the mid-1400s, and the subject was captured by a knight Hospitaller after a siege on a small village outside Jerusalem." He looked at me gravely, then lowered his voice to a whisper. "Every child in the village had been slaughtered," he said.

I shivered, my thoughts immediately turning toward my kids. "Is that why they attacked Allie? Are the children of San Diablo in danger?"

"I don't know," Father admitted. "Other than the attack on Allie, there's been no unusual activity related to children." He gestured to the police band radio on his credenza, his first purchase through his *Forza* expense account a few months ago.

"More likely she was attacked because she's your daughter," David said. "If the demon population is up to something, it makes sense to keep you off guard."

"And what better way to throw me off than to attack my kids."

"Exactly," Father Ben said.

"Which brings us right back where we were," I said. "We need to figure this out. And we need to end it." I looked at Ben. "So go on. The interview Father Corletti found. What else did it say?"

"Apparently Andramelech was trying to build his army. The reference said that the army would be 'amassed by mining the stores of kings and gathering his imprisoned compatriots.'"

"Uh-huh," I said, completely clueless. "So what exactly does that mean?"

"I'm afraid we don't know," Father Ben admitted. "The archivists in Rome are examining the collections in great detail now, hoping to find a secondary reference. Anything, actually, that might give us some insight."

"And in the meantime, we keep patrolling," I said. "Keep trying to locate new demons and pare down the operation." It wasn't a satisfactory solution, but at least it played to my strengths. Research had never been my strong suit. Unlike Eric, I'd always been much more inclined to forget the rationale and simply go forth and conquer. This time was no exception. And as much as I wanted an explanation, my blood burned to kick some demon ass. Go after my kids, and that's really the only possible reaction.

"It sounds to me like Andramelech was trying to free demons that had been imprisoned somewhere," David said.

"The prisons of kings," I said. "And any demon he freed would surely pledge allegiance to Andramelech, right?"

"Makes sense," David said. "Maybe while he was trying to free the other demons, he got trapped himself."

"But we're talking, what? Six hundred years? Wouldn't he just give up?"

"Time doesn't mean the same to a demon," David pointed out reasonably. "And if he was incorporeal for some of that time it could easily take centuries for him to not only locate the bound demons but determine how to release them."

"I suppose," I said, still a bit dubious.

"Actually, I think it's a good theory," Father Ben said.

"But how does it tie to San Diablo?" I protested. "There are no kings in California."

"Perhaps the reference to a king is metaphorical," Father Ben said. "Christ is King."

"A true relic of Christ," I said, turning the idea over in my head and deciding it had merit. "Except St. Mary's doesn't have anything like that. Do we?"

"Not catalogued," Father Ben said, shooting me a smile. "But I doubt there is something of such significance here."

"A piece of the cross?" I suggested. "It's possible something like that made its way here."

"The trouble is we simply can't know," Father Ben said. "In the meantime . . ."

"Damage control," I said. "And hope Rome comes up with something."

We all looked at each other. It wasn't much, but at least we were a bit further along than we'd been the day before.

I pushed myself up and out of my chair. "That's it, then. We'll talk when we learn more."

Beside me, David checked his watch. "I need to get back. I've got a class in half an hour."

I took a step toward the door, then paused. "Actually, Padre, there's one other thing."

"What is it Kate?"

"It's about Eric. I'm making no progress here. Can you call Rome? See what you can find out for me?"

"What did you find out from Father Donnelly?" Father Ben asked, referring to the priest that Father Corletti had referred me to. When I'd first learned that Eric had decided to train as an *alimentatore*, I'd called Father Corletti. After all, he'd been like a parent to me, and it was natural for me to turn to him when I was confused and hurt. That he might have inside information about my husband was a bonus.

He'd told me that Eric had been working with Father Donnelly but that beyond that, he had no specifics with regard to Eric's training. I'd called Father Donnelly and left numerous messages before I was finally able to get the man on the phone.

All my trouble, though, had been worth very little. He simply reiterated what I'd already learned. Eric, he'd said, had felt a calling to return to the folds of *Forza*. He'd planned on telling me, but never found the time or the words. He'd been an eager and excellent student, but as far as Father D knew, he'd only been a student. There was nothing in the teachings or their conversations that would suggest that Eric had delved into anything dangerous. And certainly not anything that would get him killed.

Father Donnelly had always believed that Eric's death

was a random mugging, just as the police had concluded all those years ago. When I shared Eric's notes with him, he agreed that Eric had fallen victim to foul play, but he had no more help to offer, only prayers that I would find the answer. Or, if not the answer, then that I would find peace.

So far, I'd found neither.

"Are you sure you really want to know?" David asked as we left the rectory with Father Ben's promise to do a bit more poking around.

I eyed him suspiciously. "Why? Are you suggesting I might not like what I find out?"

"I'm just saying that sometimes our memories are better than our reality."

"Right," I said, trying to process what he was saying. And, more important, what he wasn't saying. A shiver ripped through me, but whether merely a chill or a sense of foreboding, I didn't know. Eddie still believed that Eric was hiding within the man I knew as David. And although I believed David's denial, I couldn't quash the crumb of doubt that tickled the back of my mind.

Finally, I decided to bite the bullet. "What about it, David?" I asked, pausing in front of my car. "You told me that Eric was your friend. Did he tell you something?"

"It's been almost six years, Kate. Why reopen old wounds?"

"It's not your decision to make. It's Eric's. And he left me the notes. He wanted me to know."

"Back then, sure. But that was before you remarried. Before you had a son. Before you got a whole new life."

"But now I've stepped right back into the old one."

"Katie—"

I held up a hand. "You can't hold back on me simply because time has passed. That's not a decision you're allowed to make."

I watched his face as I spoke, saw the hesitation in his eyes. For a moment, I thought he would turn me down again. But then he nodded. "Fine, Kate," he said. "He left you those notes, so you're right. He must have wanted you to know."

"To know *what*?"

"Get in," he said, gesturing toward my car. "Give me a ride back to the school and I'll tell you while we drive."

"Start talking," I demanded as soon as I'd started the car.

"I can only tell you what Eric told me. And before you start interrogating me, let me tell you flat out that my mind is a little fuzzy on the details."

"Why?"

"I was in a car wreck, Kate," he said, thumping his cane on the floorboards. "I almost died. Sorry if that's inconveniencing you now, but . . ."

"Right. Fine. Go ahead."

"A few years back, Eric contacted Father Corletti and told him he wanted to train as an *alimentatore*. The father put him in touch with Father Donnelly, and they started from there."

This was old news to me, but I didn't want to distract David or slow down his rhythm. I kept my eyes on the road and kept right on driving.

"He studied, he researched, he did everything an *alimentatore*-in-training is supposed to do. And you know what?" he asked, turning to me. "He was really getting into it. One day he told me that he felt whole again. Like he'd lost a piece of himself when he'd given up hunting, but that he'd found it again in the research."

I pressed my lips together and forced myself not to cry. Unreasonable, I know, but right then, I felt like I'd been holding Eric back. Like he'd given up *Forza* only for me. Worse, that he resented me for it.

"It wasn't like that, Kate," David said, even though I hadn't spoken one word.

I sniffed, and brushed the pad of my thumb under my eye, drying an errant tear.

"In fact, he was planning on telling you. He wasn't sure if he wanted to be an active mentor or if he would rather take a research position. Either way, he wasn't going back into fieldwork."

"He told you that?"

"I think it's fair to say we discussed it."

"So what happened?"

"What did he decide?" David shook his head. "I don't think he ever did. He started to learn things about *Forza* that shook him up. Not about the organization itself, but about some of the people in it. *Alimentatores* and Hunters who'd turned traitor, lured by dark promises."

"Is that why he was killed?"

"Who knows?" David said. "But I do know that he was concerned about San Diablo."

I hit the brakes for a stoplight and turned to him. "What do you mean?"

"Demon activity. It seemed to be starting up again."

"Hold on," I said, ruffled. "I was here, too, remember? If there was any demon activity in San Diablo, I surely would have noticed."

"It was specific to Eric."

I turned sharply to look at him. "What exactly are you saying?"

"He was afraid he'd gotten in over his head. That some of the less-than-honorable Hunters were getting nervous about his questions. And they'd decided to focus the attention of their demon cohorts on him."

"Wait. *What?*" I tapped the brakes again, this time

causing a large truck behind me to lean on the horn. I made a rude gesture, but accelerated again. "Eric thought that he'd been targeted?"

"It was a theory," David said.

"He didn't tell me," I said, my voice almost a whisper. "And I didn't suspect a thing." I felt ice cold, and I stifled a shiver. "What do *you* think?" I demanded.

He sighed. "I don't know."

"So the notes were about what he'd learned?" I said a moment later. "That Eric had gotten in over his head with *Forza*? That he believed he'd been targeted by traitors and he wanted me to be careful?"

"That's my best guess," David admitted. "But it sounds like the trail has dried up."

"Do you know who betrayed him?"

"No," David said. "I'm not even sure Eric found out."

"What would you do if you knew for sure?"

"Anything I could to avenge my friend," he said.

Our eyes met, and I nodded in both approval and agreement. "And that's all there is?" I turned onto Oceanview, then slowed to 20 miles per hour since it was a school zone. "There's nothing more to tell me?"

"One more thing," he said. "Right before he died, he told me he had a lead."

"About *Forza*? About whoever had thrown in with the demons?"

"Yeah," David said. "More specifically, about who killed Wilson."

"Wilson?" I tightened my grip on the steering wheel, fighting the wave of unexpected grief. I'm not sure what I'd expected during this little chat with David, but a discussion of why Wilson died really hadn't been on the list.

Wilson Endicott had been my and Eric's *alimentatore* until

the day we'd retired. Where Father Corletti had been like a father to me, Wilson had been like an older brother. I'd trusted him, looked up to him, and I missed him terribly.

I'd been one day past Allie's official due date when I'd received word that Wilson's car had been run off the road. I'd always assumed his death had been caused by demons. Now, I wondered if *Forza* traitors had been behind it.

"What did Eric tell you?"

"Just that he'd been contacted by a Hunter who'd known Wilson. She had some information she wanted to share about his death, and she'd been poking around, trying to figure out who was safe. Apparently she stumbled across Eric's name."

"And?" We were in front of the school now, and the bell had obviously already rung, as kids were scurrying from one side of the campus to the other. I, however, wasn't letting David out of the car until I'd heard it all.

"And that's all I know. Wilson had sent Eric a few things not long before he was killed. Books, relics, kind of thing. He told Eric to keep the things safe, and that he'd be coming to California in a few months to retrieve a few of the items. Obviously, he never made it."

I fought to keep my expression bland. Eric had never told me about a package from Wilson.

"At any rate," David continued, "the girl used to be one of Wilson's Hunters, and she knew that Eric had received the package. She thought there might be a clue in the belongings. A clue about the betrayal."

"What was in the package? Did you ever see it?"

"Once," David said. "It was just an amalgamation of stuff. Some journals. A crucifix. A vial for holy water. A ring. A scapula. Even some photographs." He smiled at me. "Some were of you and Eric. Photos that Wilson had taken of the two of you training."

"Oh," I said, then closed my eyes. "I never saw them."

"I think he took them with him when he went to meet the girl."

"He gave her our photos?"

"Honestly? I don't have any idea. All I know is that he finally decided that it wouldn't hurt to meet with her."

"He didn't tell you what happened at the meeting?"

"Kate," he said gently. "He was going to meet her in San Francisco."

I should have seen it coming, but his words blindsided me. I closed my eyes and held tight to the steering wheel, wishing Eric had told me back then, before he died. If he had, I wondered, would he still be with me?

A ball of rage swelled in me, and I slammed my fist hard against the steering wheel, anger exploding from me. Anger at Eric for keeping his secrets, at myself for being so tunnel-visioned that I hadn't seen anything beyond the house and the child. And at David, because he'd known my husband in those last days better than I had. And six months ago, that was something I never would have believed.

The girl, though, wasn't the subject of my rage. To her, I turned cold, dispassionate speculation. "Did she kill him?" I asked. Because if she did, I would find her. I had no idea how, but somehow, I would manage it.

He searched my face, undoubtedly searching for my purpose. "I don't know," he finally said. "Believe me, Katie, I wish I did."

Nine

"A whole lotta nothing," Eddie said. "That's what you got. A great big barnyard full of nothing."

"Thank you for that insightful assessment," I said, giving the leasing agent a friendly smile. "Maybe we should talk about this later."

Eddie had wanted to show me two furnished apartments he'd discovered near the beach. I was completely opposed to his moving out, but there's no arguing with Eddie when he's in one of his moods. And for months he'd gotten it into his head that he had to find a place of his own.

To be fair, the seeds for that delusion were planted by my husband, who had only agreed to let Eddie camp in the guest bedroom until we could find a new assisted living community for him. But lately, Stuart has backed off and was willing to let Eddie stay. Eddie, on the other hand, was apparently pining for his freedom. "Too much goings-on in that house of yours," he said. "And how am I supposed to have a social life if I got four people under the same damn roof?"

Since I didn't have a good argument, I gave up and let him drag me to apartment after apartment. On this particular occasion, I'd picked him up after I dropped David off. In the car, I'd brought him up to speed, fully expecting that the conversation would be put on hiatus while we investigated square footage and closet space.

Eddie, though, wasn't clued in to the whole hiatus plan.

"Maybe you'd like to look at the kitchen again," Belinda, the leasing agent, suggested.

" 'The prisons of kings,' " Eddie said to me. "What kind of bull-honky is that?"

"Eddie—"

"And that boy knows who killed him." He aimed a bony finger my direction. "You mark my words, girlie."

"Eddie," I muttered, but with a smile for the agent. "Please."

"Humph." He turned to our bewildered companion. "Okay, missy. Show me what you got."

An expression that could only be relief wafted over her face. "Right this way."

I trailed after, almost slamming into Eddie's back when he stopped just shy of the kitchen. "I take it back," he said. "You don't have nothing." He waggled his eyebrows. "You got trouble."

"Thanks, Eddie," I said. "You're being so helpful."

He snorted. "Ain't my turn to be helpful, now is it? That's why I brought you along."

"Right. Fine. No problem." I shoved past him into the kitchen, telling myself that this was a good thing. Once he signed the lease and moved in, I would no longer have to deal with his orneriness or his disdain for David. Or, for that matter, his grudging acknowledgment of my husband.

All good reasons for getting him a place of his own, and

yet the thought of him moving out left a sad little scar on my heart. I'd grown up in the company of other Hunters, in a dorm filled with people who knew about my life, both its risks and its joys.

I honestly hadn't realized how much I missed that until Eddie had moved in. He was a complete curmudgeon, but in the short time he'd been with us, he'd become family, too.

And I liked the idea of another Hunter in the house. A Hunter who could keep an eye on and help protect my kids. Even one who claimed to be totally out of the game.

"As you can see," Belinda said, "the kitchen is as well-appointed as the rest of the house. Refrigerator, dishwasher, trash compactor." She indicated each item in turn. "The pantry is quite substantial, and I just love the way the darling little breakfast table tucks neatly into this alcove." She smiled at Eddie. "The perfect place to sit and drink your morning coffee."

"You'll need to buy a coffeemaker," I told him. "The kind that shuts itself off. I've lost count of how many times you've left ours on after you took the last cup of coffee."

He waved my criticism away with a rude noise.

"I'm serious, Eddie. You could start a fire."

"We have excellent smoke alarms installed throughout," Belinda assured me.

"Wonderful." I managed to work up a modicum of enthusiasm.

"My favorite feature is the side door," she said, moving efficiently to a door tucked in behind the breakfast table. "You have your patio, of course, with a view of the ocean. But just go through here; it opens up on the walkway that leads directly to the beach."

"That's awesome," I said. "Although . . ."

Eddie peered at me. "What?"

"Well, that's a lot of traffic traipsing past your apartment. I imagine your neighbors will be going up and down the stairs quite a bit. What if they're noisy? And is there any sort of gate between the complex and the beach?" I asked Belinda.

"Of course," she said with a tight smile, apparently deciding I wasn't quite the ally she'd hoped for. She stepped into the concrete-and-wood-foyer and gestured for me to follow. Between the walkway and the beach, I saw a low iron fence with a keypad mounted onto the gate. "It's very secure."

"It's jumpable," I said to Eddie. "Anybody could get in."

"Don't you mean any*thing*?" he countered.

I shrugged. "I'm only trying to be helpful. It's such a hassle to move; you really need to think about the pros and cons before you pack up and move in."

"Uh-huh." His expression reflected total disbelief, which made sense, I suppose, since the entire sum of his worldly possessions wouldn't even fill a duffel bag.

He went back inside and plopped himself down into one of the chairs at the "darling little breakfast table." "Anything else on your mind?"

"I'm only being practical. It's a great apartment"—I aimed that comment toward Belinda—"but it's awfully far away. Allie won't be driving for another year, and it's too far to ride her bike. And since you don't have a license . . ."

He'd been off the grid for so long before moving in with us that he'd managed to get lost in the system. He could probably have gotten a new license if he wanted to, but I think he liked the idea of me chauffeuring him around. I was fine with it, too. I'd rather that than have him fall asleep at the wheel. And Eddie was notorious for falling asleep at the drop of a hat.

I mentioned that little fact to him as well. "Under the circumstances, I'm not so sure it's a great idea. You living alone, I mean."

"You want me to stay, girlie, just come right out and say so."

On the other side of the kitchen, Belinda glowered at me. Beside me, Eddie looked extremely amused. I felt like I was living in one of those dreams. The kind where you're forced to make a speech. On stage. Naked.

"Fine. I want you to stay."

He snorted, satisfied. Then turned to Belinda. "You got one of them lease forms handy?"

I gaped at him, baffled.

"You may want me in the house, but I got my standards, you know."

"'Standards'?" I repeated, brows raised.

He started ticking off on his fingers. "Cable, for one thing. Can't watch my shows if that damned Nickelodeon is blaring."

"There's no television in that room, Eddie."

He held up his second finger. "I was just getting to that." Another finger popped up. "And an extra phone line. Got a lady friend now. Can't have folks picking up the extension and interrupting my conversations. A man needs his privacy."

"You could get a cell phone," I pointed out, but he waved that off as one of "them damned techno gadgets."

Considering Eddie was remarkably well-versed in current technology, I considered the demand more form than substance. Not that it mattered. I was willing to agree if that meant he'd stay.

"The furnishings," he said. "Gotta do something about the furniture. That dark stuff is butt ugly."

I bit back a smile. "And I suppose the room needs a paint job, too?"

"It is a big dingy."

The phone, cable, and paint I could agree to on my own. Furniture, however, got us into serious bucks. Which meant I needed Stuart's agreement, too. I was pretty sure he'd say yes just to make me happy, but pretty sure wasn't good enough. I needed the odds stacked in my favor, and I knew exactly how to do that.

I checked my watch, then did a fast mental adjustment of this month's budget. What the hell. We'd eat a lot of hamburger this month, but it would be worth the sacrifice.

As Belinda handed him a pen, I snatched the lease form off the table. "He'll fill it out at home," I said, "and give you a call." To Eddie, I said, "We need to get going. I have to run by the mall before we go get Allie."

Because I needed to buy a new dress. Low-cut and sexy. The kind of dress that can entice a husband to agree with just about anything.

Since Eddie informed me that he would rather "have his toenails ripped out by a pissed-off succubus than go to the mall," I dropped him back at the house and then enlisted Laura. Not that I couldn't shop by myself, but I wanted her input on the dress issue. Plus, I wanted to know if she'd managed to scrape up any info on our new pal Andramelech.

"Any progress?"

"Maybe," she said, using her good arm to hold up a clingy bloodred number and a slinky purple cocktail dress.

"Which?" I asked. "The dress or the demons?"

"Both, actually." She passed me the red one. "I don't think purple is good for your complexion."

Being somewhat fashion challenged, I had to take her word for that. So I took the dress and headed into the dressing room in which the salesgirl had hung the pile of dresses I'd already tagged for consideration.

"What about the other?" I asked. "Do you mean that maybe you've found something else?"

"Hold on," she said, from the other side of the door. I already had my jeans off, but I opened the dressing room door just enough to see what she was holding up. I found her creeping slowly through the dressing room, peering under stalls for legs, which presumably, were attached to ears.

"No one here," she said, seeing me peeking out at her.

"I know," I said, amused. "I checked when we came in."

She rolled her eyes. "Damn."

I laughed. "But it's good of you to double-check me. And you get brownie points for remembering in the first place."

"I'd rather have the brownies."

"That," I said, "you get if the information's good enough."

"Then I'm probably stuck on my diet. I learned a few things, but everything is so vague that I'm not sure how much use it's going to be."

"At this point, every little bit helps." I was out of my shirt now and shimmying into the dress. "Zip me?"

I pushed open the door, and as Laura zipped the dress, she told me what she'd learned. "First of all, can I just say that typing with a broken arm is tricky business?"

"Your dedication to your job is noted," I said. "Definitely deserving of brownies."

"Exactly what I wanted to hear," she said with a laugh. "Anyway, I think I've set myself up to get the creepiest spam on the planet. When you research demons on the internet, you come across some pretty disgusting websites."

"Anything both relevant and disgusting?"

"Maybe." She stepped in front of me, looked me up and down, then gave a sad little shake of her head.

"Really? It's so comfortable."

She waved at the three-way mirror at the end of the dressing room. "See for yourself."

I did, then immediately reached back to try and unzip the thing myself, disappointed to say the least. For months now, I'd been working out, burning calories at an exceptional pace and toning muscle like you wouldn't believe. Twenty years ago, after one week of that kind of regimen, I would have dropped two sizes. Now, though, with forty creeping closer and closer, the effects weren't quite so dramatic.

"I guess I'm not quite a size eight yet," I said, patting the area where the dress clung tenaciously to my thighs. Nicely toned thighs, I might add. But definitely still size ten.

"I'll get you the next size up," Laura said.

I shook my head. "No way. I've got dresses in here with flouncier skirts. Lets see if one of those fits."

She held up the red garment, which had just wreaked such havoc with my ego. "But this is darling," she said. "You're going to pass on it just because you need something bigger than an eight?"

"Absolutely," I said. "And don't look so indignant. You know damn well you'd do the same thing."

She shrugged and tossed the dress over the door of a nearby dressing room. "Good point."

"The Internet?" I prodded, shutting the dressing room door in case someone decided to walk in and join our little party.

"Right. Well, I poked around and I found some guy's blog. At least, I think it was a guy. Doesn't matter. He's going on and on about all these various demons and what they want and who worships them. Honestly, Kate, it gave me the creeps."

"I can see why. So what did it say about Andramelech?"

"Well, I can't tell how much of this has any real basis, you know? I mean, for all I know, everything on the site is fake. Fodder for a bunch of guys doing role-playing games or something."

"You're totally off the hook for any incorrect information," I said, opening the door and trying not to laugh. "I absolve you of all accountability. But what did you find out?"

She made a face, but I ignored it, hiding back in my dressing room instead and moving on to one of the flouncy dresses.

"According to this guy, about seven years ago, Andramelech spoke through some of his followers, and told them that he was building an army of Hell on earth."

"Right," I said. "We got the army part."

"Dammit," Laura said. "I'm always one step behind the Vatican."

I laughed. "Trust me," I said. "Your efforts are totally appreciated. What else did you learn?"

"Well, the army thing was a biggie," she admitted.

"Don't any of these demons start small? A whole army? Why not start with a small club?"

"Very funny," Laura said. "How's the dress?"

"Flouncy," I said. "And very, very cleavage-y." At that moment, in fact, I had my hand down my bra, trying to shift myself around so that I'd end up with the illusion of even more cleavage. I can't say my efforts were successful, but I figured a trip to Victoria's Secret could help me out.

"Let me see," she demanded.

"Tell me what else you found."

"What does it matter? *Forza* probably already knows it."

"Laura . . ."

"Right. Anyway, apparently Andre wanted some big-shot demon dude to be his generalissimo or something. He'd been trying for centuries to get this other demon on board, in fact. But the big-shot demon had been—how did they put it?—bound. And Andre never did manage to get the demon free."

"This is good. And new. Did it say the name of the generalissimo demon?"

"No," she said, looking pleased, "and I looked for hours to try and find out. Nothing. It was almost as if the blogger was talking in code, you know? Wanting to talk about it, but fearing retribution if he accidentally clued anyone in to what Andramelech was doing."

"Makes sense," I said. "Anything else?"

"One thing I thought might be helpful," she said. "Apparently to get to the bound demon, Andramelech would have to challenge the power of the archangel himself."

"*That's* interesting," I said, as I stepped out of the dressing room and did a little twirl, the full skirt flaring in a way that made me feel absolutely sexy, even in my Keds. And, yes, my narcissism was fueled by the fact that *this* dress was an eight. "Did it say which archangel?"

"Nope," Laura said.

"I'll tell Father Ben. Maybe this will lead somewhere."

"Well, *that* will lead somewhere," Laura said, indicating my dress. "Any chance I can borrow it after you seduce your husband?"

"Oh, really?" I asked, my voice rising with interest. "And why exactly do you need an ultra-sexy dress?"

"No reason," she said, but her smile told a different story. If she'd been a cat, there would have been tiny yellow feathers peeking out from between her lips.

I let out a low whistle. "What are you up to?"

"Just dinner," she said. "No big deal."

"If it's no big deal, then wear your black jeans and Coronado Beach tank top."

"A little bit bigger deal than that," she said. "Okay, a lot bigger."

I twirled my hand, urging her on.

"Dr. Meyer," she said. "From the ER, remember?"

"The cute one? The one who did your cast?"

"That's him. He called this morning. Wanted to know if I wanted to have dinner with him tomorrow."

"On a Wednesday, no less," I said. "That's a good sign."

"Do you think so?" she said. "I wasn't sure. Maybe that means I'm not good enough for a Friday or Saturday night."

"Nonsense," I said. "It means that's his first free evening, and you're the one he wants to spend it with."

"Really?"

"Absolutely." I nodded to emphasize the point, and when I saw her smile, I was glad I did. Laura had been through her own hell recently. I was glad to know that maybe she was starting to come through it.

"What does Mindy think?"

"I haven't told her," Laura admitted, after the briefest of hesitations. She lifted a hand to ward off my inevitable sarcastic remark. "Spare me," she said. "I'm going to tell her. I'm just going to do it after."

I kept my lips pressed together, trying very hard not to laugh.

"Oh, shut up," she said, but her shoulders were shaking with laughter, too.

"Okay," I said, trying to catch my breath. "Okay, here's the deal. If this dress does its job—if Stuart agrees to Eddie's list of residential accoutrements—then I will personally deliver it to you tomorrow morning."

"Oh, it'll work," she said. "Believe me. If that dress doesn't bend him to your will, your husband isn't looking."

By the time I got to the high school, I was officially running late. I had to pick Allie up, get in an hour of training with her, retrieve Timmy from day care, shower, do my hair and makeup, and pour myself into my fabulous new dress. All before Stuart made it home. And it wouldn't be the same if I was still dressing when he arrived. Trust me: The impact of a sexy dress is significantly lessened if your husband gets a look at the tummy-control panties you're wearing underneath.

Fortunately, Allie was waiting on the campus, talking with a boy in the shade of a large oak tree. At least, I thought she was waiting. As I pulled closer, I saw that my daughter was agitated, her hands moving as she talked, a sure sign that she was upset.

I slammed on the brakes and shifted into park, leaving the Odyssey in the circular driveway, much to the consternation of the Toyota Sequoia that had pulled in behind me. I didn't care. Whether it was mom-sense or Hunter instincts, something told me to get to my daughter—and if that meant blocking traffic, then so be it. I'd endure the other mom's wrath at the next PTA meeting.

While the Sequoia honked, I jumped out of the van, then hurried toward the tree. Allie and the mystery boy were still talking, with Allie gesturing madly and the boy leaning in just a little too close for my Hunter—and mom—sensibilities.

I'd been on edge from the moment I got out of the car, but as I got closer, my sense of urgency increased, reaching the boiling point when they turned toward me. That's when the boy reached into his pocket, pulled a stick of gum out of a bright red package, and popped it into his mouth. And if that weren't bad enough, Allie's right eye had a doozy of a shiner, which looked all the worse with the smear of mascara left in the wake of her tears.

Shit, shit, shit.

I picked up speed, trying to look both determined and nonchalant. Like a concerned mom, not a terrified Hunter. As I race-walked, though, I was plowing through my purse, and by the time I reached my daughter, my fingers had found the travel-size hair spray bottle no longer filled with medium-hold spray.

Instead, I'd filled this puppy with holy water.

I pulled it out, aimed it, and was just about to give the boy a solid squirt in the face when Allie slapped my arm down.

"Mom! Hey! Chill out, okay?" She turned to the boy. "My mom's on a hydration kick. She's always squirting me with Evian. It's totally lame, but what can you do?"

I stood there dumbstruck as she took the spritzer out of my hand, then squirted herself in the face.

"It is refreshing, though," she said to him. "Want some?"

"Um, okay." He glanced sideways at me, then took a step in the opposite direction. Whether he thought I was a loon, or whether he anticipated the pain associated with holy water I didn't know. But I readied myself to tackle him just the same.

Allie pushed the plunger and squirted him in the face. He blinked, then wiped the mist off his eyes and cheeks. He managed a forced smile. "Wow. Gee. Yeah. That's, um, great." He hooked a thumb over his shoulder. "Well, I gotta go. See you in class tomorrow?"

"Totally," Allie said.

"Sorry about the eye," he said. "Don't forget what I said. My grandpa's all about putting steak on it."

"Right. Got it. Thanks."

She kept a cheerleader-quality smile plastered on her face until he disappeared back into the building. The second he was gone she laid into me. "*Mom!* What were you thinking?"

I let the question hang in the air since, really, it was pretty obvious what I'd been thinking.

She rolled her eyes and huffed a little. "He is *so* not a demon," she whispered. "I mean, why would you even think that?"

"Why?" I countered. "I don't know. Could it be the fact that you have a black eye? That you looked like you were arguing with him? That he was in your face? That the second he saw me he popped a stick of gum in his mouth?"

"He's *not*," she said.

"So I saw," I said. "But how could you be so sure?"

She made a face. "Because I got him with holy water this morning," she admitted sheepishly. "He does totally stand too close and, honestly, his breath isn't that great. So . . ." She trailed off with a shrug.

"So I'm not quite the embarrassing idiot you make me out to be?"

"Embarrassing, yes. But maybe not an idiot," she admitted, though reluctantly.

"Who is he?" I asked. "And what happened to your eye?" I reached to touch it, but she jerked away.

"Just a new guy," she said. "His name's Charlie. And the eye is from cheerleading. Bethany accidentally kicked me in the face."

I winced. I'd been kicked in the face on more than one occasion, and it wasn't an experience I wished on anybody. "How does it feel?"

"Better than it did," she said with a grimace. "Don't worry. I'll live."

"Are you still up for working out?" I asked. "Because if you want to put it off . . . No," I added, correcting myself. "Never mind. Unless you're sick in bed, you train." After last night, that was the rule. And I intended to stick to it like glue.

Ten

An hour later, I realized that the "stick with it like glue" plan would have to be amended. We'd arrived at Cutter's studio only to find that both of his practice rooms were full, which left us without a place to work out.

No problem, right? We could just do weapons training today.

But since we'd already stopped by KidSpace to pick up Timmy, I wasn't too keen on practicing knife throwing in the backyard. I also wasn't keen on leaving him alone in the house while we practiced, especially since Eddie wasn't home to keep an eye on him. A few minutes, sure. But for the hour or so of practice time that I wanted to get in? Just not practical.

In retrospect, I probably should have left him at day care for another hour, but it was inconveniently located on the far side of town, and I just didn't have enough time today to make two trips out to pick up kids.

Which meant that our day's training ended up being

theoretical only. I took Allie up into the attic and ran her through the parts and operation of the crossbow.

"But when do I get to *shoot* it?" she whined.

I felt her pain. Now that I'd made the decision to train her, I wanted to get on with it, already.

"Soon," I promised. "But only in training. A knife, you can hide in a pocket or a purse. A crossbow? Not so much."

"You'll still teach me how to shoot it, though, right? I mean, it's totally cool and I want—"

I cut her off with a laugh. "I know you want, Allie. We just have to find some place to practice."

"Yeah, right. Like that's going to be easy."

She had a point, but I did have one idea. "Hang on," I said, then pointed to the array of weapons I'd spread out. "And don't hurt yourself."

I left her in the attic, then went downstairs to call David, checking on Tim as I passed through the living room. I'd left him with a pile of LEGOs, then taken the baby monitor with me. As far as I could tell, he was busy studying for a career in architecture, and his skyscraper towered almost as tall as my boy.

"Look, Mommy! I build a tower."

"Good job, kiddo," I said, as I grabbed the phone and dialed David's cell number.

"Watch, Mommy, watch." He grabbed a handful of blocks, then jumped up onto the couch. Carefully, he leaned forward and gently put one block on top, then another. The tower wobbled, but didn't fall, and Timmy bounced on the couch, squealing and laughing with pride.

"Awesome, kiddo," I said, as David's phone rang on the other end of the line.

"No, Mommy. Watch *this*." And he hauled his little leg

back and kicked as hard as he could, sending blocks clattering to the ground and then bouncing across the hardwood floor. He squealed and screeched and I amended my earlier assessment. Not an architect. A demolition expert.

"Kate!" David's voice rang in my ear. "Kate, are you okay?"

"I'm fine," I said. "My living room will never be the same, but I'm fine."

"Thank God," he said, the relief in his voice palpable. "I saw the caller ID, and when I heard . . . Well, anyway, I'm glad you're safe."

I basked a bit in his concern, but assured him that I was just fine. And then, as Timmy started to build his next masterpiece, I explained my problem to David.

"You're sure you want her to train?" he asked.

"David," I said, a warning note in my voice.

"Right. You're the mom. Your call."

I sighed. "I'm not going to let her Hunt," I said, feeling the need to explain my decision to him even though it was none of his business. "But after everything that's happened, I want her prepared."

"Fair enough," he said. And then, "I'm sorry."

"So will you help me or not?"

"You need a place to train? I'll see what I can do. Maybe we can find a loft to rent downtown or something."

"Right," I said, my voice sounding far away even to my own ears. "Good."

"Kate?"

"Sorry." I shook off the melancholy. "I'm fine." And I was, too. I'd just stumbled a bit at the idea of leasing a loft.

Because no matter how fervently I believed that Allie needed these skills, signing a lease made the whole thing that much more real.

* * *

What *also* made it real was what I found in the attic when I returned to my daughter: my stiletto, embedded in one of the rafters, and my daughter standing under it, a wide grin on her face.

"I totally missed the target," she said. "But I did get it to go in the wood. It took ten tries, but I got it."

"Awesome," I said, then laughed when I saw the red X she'd drawn with a marker on the wall—a good five feet away from where the knife had actually landed. "You're doing great, kid."

She shrugged, and I retrieved my knife, saying a silent prayer that she'd remembered how to open the thing. "Be careful with this," I said, unable to help myself. "You don't want to slice your hand."

She rolled her eyes. "I got it open just fine."

"Yes, you did," I admitted. But at the same time I made a mental note to go over the operation of each and every one of my weapons with her on a daily basis until I was absolutely sure she wouldn't impale herself in her enthusiasm.

Today, however, we were done. At least with training. The mystery of Eric's death, though? As to that, Allie assured me that she was just beginning.

"I've been reading all of Sue Grafton's novels," she said, referring to the mystery series that begins with *A Is for Alibi* and continues on through the alphabet. "And in all of them, Kinsey does tons of research about the victim's jobs and stuff. So I thought I would call the library. You know. Just see if maybe somebody remembers something."

"It's been over five years, Al. How much could they remember?"

"I don't know," she admitted. "But it can't hurt."

I had my doubts that it would help, especially since we were pretty sure that Eric's death stemmed from his *Forza* training—and I sincerely doubted Eric would have been foolish enough to have let that part of his life leak over into his job.

Still, I didn't want to dim Allie's enthusiasm. So while I showered and dressed, she pulled out the phone book and started making calls. By the time I'd cleaned up, put on my dress, and dried my hair, she had a full report for me.

"The rare books room is closed now," she said as I bent over Timmy to receive a wet, slobbery kiss. "I forgot it closes at five. But the research librarian used to work with Daddy, and she talked to me for a while."

"Betty?" I asked, tickling Timmy. "I remember her." A nice older lady who'd never forgotten Allie's birthday, and had brought me casserole after casserole after Eric's death.

"Yeah? Well, I told her what I was doing—"

"Allie!"

"Not the demon thing, Mom. Jeez. I told her that I didn't believe Daddy had been mugged, and that since I was almost fifteen, I was going to figure out what happened to him."

"Did she have anything to tell you?"

"No," she said, the enthusiasm draining from her voice. "She didn't remember anything suspicious at all. And she said that you already had all of Daddy's papers and stuff."

"She's right. Most of it's in the storage shed. I actually looked through some of it last night."

"Without me?"

"Trust me, there are still plenty of boxes to go through."

She shot me a sour expression. "Whatever. Did you find anything?"

"I haven't had a chance to look through the papers closely

yet," I said. "But I did find an address book. One I'd never seen before."

"Yeah? Can I see?"

"Of course. I flipped through it already," I said. "And nothing jumped out at me, but you're welcome to put your detective hat on and give it a go."

She raised an eyebrow. " 'My detective hat'? What am I? Nine?"

I laughed. "No disrespect intended."

"So where is it?"

"Let me finish getting dressed, and I'll get it for you. I want to do my makeup before Stuart gets home."

Not that I had the chance. Because Laura and Mindy arrived at the back door, ready to spend the evening at our house, Mindy hanging out with Allie and Laura playing babysitter to Timmy.

Just to be on the safe side, I'd also asked David to come by, scheduling his arrival for a half hour or so after Stuart and I left. I was probably being overly concerned, but if any demon tried to get into my house and close to my kids, I wanted a surfeit of Demon Hunters there to protect them.

"Wow," Laura said, when I did a pirouette for her and Mindy. "Definitely worth spending the extra money to buy those shoes."

I pointed my toe and silently agreed. Not that she'd had to work too hard to convince me. After spending a small fortune on the dress alone, adding the shoes to the grand total was merely a drop in the bucket. And so long as I offered to take care of paying the bills for the next two months, Stuart need never know.

Laura had come bearing a lasagna, and she disappeared into the kitchen while the girls headed to the living room to choose a movie from the totebag full of DVDs that Mindy had brought. After eliciting a promise from them that they would watch only a toddler-friendly movie, I retreated upstairs to finish my makeup.

My standards are eyeliner, lip gloss, mascara, and powder, but tonight I pulled out the big guns. Foundation. Eye shadow. Eyelash curler. Blush. And, yes, even concealer under my eyes.

When all was said and done, I looked pretty damn good, if I do say so myself.

There's never much hope for my hair, but I gelled, curled, and sprayed it. Then I twisted it on top of my head and secured it with a clip. Not half bad, actually, although I knew it would lose its curl the second I stepped out the door. At least Stuart would see me before that. And with any luck, the image of his wife in a sexy dress with sexy hair would stay burned in his brain. At least long enough for me to bring up the rather explosive subject of Eddie's living arrangements.

I did one last check in the full-length mirror, decided I was as good as I was going to get, then trotted to my jewelry box to get the diamond drop necklace Stuart had given me for Christmas. Lately, I'd taken to wearing the small silver crucifix that had been a gift from Father Corletti on my sixteenth birthday. Tonight, though, I was dressing to please my husband.

I fastened the necklace, then opened the small drawer on the bottom of the jewelry box where I'd earlier put Eric's address book. As I'd told Allie, I'd looked through the thing myself, but nothing had jumped out as foreboding. I hadn't called all the numbers listed, but I'd examined the names, frustrated merely by the fact that I didn't have a clue what I was looking for.

Now I grabbed the book, a small knife, and a miniature

vial of holy water. The knife and the water I put into the tiny beaded evening bag I'd earlier laid out on the bed. The address book I held on to, planning to leave it on Allie's dresser.

I wasn't two steps out of the room when Stuart came up the stairs. He took one look at me and let out a long whistle. I immediately blushed, which was ridiculous considering that was exactly the reaction I was hoping for.

"Well, hello," he said. "I was coming upstairs to look for my wife. I don't suppose you've seen her around anywhere?"

"The fashion police took her away," I said, sidling up to him and hooking my arms around his neck. "Will I do as a replacement?"

"I think I can suffer through," he said, then kissed me hard. The kind of kiss that makes a woman sad that the kids are in the house and a dinner reservation is looming.

"Wow," I said, coming up for breath. "Your wife is one lucky woman."

He stroked my cheek. "On the contrary. I think I'm the one who's lucky." He gave me another kiss, this one not quite as toe tingling. "Just give me five minutes, and we can get going. We'll be early, but it will give me a chance to show off my wife in the bar before we're seated."

"It's a date," I said, and while he went into our bedroom, I continued on to Allie's, realizing along the way that I was smiling.

Miraculously, the smile didn't fade when I hit her room. Because what was usually a disaster area had actually been straightened. I'm not sure if she'd simply gotten tired of living in a flurry of belongings, if *Teen Vogue* had announced that boys think a girl with a clean room is sexy, or if she was trying to prove something to me. Honestly, I didn't care. I was just happy to be able to see the floor.

In this newly clean state, I could have left the address book anywhere and been reasonably sure she would find it. But old habits die hard, and I crossed to the princess-style desk I'd bought her when she turned eleven. It sported a small hutch with tiny drawers accented by rose-shaped pulls. Whenever I had something that I didn't want her to miss, I put it on the ledge of the hutch, just above the right-hand drawer.

Today was no exception, but as I put the address book down, I noticed that the drawer was open—and inside, I saw Eric's ring, a simple gold chain coiled beside it.

Slowly, I reached for the ring, then slipped it on my finger, wanting in some small way to be close to Eric for just a moment. I held my hand over my heart, lost in memories and fighting tears.

And then I drew a breath, took the ring off, and put it safely back in my daughter's drawer.

"To us," Stuart said, lifting a champagne flute and waiting for me to lift mine.

This was at least our tenth toast, and I was feeling more than a little giddy. "No, no, no," I said. "We've already toasted to us. But this is the night before your big announcement. We need to toast you."

"All right," he said agreeably. "To me."

We clinked glasses. "To my wonderful husband," I said. "Who's going to make a damn fine county attorney."

"That's the plan," he said, then reached across the table and took my hand.

I smiled at him, then looked out over the dance floor. He'd brought me to the Blue Note, a popular restaurant and club that had opened in San Diablo to much fanfare about three years ago. The club sported a big band and required its customers to dress for dinner. The food was as good as the music, and the place was always packed.

We'd been here twice before, both on special occasions, and I was enjoying being back now. I had even forgiven Stuart the usual political chitchat, him shaking hands and making small talk in the bar before the maître d' had led us to our table. After all, we were here to celebrate politics; I could hardly ask that political banter be stricken from the agenda.

Our table was right off the dance floor in a prime location, and as we sat drinking champagne and eating our appetizers I inevitably found myself watching the dancers. Couples with a grace and style that I could never mimic. Not on a dance floor, anyway. In a fight, though . . .

Well, a fight was a totally different story.

Stuart, of course, didn't know that side of me. He only knew the girl who stepped on his feet on our first date. At our wedding, though, I was the belle of the ball, and all because of Stuart. I had no idea how he'd manage in hand-to-hand combat, but on a dance floor, he's pure magic. One of those men who can make even the most uncoordinated woman look like Ginger Rogers.

And fortunately, he was all mine.

Stuart saw me eyeing the dance floor and stood. "Shall we?"

"You're announcing tomorrow," I reminded him. "Do you really want the papers reporting that your wife can't dance?"

"The news will garner me the sympathy vote," he said, holding out his hand for me.

I took it and let him tug me to my feet. "Okay," I said. "But just one."

Naturally, one faded into two, and two into three. I was just about to beg off of the fourth turn around the floor when a trim octogenarian in a finely cut suit approached us.

"May I cut in?"

I froze, because I knew that face. All of it, including the nasty cut under one eye. I ought to, since last night he'd attacked my daughter.

Stuart, who knows I won't dance with any man except him, shook his head. "I'm sorry. This is a celebra—"

"Yes," I said, easing closer to the demon. "Of course he can. One dance with the gentleman can't hurt."

I was taking a risk, but not much of one. I couldn't believe that the demon had come to kill me. That would draw too much attention. Instead, he'd come to deliver a message. Or a warning. And I wanted to know exactly what the creature had to say.

And if I was wrong? Well, my purse was on my shoulder, my knife and my holy water within reach.

As Stuart stepped back to the table, his expression more than a little befuddled, I moved in closer to the beast. "How's the eye?" I asked sweetly.

"Do not think you are so clever, Hunter. This is one battle you will not win."

He grinned, showing off brown teeth that hadn't been brushed in weeks. This was no newly made demon; he'd been living among humans for a while now. And considering the cut of his suit and the odor of Listerine that covered his wretched breath, I had to believe he'd been doing it successfully, too.

Something important had pulled him out of hiding. And twenty points to me if I guessed right.

"Andramelech sent you," I said, even as the demon led me across the dance floor in perfect time to the music. As if

I hadn't already believed my dancing skills were pathetic, now I'd been shown up by the scourge of Hell. Wasn't that just peachy?

"Fool," he said. "Andramelech speaks to no one. His followers speak for him."

"Then speak," I said, silently congratulating myself. He'd just confirmed that wherever Andramelech was imprisoned, he was incommunicado. His minions were operating on their own. What exactly they were doing—and what they needed—*that* remained a mystery.

"What do you want?" I asked, going straight for the point. "And let's forget the riddles."

"There is no riddle," he said. "There is only our demand."

"You want the stone," I said. "Yeah, I got that. Why don't you tell me what stone?"

"Don't play games with me, Hunter. Do you think I'm newly made? Free Andramelech from the stone that binds him, for if you do not, you will surely suffer his wrath. Release him, and release the old one who would walk with him."

"How?" I asked, desperate for any tidbit of information. "How in the hell am I supposed to do that?"

"Bring the vessel," the demon said. "Tonight. To the field behind Coastal Mists."

I shook my head, even more baffled than before.

"The vessel? You mean the stone? Where Andramelech is trapped?"

"Bring it," he hissed, "or your daughter will never be safe."

My skin prickled as if I'd just been dropped in a freezing ocean. "You stay away from my daughter," I said, my voice low and dangerous. But I was scared, and I think he could hear the fear underneath.

"Bring the stone," he said. "Bring the vessel. Tonight. You and the one you call David."

"What do you want with David?" I demanded.

"*Tonight,*" he said. "Tonight, and all will be well."

"I don't know what stone you're talking about," I said, my voice filled with frustration. "At least give me a damn clue!"

From the edge of the dance floor, Stuart watched us, his forehead creased with concern. I realized I was scowling, and plastered on a smile. "How the hell can I bring you something if I don't even know what you want?" I asked, my face almost cracking under the strain of my happy expression.

"Do not toy with me, Hunter. If you do, you will not live long enough to regret it."

"Dammit," I said, not even bothering with the smile anymore. "I already told you I don't know what the—"

Smack.

The words died on my lips as the demon's hand cracked against my cheek. I'd expected an attack in a dark alley—not a crowded dance floor. And it took me a split second longer to react—probably a good thing in retrospect, as my instinct was to rip out my hair clip and slam it through his eye.

Instead, I caught myself in time, my hand stilling just as my hair fell, and my foot catching him just under the kneecap with a nice solid kick.

He fell to the ground, his face a mixture of pain and fury. Around us, everyone on the floor stopped. Even the band went silent, the notes from the various instruments fading out, leaving only the sound of ice tinkling in glasses and the electric hum of neon to fill the intimate dance hall.

Stuart was already at my side, and he looked me over before rounding on the demon, still on his ass on the floor.

"What the hell were you doing?" he demanded. "Why the hell did you slap my wife?"

The demon's eyes turned to slits, his pupils turning red as he fought to keep his true form confined within the human shell. I hoped Stuart was angry enough that he wouldn't notice. And I also hoped he wasn't stupid enough to take the demon on. Considering the demon looked like an old man, I guess I hoped he was chivalrous enough not to assault an octogenarian.

"Your wife?" he spat, climbing to his feet with far more grace than your average eighty-year-old. "You mean your whore."

"Now wait just a—"

"Do you have any idea what she is? What she does?"

I'd never seen Stuart turn that shade of red before, and I closed my hand tight around his upper arm. "Just let it go," I said.

"The hell I will."

"Stuart. Please."

"Maybe we should take this outside," he said to the demon, ignoring me.

"The only one I'll take outside is her," the demon said, his hate-filled eyes looking right at me. He licked his lips. "Oh, yes," he moaned, his voice low and guttural. "I'd love to take her outside."

Honestly, the feeling was mutual, and it was everything I could do not to reach into my purse and pull out my knife.

"That's it," Stuart said, jerking his arm free of me and lunging forward, catching the demon right in the jaw with an amazing left hook. The demon wobbled for a second, his expression startled as cameras flashed all around us. Then the demon turned and sprinted toward the exit. Stuart started to follow, but I grabbed the hem of his jacket and tugged him back even as onlookers and media hounds surrounded him. A brawl with a local political candidate is big news in San Diablo.

As I moved away from the flashing cameras, I noticed that the demon had paused in the doorway. "He will come forth," the demon said, his words clearly meant for me, the only one in the room watching the demon and not my husband. "And when he does, he will punish those who failed to help him. Nadia knew," he added, then turned and disappeared through the doorway, his words echoing behind him. "Nadia learned."

Nadia.

I latched on to the demon's words, hoping that somehow, even inadvertently, he'd left me a clue. Because clearly Nadia had learned something important. The question was what. More important, had the knowledge gotten her killed?

Eleven

While Stuart got sucked into a mini press conference, I called David to bring him up to speed on the demon's demands. After that, Stuart and I headed home, and I spent much of the drive assuring him that by the time the election rolled around no one would even remember the incident.

"You were sticking up for me," I said. "Chivalry. Machismo. Grand romantic gestures. All that stuff wins votes, right?"

He stopped at a red light before turning in to our neighborhood. "Do you really think I care about that, Kate?"

I stiffened, startled. "Well, yes. Considering all the time you've put into this campaign, I assumed you cared a lot."

He reached over and took my hand. "I care about you more," he said, squeezing my fingers and sending all sorts of little trills shooting through my body. "Anybody treats my wife that way, they get pummeled. That's just the way the world works. And if that means I don't win the election, then so be it."

"Yeah?" I smiled, both surprised and pleased. Maybe now was the time to ask about Eddie.

"Yeah," he said, and then stroked my cheek. "So who was that guy?"

My warm fuzzy feelings disappeared like so much smoke. "I wish I knew."

He looked at me sideways. "He certainly seemed to know you."

"And he certainly seemed interested in picking a fight with you," I said, my snappy tone probably originating with my guilt at getting Stuart involved in a brawl. "Honestly, Stuart, if you're not going to believe my answer why even bother asking the question?"

He didn't answer that, instead concentrating on navigating the short distance to our house. As soon as we reached our driveway, he hit the button for the garage door opener and the mechanism began its slow and steady grind.

We stayed silent in the car, the air thick between us, with me cursing demons, my husband, myself, and the damn garage door that had been on its last legs for months, but which Stuart never got around to repairing.

Finally, as the door clicked open into place, Stuart pulled into the garage, and then turned to me. "I'm sorry," he said. "It's been a long day."

"I know," I said. It had been a long one for me, too.

As soon as we were inside, Stuart made himself a drink and headed upstairs to watch the news in bed. The romantic interlude that had begun in the car had faded in the wake of my denials about knowing the demon. Which, of course, made me feel even guiltier, and did nothing for my mood. Nothing good, anyway.

I puttered around until the house was quiet, and then I crept into the attic and retrieved my stiletto and crossbow.

By now, my mood had shifted to determined. This demon had messed with my husband and my daughter, and he was going down.

The hard part was getting out of the garage—I'm going to break down and fix the damn automatic door by myself—but once I was in the driveway, I breathed a sigh of relief. That is, until I almost ran over David, who'd rushed behind me and held up a hand, signaling me to stop.

I muttered a curse, then rolled down the passenger-side window.

"Go home," I said.

"I'm coming with you."

"The hell you are. They seem to want you as much as they want this damned stone. There's no way I'm going to let you walk into a trap."

"Then I'm not letting go of your van."

I weighed my options, decided that I really couldn't bring myself to run over his foot, and unlocked the door.

To his credit, he didn't comment on my change of heart, but opened the door and climbed inside.

"It's too risky," I reiterated, keeping my foot firmly on the brake even as he settled into the passenger seat and fastened his seat belt.

"Just drive," he said. "This isn't an argument you're going to win."

"*David.*" Honestly, the man was exasperating.

"They want me. We don't know why. We can guess why they want this stone, this *vessel*—because Andramelech is trapped in it. But the rest is a mystery. And unless I go with you, there's no chance they're going to tell us."

"But if you do go, there's a good chance you'll get yourself killed," I said.

"Kate, think. You don't have the stone. I'm your only

bargaining chip. If you go there without something they want, you know damn well that they'll follow through on their threats."

"Allie," I said, my voice barely a sigh. I'd recruited Eddie to sleep in the hall outside her door. If Stuart woke up, that would require some explaining, but I'd rather dump a fabrication on my husband than keep my daughter unprotected.

And just in case Eddie wasn't up to the task, I'd called the police and told them about the encounter at the Blue Note. An assault on my husband and a threat to my daughter. That was serious business, and the officer I spoke to assured me they were on the case.

I didn't like getting the police involved in supernatural problems, but if that's what it took to keep Allie safe, then that's what I had to do.

"I'm not doing this for you," David said, following my line of thought. "And I'm not on some idiotic heroic crusade. But the sooner we end this, the sooner she'll be safe."

I drew a breath and counted to ten. I didn't like it, but I had no better plan. Worse, I had the sinking feeling that time was running out.

"All right," I said. "But if you die on me, David Long . . ."

"Cross my heart," he said. He reached toward me, then gently tucked a strand of hair behind my ear. I let out a shaky breath, my emotions a confused swirl. David was a friend, nothing more. And yet right then, I knew that if I lost him, a piece of me would die, too.

We finished the drive to Coastal Mists in silence, and I killed the headlights as I maneuvered the driveway, then parked near the main door.

This late, the nursing home was dark, but we weren't going inside. Instead, the demon had told us to come to the open area on the far side of the building, an area off limits to residents since there was no barrier between the landscaped field and the cliff onto which it opened. Anyone who tumbled off that cliff would drop fifty feet to be battered on the sharp rocks below. Survival really wasn't an issue.

So instead of providing a nice place for the residents to walk and picnic, this section of the Coastal Mists property was limited to merely providing a view from the media room. Now, I went to that window and peered inside. I didn't mind battling demons, but I'd rather do it without an audience cheering us on.

As I'd hoped, the media room was empty, the residents long ago tucked into their rooms. The whole place seemed to be sleeping, and I saw neither residents nor staff. For that matter, I saw no demons. Either in the building or on the grounds.

Except for the fact that the demons had invited us here, their absence was a good sign. Once upon a time, Coastal Mists had essentially been a demon-manufacturing plant, the human staff more than willing to help the demons find a fresh body or two.

Fortunately that was no longer the case, but death still came regularly to Coastal Mists, and that meant demons would always have at least a minimal toehold. I made it my business to come here regularly, just to keep the vermin population under control.

Normally, then, I'd be thrilled to come here and discover a dearth of demons. Today, though, I wanted one or two. I wanted to kick ass. And I wanted answers.

David walked the length of the grounds, turned, and came back to me. "Nothing," he said. "I don't see a thing."

"It's been hours since the Blue Note incident," I said. "Maybe they decided we weren't coming?"

"Or maybe this was a different kind of trap," David said.

I met his eyes, seeing my own fear reflected there. "Allie."

That was all it took, and we both sprinted for the car. We hadn't made it ten feet, though, when a scream pierced the air. An inhuman wail. I turned in the direction of the sound and was immediately knocked to the ground by a huge black crow.

"David!" I cried, as the crow pecked at my face. I thrust my arm up, trying to block its assault. There wasn't a damn thing I could do offensively. With the powerful beating of its wings and the violent jabbing with its beak, it was all I could do to defend myself and keep my eyes from being pecked out.

"Hold on!" From somewhere behind the howl of wind from the demon-bird's wings, I heard David's voice, followed by a huge grunt and then a gut-wrenching squawl as the bird was ripped away from me, his claws grasping my hair so that it felt like huge chunks were being ripped out of my head.

I fell back, smashing against the hard ground, my vision filled with the image of a bloody blackbird, wings spread, a knife slammed from the back straight through its heart. In an instant, it burst into a swirl of yellow and red fire that spun faster and faster until, like a cyclone, the bird's remains were sucked inside the vortex and nothing was left but the stars shining in the sky, and David, standing there with his knife still clenched in his hand.

He sheathed the knife and reached down, pulling me to my feet. "A familiar," he said, referring to the hell-birthed creatures that often assist demons as they torment humans on earth.

I nodded, then turned and looked over the rest of the area and the sky as well, searching for the crow's companions, be they birds, hellhounds, or demons of the two-legged variety. I'd encountered hellhounds once during my time in San Diablo, and I'd rather take on a walking, talking demon any day of the week.

Tonight, I saw nothing, though the encounter had put me on edge. I turned to David. "Was that a warning?"

"No," David said, his eyes suddenly going wide. "I think that was the first act."

I whipped around and saw what he was looking at: my friendly neighborhood dancing demon astride a giant mastiff. A hellhound, complete with fangs, bloodred eyes, and quite the nasty temperament. A second beast thundered beside the first, this one without a rider but just as determined.

Not actually canines, hellhounds are demon manifestations, pulled from the depths of Hell to do a demon's bidding.

The ground shook as the mastiffs barreled toward us. I half considered running, but honestly, where would we go? Not only were we cut off—with the demon filling the space between us and the parking lot, and a deadly dropoff behind us—but running would only postpone the inevitable confrontation.

And I wanted that confrontation. I'd been seething since the demon attacked David on the beach, but my blood had reached the boiling point when the demons had pulled my daughter into the quagmire.

Beside me, David unsheathed his saber from the cane casing that camouflaged it.

I reached over my shoulder and pulled my crossbow into attack position. One hellhound raced forward, straight for me, saliva dripping from its jowls, its eyes glassy with bloodlust.

Closer, closer. I stood stock-still, waiting, knowing I had to get the best possible shot. Tangling with these beasts was never a good idea, and the idea of going home mauled did not appeal.

Finally it sprang, using its massive haunches to push off the ground, its eyes never leaving me. As it soared toward me, I saw the other leap for David, its gut sliced open by the point of his sword.

I heard the mastiff's howl of pain, and then heard nothing else but the ravenous cry of my own attacker seeking blood.

It was right upon me and desperate, and at the last possible second, I released the spring on the bow, sending the arrow flying home. A perfect shot, and it pierced the hound's heart, causing a thick black goo to leak out, taking with it the mastiff's life.

I didn't waste any time catching my breath. A few yards away, closer to the cliff, David was still tangling with both the injured dog and my demon friend.

That the dog was no ordinary canine was obvious: It was still going strong, despite the fact that entrails were hanging from a fresh gash in its belly.

The mastiff was on top of David, pinning him down as the demon stood over him, the tip of David's own sword pressed against his jugular.

"*No,*" I cried, rushing forward. The demon's head jerked up, but he only smiled at me, a vile, evil expression that came very close to unnerving me. And after all I've seen in my life, it takes a lot to make me stumble.

I didn't, though. I pressed forward, determined to get to David. When I was about ten feet away, I was pulled roughly back, something tight and sharp gripping my shoulders. I couldn't turn to see it, but I could see the huge black wings beating and feel the pecking of the monster's beak, so hard as to feel like it was drilling through my skull.

I flailed, trying to release myself, but the creature's strength was amazing and it managed to pull me back, farther and farther, even though I dug my heels in and stabbed backward with my knife, trying desperately to get my footing or to cast a mortal blow.

No use. I was helpless as a rag doll.

In front of me, David was having problems of his own, but so far he hadn't succumbed. "Kate!" he yelled. "Hold on!"

At the moment, I didn't have much of a choice, and I was about to try one more blind slash backward when the bird suddenly released me. I teetered a bit, my balance precarious, and then the beast swooped over me, its massive black wings beating against my face.

I stepped backward out of instinct, and as I did I realized my mistake—and what the bird's goal had been. The ground under my feet disappeared, and I was tumbling down. I reached out, grabbing at the rough cliff face as I fell, my body battered by the jutting rocks and vegetation.

My fingers closed around a root and I held tight. I was below the field, though, and I could see nothing. Worse, I had no footing, and in the dark I could see nothing else to grab on to.

I was trapped there, and all I could do was hope that David survived . . . and that he did it soon enough to come save me.

Minutes ticked by, my arms aching from the strain of keeping my body from crashing to the rocks below. A blood-curdling scream ripped the air. "David!" I cried.

No answer. Only deathly silence, which seemed to fill the air like cotton.

No, I prayed. *Please, God, no.*

A faint scratching sound from above. I stiffened, afraid it was the crow, come back to finish its work. Or the demon, come to do the same.

"Katie?"

I exhaled, relief flooding my body even as tears streamed down my face. "David. Thank God. I thought you'd . . ."

His face appeared over the edge. "I thought the same thing," he said. "Here." He took off his belt and lowered it down to me. I wrapped it around one wrist, then as he pulled me up, I used my legs against the side of the cliff, as if rappelling, to help the process.

I was sobbing when I reached the top and saw the dead demon carcass near a pool of black goo that had once been the hellhound. "I thought . . . I thought . . ."

"It's okay," he said, and then he kissed me. Not a friendly kiss. Not a thank-goodness-you're-safe kiss. But a real, live, honest-to-goodness how-I-want-you kiss.

And so help me, I kissed him back.

Twelve

I actually kissed him back.

I told myself to take deep breaths and calm down, which was what I'd been telling myself for the last four hours. I'd spent the remainder of the night pacing the kitchen, drinking coffee, and telling myself that I'd almost died. That my emotions had been scraping the surface, and that it didn't mean a thing.

I loved my husband. I didn't love David. And I would never in a million years do something to hurt my marriage.

So why the hell had I kissed him back?

The glow of the morning sun started to fill the house, and all around me, I felt the day begin to bustle to life, even as I started to fade. I'd been running on fumes for days. I was tired and on edge. And while that might not be an excuse, at least it was an explanation.

"Hoo-boy," Eddie said, wandering into the kitchen in his bathrobe, the newspaper clutched tight in one hand. "If that doesn't shake things up a bit."

Immediately, I blushed, the heat starting at my toes and shooting straight up to the roots of my hair. "What? What's shaking things up?"

He squinted at me, then padded toward the coffeemaker. "That," he said, tossing the newspaper onto the counter. And there, on the front page, was a close-up picture of my husband, his fist connecting with the demon's jaw. "Boy's got more life in him than I thought."

"You don't really think it'll hurt his campaign, do you?" I asked, feeling guiltier by the second. The demon brawl was my fault, no matter how you looked at it. "Surely this will blow over." If I'd kissed David *and* ruined Stuart's career, I really didn't think I could live with myself.

"Hopefully it will," Stuart said, as he walked into the kitchen wearing one of his best suits and his favorite tie. He came over and kissed me on the cheek. "But I was defending the honor of my beautiful wife against an aggressive stranger, and I wouldn't change a thing."

I tilted my head. "Stranger?"

He shrugged. "I'm sorry. I was on edge afterward. You said you didn't know him, and I should have believed you."

I nodded, my chest tight, as Eddie silently watched me. "Thanks," I said, fighting the word out past the guilt. "Apology accepted."

"So today's the big day, eh?" Eddie said, as Stuart reached past me to pour a cup of coffee.

"It is," Stuart said.

"Do you need me there today?" I wasn't entirely sure what the announcing process was, but I remembered that Stuart had mentioned a press conference.

"It'll just be a two-minute deal, but I'd love to have my wife next to me on the podium."

"I'll be there," I promised, scribbling a note as to time and place.

And then he headed out, leaving me at home with Eddie and my guilt.

Or rather, with Eddie and my kids and my guilt.

I'll say one thing for parenthood: Once the kids are awake, there's very little time to wallow in your own guilt-filled cesspool.

The next hour was a flurry of blessedly mindless activity as I got Timmy dressed and fed, helped Allie find a purple T-shirt that had mysteriously disappeared, and then got Timmy dressed again after an accident involving a glass of milk and a strawberry Pop-Tart.

I had one moment of panic when Allie declined my offer to stay home for the day. I didn't tell her about the dancing demon's threat, because even though she now knew about the demons, I didn't want her seeing danger around every corner. I wanted her safe and careful, not terrified.

And, of course, the fact that David had killed that particular demon made me feel a bit safer about the prospect. Even so, just to be sure, I sucked in a breath, steadied my nerves, and dialed David's number.

He answered on the first ring. "Kate, I—"

"I need you to watch Allie," I said from my hideaway in the upstairs bathroom. "Make sure she's safe at school today. Hang around cheerleader practice after if you have to."

"Of course," he said. "Of course I will."

"Thank you," I whispered, realizing suddenly how nice it was to share responsibility. "Thank you."

"Katie, about last night. I'm so sorry. I shouldn't have—"

"No. It's okay. It was a mist—" I cut myself off and started again. "It wasn't something we should have done. Stress and fear and too much adrenaline. You know as well as I do that's a bad combination."

"Very bad," he said. "So we're okay?"

"Absolutely," I said with more certainty than I felt. "Totally okay."

"This is so not okay," I said to Eddie and Laura after I got back from taking the kids to school. "Hellhounds and demon birds." I shuddered. "I almost got killed."

"And he called it a vessel this time," Laura said. "Instead of just *the stone*. Do you think that's important?"

"I don't know. I'm guessing Andramelech is trapped in the stone, and so they call it *the vessel* because it holds the demon. But maybe there's some other significance?"

I looked at Eddie, who lifted his hands. "Not my area," he said. "Only vessel I got my hands on holds whiskey."

I caught Laura's eye and grimaced. I could tell she was trying hard not to laugh.

"So we've got the threat, the vessel thing, and the mention of Nadia," Laura said. "Anything else significant?"

I thought about the kiss, and firmly shook my head.

"Like hell," Eddie said. "David survived. I'd say that's damn significant."

"Yeah, well, I feel the same way about me surviving," I said.

"You didn't see how he got away. Said yourself you were hanging from a cliff. Said the demon was on top of him and the hound about to rip his throat out. So why didn't they, Kate? Why didn't they?"

"Because David fought," I said. "Just like any Hunter. He fought, and he won."

Eddie snorted. "Once, sure. But three times? The beach, his apartment, and now this? Sounds to me like the man's charmed, eh? Either that, or these attacks are all a ruse to make us trust the boy."

"Eddie, would you drop it already?" I said. "I *do* trust him. And if surviving a demon attack is your indication that a Hunter's gone bad, then I must be a minion of Hell, too."

My logic was perfectly fine, but Eddie snorted anyway.

"He *saved* me," I said. "There's nothing nefarious going on," I insisted. "Not with David, anyway."

"You ain't thinking with your brain," he said, his gaze dropping to right about my crotch.

"Eddie!"

He snorted. "Just calling it like I see it. And if you were using your head, you'd see what's going on, too."

"You're wrong," I said, but I'm afraid my words lacked the proper conviction, because my mind was already off and running elsewhere.

Eddie's belief stemmed from his continuing conviction that Eric had used the black arts to become David. Now, I took that a step further. Because if David really was Eric—if he'd lied to me that day on the beach—then I was off the hook for kissing him.

Wasn't I?

I closed my eyes and counted to ten, telling myself that not only was I being ridiculous, but that I had more important things to worry about at the moment. When I opened them again, I saw Laura staring at me, her head tilted curiously to one side. Because I was in that kind of a mood, I was just about to snap at her and ask what she was looking at. Fortunately for me—and our friendship—the doorbell rang. I sprinted to the front hall faster than I usually did when anticipating door-to-door solicitors, and pulled open the door.

"Cutter!" I said. "Thank goodness."

"I like your enthusiasm," he said, stepping not only inside my house, but also into my personal space.

I took a step backward. "I thought you were some obnoxious salesman."

"I'm not obnoxious," he said, then grinned lasciviously. "But are you in the market?"

I ignored him and cocked my head toward the kitchen. "Come on in."

"You're not going to correct me about the obnoxious part?" he asked.

I paused and turned, flashing him my brightest smile. "There's nothing to correct," I said.

"You're wicked, Kate."

"Trust me, Cutter. You don't know wicked."

He returned my smile, watt for watt. "Oh, but Kate, I'd like to."

I couldn't help but laugh. "Sit," I said, indicating a chair by Laura. "Coffee?"

"Sure." Then, "Hey, Laura. Eddie."

Laura greeted him back, but Eddie just made a strange noise in the back of his throat. As a rule, he likes Cutter, so I could only assume that was some sort of indicator of approval.

"Not to sound like a poor hostess," I said, putting a cup of coffee in front of him, "but why are you here?"

Cutter had never been to my house before, and there was something surreal about seeing him now, sitting casually at my table, his denim-clad legs stretched out in front of him and a black T-shirt doing only an adequate job of covering up the bulk of his muscular arms and chest.

"I have some news for you, so I thought I'd bring it by. You seemed anxious, so I thought you'd rather have it now than wait until our next session." He shrugged. "And I thought in person seemed more appropriate than by phone."

"You have news? About Eric?" I couldn't believe he'd actually learned something.

He shot a quick glance at Eddie and Laura, as if questioning whether it was okay to talk in front of them.

"Go on," I said. "They know the story."

"Turns out Eric had a P.O. box at one of those private mailbox places. The one on Main."

"Oh," I said, a bit taken aback. Because even though I'd known that my husband had been up to something, the revelation that he'd gone out of his way to set up a mailbox away from work and home stung. "Was there anything in it?"

"Unfortunately it's a mailbox, not a safe-deposit box. The mail that came in after he died just stayed in there until the lease on the box expired."

"And then?"

"Then my friend didn't know. He assumed the previous owners shipped it back to the post office. Or shredded it."

"Your friend?" Laura asked.

Cutter nodded, then took a sip of his coffee before answering. "Yeah, he bought four of the PostPlace franchises about two years ago. But by the time he took over, the box was empty." He looked at me. "And he had no memory of Eric at all. He did pull the old records for me, though. According to the fax log, he used their location to send and receive a few faxes."

"Did they keep incoming and outgoing fax numbers?" I asked.

"Indeed they did," he said, his expression more than a little smug. "Apparently he received and sent mostly to Rome and Los Angeles. But then around December and into early January, he started communicating with someone in San Francisco."

I pressed my lips together. Eric had been killed the second week of January.

"Any chance of getting the fax numbers?" Eddie asked.

"Already did," Cutter said. "The calls to Rome go to an office in the Vatican." As he said that, he looked at me, and I tried hard not to react. It had never occurred to me that by asking him to help with the Eric mystery I'd be drawing him closer to my own secrets, too.

"That's odd," Laura said, obviously trying to cover for me.

"Eric was an expert in rare books," I said, which was actually true. He'd been trained by *Forza*, and that training had come in handy when he'd gone to look for a civilian job. He'd even been able to put the Vatican on his resume, although the *Forza* connection was conspicuously absent.

"The Vatican has a massive library," Cutter said. "That could be what the calls were about."

He didn't sound convinced, though. "What doesn't fit?" I asked.

"Not sure," he admitted. "The faxes to Los Angeles were to the St. Ignatius Catholic Church."

"Which also has an impressive collection of relics and ancient texts."

"You seem to know a lot about that," Cutter said.

I smiled, then turned my back to him, ostensibly to pour myself more coffee. "Yeah, well, when you live with a guy who knows so much about ancient books, you pick up a few things here and there."

"I'm just impressed you found all this information," Laura said, jumping into the conversation, probably to distract Cutter. "You've totally put me to shame."

"To shame?" Cutter said. "What are you talking about?"

Laura turned pink as she realized her mistake. "Oh. Nothing. Just that I was trying to help Kate, too. You know. Figure out what happened to Eric. That's all." But from the twelve shades of red she was turning, I think Cutter knew that wasn't really "all" at all.

"What about San Francisco?" I asked before he could interrogate Laura. "Did you get a number there?"

"Dead end," he said. "The number went to a Mail Boxes Etc. And they had no records on their end about who was sending or receiving the faxes."

"Damn," I said.

"Still, it tells you something." He looked at me intently. "Your husband was corresponding with someone. And from what you told me about the letter you found in the safe-deposit box, it wasn't something he wanted to keep from you forever."

"Yeah? Well, that plan didn't go over too well. After five years, I'm having a hard time learning anything."

"Still, I don't believe he would have gone to the trouble of leaving you a note, and then left nothing concrete for you to find. If the letters and faxes were important, he probably would have saved them."

I looked at Laura. "I haven't finished going through the boxes in the shed yet. I don't suppose you're up for a little dusty investigative work?"

Laura sighed. "Why not? I've got nothing better to do except stick straight pins into my Paul voodoo doll."

"Don't look at me," Eddie said. "I've got two more

apartments lined up to look at. Got a real estate agent coming by to pick me up in an hour."

"Eddie . . ."

He held up his hands. "You tell me it's copacetic, and I'll quit looking. Meantime . . ." He trailed off with a shrug.

I frowned, because I hadn't had time to discuss Eddie with Stuart, for obvious reasons. And since Stuart was announcing his candidacy later this afternoon, I really didn't think a phone call would be appreciated.

"There's another possibility," Cutter said. "Other than his work papers, I mean."

I looked at him curiously.

"I'm still trying to find out if your husband had another safe-deposit box. If he did, that might have all your answers."

And if he didn't, I thought, the mystery of Eric's death would just keep getting deeper and deeper.

After Cutter and Eddie left, Laura and I parked ourselves on the back porch and started plowing through the boxes filled with Eric's old stuff. The day was cool, with a nice breeze blowing in off the ocean, and we worked quietly for a while, but it was a noisy kind of quiet, and after a few minutes, I couldn't take it anymore.

"What?" I demanded.

Laura looked up at me from her bent-over position, where she was trying to tug a file folder out with her one good hand. "Excuse me?"

I leaned over and grabbed the folder for her. "Something's on your mind," I said. "You might as well come out with it."

Her lips twitched, then she cupped a hand over her mouth as if hiding a smile.

I sighed. "Okay. Now what?"

"Kate, there was nothing on my mind, I swear. But now . . ." She trailed off, her eyes dancing. "Now, I'm definitely intrigued. So spill."

Inside, I cringed, because I'd royally blown that one. "There's nothing to spill."

"Kate, I have a teenager. Out with it."

I closed my eyes, trying to decide what to say. I didn't want to tell her what happened. The moment had been too surreal, too intimate. And somehow telling Laura would make it seem all the more real.

At the same time, though, Laura was the first truly close non-Hunter friend I'd ever had. We'd shared problems with our kids and with our marriages. And, yes, I wanted to know what she thought. From a psychological perspective, Laura was right; I'd practically been jumping up and down, begging her to ask me.

So I told her. I kept my language matter of fact, just as if I was relaying a fight or a kill. But when my recitation was over, I couldn't help it. I ended on a sigh.

"Wow," she said, sighing a little bit herself.

"It was just an in-the-moment thing," I said. "I don't think he even realized what he was doing beforehand."

"But you kissed him back."

"I know," I said, my voice choked with agony. I slumped in my chair, feeling lower than dirt. "I'm pathetic, Laura. I feel like I'm going to drown in the guilt."

"No." She shook her head, her emotions rolling off her in forceful waves. "From someone who just went through the unfaithful thing, trust me. You are fine. Extenuating

circumstances and no lust aforethought. Your Honor, my client is completely innocent."

"And David?"

She leaned back in her chair. "Him you'll have to watch like a hawk."

"Great."

She laughed. "Oh, Kate, I'm kidding. You almost *died*. The whole situation was emotional. He got a little carried away, that's all."

"But the thing between us," I said. "That's not going to go away."

She looked at me, her eyes warm and appraising. "You've been attracted to him from day one, Kate. And he's been hot for you, too. You know it, he knows it. Even I know it."

I could feel my cheeks heat.

"It's human to be attracted to other people, Kate. So long as you don't do anything about it, you haven't broken your vows."

She was right, of course. And yet I still felt as though I'd crossed a line. But since it was never, *ever* happening again, best to not dwell on it and simply move on.

I bent down and pulled a fresh stack of file folders into my lap. Laura followed my cue and started leafing through her own pile. "Nothing personal," Laura said after a few minutes of silence, "but Eric kept a lot of crap at his office."

"No offense taken," I said. She was right. The boxes were filled with page after page of nothing. Eric's notes about acquisitions and the provenance of books the library had acquired. A few scribbled references to things we had done as a family or that he hoped to do: notes about the hotel we stayed in when we took Allie to Disneyland, notes about the cost of taking a whale-watching cruise, and papers on which he'd scribbled various confirmation numbers for our vacation trips. All hopelessly out of date now.

"We have to go through them all, though," I said. "Or I do, anyway."

"I don't mind helping," she said. "Even if it is a pain to rummage through with only one good hand. It keeps my mind off tonight."

"Nervous?"

"A tad," she admitted. "Thanks for the dress. Especially considering what happened."

"Extenuating circumstances," I said. "Trust me. I saw the look in his eyes. If I'd asked about Eddie before the whole demon incident, I would have been golden. And you're going to look fabulous tonight."

Her nose wrinkled. "I've been out of the game a while." She pondered that. "Actually, I was never really *in* the game. I married Paul right after high school."

"I know the feeling," I said. "When I started dating after Eric died I had no clue what I was doing."

"And everything turned out okay for you," she said. Then her face clouded. "Well, I mean—"

"Never mind," I said. "I know what you mean."

Since she apparently didn't want to revisit the whole David issue any more than I did, she bent down and grabbed another handful of file folders from the box, using her good hand to pull them out and plop them on her lap. "You owe me big time."

"Believe me, I know I do."

I was about to offer her a lifetime supply of brownies when the phone rang. I hurried into the kitchen and grabbed it up, only to find Delores Sykes, the cathedral's volunteer coordinator, on the other end.

Immediately, I regretted not checking the caller ID.

"Delores," I said. "Hey, listen, I'm sorry I haven't been in to get any more inventories to type. I've been crazy busy, but I do plan to come in soon and pick a few more up." That much was true. I needed to see if the cathedral archives had any reference to our mysterious stone. And wasn't *that* going to be a fun endeavor?

"Oh, sweetie, I understand. What with the holidays and school starting back up, you must be a basket case."

"Pretty much," I acknowledged. "What can I do for you?"

"Well, I'm not really sure. Father Ben is on the other line, but he asked me to call you. He was hoping you could come to the cathedral and have a little chat with him."

"Now?"

"If you can. He seemed to think you'd be very interested in what he had to say. He said to tell you it was about your mutual friend. Andre, I think he said his name was. Does that ring a bell?"

"Oh yeah," I said. "That rings a very loud bell."

Usually it takes fifteen minutes to drive from our house to the cathedral. We made it in ten, with Laura clutching the dashboard with her good hand and muttering the entire time about how she really couldn't manage with two broken arms and would I please try to get us there alive.

"Kate," Ben said, as soon as I plowed through his office door. He crossed himself, then looked at me gravely. "The trouble that has come to San Diablo," he said. "If we are right, it is almost unimaginable."

That didn't sound good. I swallowed and sat in one of the chairs. "What is it? Do you know what the stone is? Do you know where Andramelech is imprisoned?"

"The Stone of Solomon." He looked to Laura. "It was your research that turned the tide. The mention you found of the archangel focused the research in Rome on Saint Michael and—"

"Wait, wait," I said, holding up a hand. "I appreciate that Laura did a great job, but can we back up a second? *What* stone of Solomon?"

"Like King Solomon?" Laura asked.

"You know this stuff?" I was impressed.

She shook her head. "That's the only Solomon I've heard of. Back in Old Testament time, right?"

"Exactly," Father Ben said. He leaned back in his chair, apparently realizing that as bad as the news was, neither Laura nor I were going to be suitably impressed until he'd brought us up to speed on the whole Solomon thing.

"When Solomon was building the temple at Jerusalem," Father Ben began, "the demon Ornias pestered and harassed so much that no work would get done. When Solomon learned of the demon's interference, he prayed that God would give him authority over the demon."

"Wait a sec," I said, interrupting. "I do know this story. The archangel Michael helped Soloman bind the demon and forced him to do the work. To build the temple instead of bothering everyone so they couldn't get any work done."

"That's the story," Ben said.

"But there's more."

"Indeed there is." He looked from me to Laura. "After the temple was built, the demon was no longer needed to work. So he was trapped in the stone, again with Saint Michael's help, to be left there for all eternity.

"But? I'm definitely hearing a *but* in this story."

"Actually, no," Ben said. "That was essentially the end of Ornias."

"Oh." I frowned, considering that. "Nice to know that some trapped demons stay trapped."

"Except Andramelech was trying to untrap him," Laura put in.

"Exactly," said Father Ben.

"That's all well and good," I said. "But so what? We still don't know about this damn stone. Is it the stone they used to build the temple? And if it is, why are the demons congregating in San Diablo? Or have we just become the chic new demon destination?"

Father Ben smiled despite himself. "I don't know where the actual stone is," he said. "But I do know that it is not mere rock. It's a gemstone. And once Ornias was bound, King Solomon had the stone cut down using the exact method told to him by the archangel himself."

"Because?"

"Because then the demon's space would be confined."

"Cramped quarters," Laura said.

Father Ben smiled at her. "Once we had Laura's information about the archangel Michael, the *Forza* archivists were able to find additional references."

I gave Laura a pat on the back as she preened a little.

"So what do we know?" I asked.

"The stone was imbued with the power to trap and bind demons. King Solomon, of course, originally trapped Ornias, but many lesser demons soon followed."

"How?"

"The stone is a trap—don't ask me how it works, I don't know. All I know is that throughout the years it has been infused with demonic entities. Trapped there, for all eternity."

"But there must be a way out," Laura said. "That's why Andramelech was so hot to get it."

"Until he got trapped himself," I said.

"Exactly," Ben said. "The stone has been well protected through the years, passed down as a treasured and guarded secret. But even so, Andramelech believed for centuries that he could not only find it, but that he could free his compatriots and they would become his loyal followers."

"Right," I said, because that part I knew. "Go on."

"He came and went in human shape, rallying his human followers, telling them his secrets and promising them great things."

"His secrets?" I asked. "What secrets? And how do you know?"

"Because we know what else he told them," Father Ben said. "A few who turned to the church after Andramelech's grip on their soul faded a few years ago have since revealed some details. None knew the particulars of the ceremony to release Ornias—although they intimated that other humans might have such information—but they did reveal other key information about the stone."

"Like what?" Laura asked.

"Like how it worked. And how they intended to use its inherent nature to locate and claim it."

"Okay," I said. "I'll bite. How does it work?"

"It is a magnet," he said. "A demon magnet."

Laura looked at me. I shrugged.

"With the archangel's help, King Solomon had the stone set into a ring," he explained. "And when a human wears it," he explained, "it lures demons to them. The ring causes a shimmer in the ether, and the demons can see where the ring is. Maybe even who has it. The purpose, of course, is to allow the wearer to trap the demon in the ring. The dark trick, as the writing calls it, is to be performed only by a soul willing to make the greatest sacrifice."

"What does that mean?" I asked.

"I'm afraid we don't know," he said. "But don't you see the significance? Andramelech intended to turn the tables on the wearer. Somehow he planned to be drawn to the ring, and then instead of being trapped, he intended to capture the ring for himself."

"But his plan failed," Laura said. "And we still don't know where the ring is."

I didn't say anything. My body had gone completely cold as Father Ben's story filtered through my mind. *Wearing the ring attracts demons. And once the demons knew where the ring was, they'd stop at nothing to get it back from its new owner.*

I blanched, feeling suddenly nauseous. "Eric's ring," I said. "Dear God, all this time the demons have wanted Eric's ring."

"You have the ring?" Father Ben asked, clearly astounded.

"No," I whispered, my whole body icy with fear. "Allie does."

Thirteen

As I maneuvered the car at a breakneck speed toward the school, Laura called the house. On the third try, Eddie finally decided to answer the phone, and when Laura switched her cell phone over to speaker, I heard his gruff, "Whoever the hell this is, it damn well better be important."

"Allie's room," I yelled. "The right-hand drawer of the hutch on top of her desk. Go see if there's a man's ring in it."

I heard him shuffling toward the stairs. "Dammit, Eddie!" I yelled. "Faster!"

"Keep your panties on," he shouted back, but I could hear the tempo of his steps increase, and his breath started coming in puffs. "Damn frou-frou furniture," he muttered. "Where am I supposed to be looking?"

"Her desk. By the window. There's a little drawer on the right-hand side. There's a ledge on top of it that might even have a small black address book."

"I see it," he said, and I silently prayed that she hadn't taken her father's ring to school. "There's no ring in here, though," he finally said.

I looked at Laura as I approached a red light.

"Run it," she said.

And I did.

"Allie!" I yelled, racing through the halls. Coronado High is a closed campus, and parents are supposed to check in at the front office. Fortunately, the school hasn't yet started locking its doors against outsiders, and I was able to barrel inside, ignoring the signs reminding me to get a visitor's pass.

The bell had just rung, and all around us, students stopped and stared. I didn't care. I needed to find my daughter.

I stopped Bethany, one of the cheerleaders. "Have you seen Allie?"

Her eyes widened, and she pointed down the hall. "She just got out of P.E. I don't know what she has next. Are you okay?"

"Fine," I called, sprinting toward the gym. "Family issue. No worries."

I barreled through the double doors that led into the gym, then paused to get my bearings.

"That way," Laura said, pointing off to the left. We'd both been in the gym dozens of times, but only for school events. The locker rooms had never been part of the equation.

"I'll go check," I said. "You go back to the office. Find out what her next class is, just in case she's not here."

"Check," she said, then sprinted toward the door.

"*No,*" I called. "You're not her mom and we're not supposed to be here. Forget the office. Just go find David."

She waved with her good arm, then clutched her injured wrist close to her chest as she raced across the basketball court, her loafers clattering on the polished floor.

I sprinted in the opposite direction and found the girls' locker room. I burst through the doors, calling my daughter's name.

"Mom!"

I found her huddled in a towel on the floor in front of her gym locker. My heart split in two, and I rushed forward, desperate to hold her and make sure she was all right.

Mindy was with her, holding her hands and telling her it was going to be okay.

"Allie!" I knelt in front of her, grateful when Mindy moved aside so that I could fold my daughter into my arms. I held her tight, hugging her so close I probably injured a few ribs. After I'd soaked her in, I pulled back, then turned to Mindy. "Your mom went to get Mr. Long. Can you go find them and tell them we're down here and that Allie's all right?"

"Um, yeah, sure. But—"

"Mindy!"

"Okay, okay! I'm going!" She sent one pitying look back toward my daughter, then disappeared into the gym.

I turned back to Allie, my hands grasping each shoulder as I looked her over once more, anxious to prove to myself that she really was in one piece.

She put up with my examination until I tugged at the towel. That's when she slapped my hand away. "Mom! What is with you?"

"Are you okay? You're not hurt?"

"I'm fine. Why would you think— Oh. Did something happen?" She turned her head, scoping out the empty locker room for stragglers. "Is it about demons?" she asked in the world's quietest whisper.

"Well, yes," I said. But now I was the one confused. "But weren't you—"

I cut myself off, realizing with a start that we'd been at cross-purposes here. Allie hadn't been attacked by a demon at all. But if she hadn't been attacked, then what had happened?

I indicated the way she was sitting on the floor, still wearing her towel. "I thought something had hurt you."

"I'm not hurt," she said. "I'm just . . . I'm just . . ." She trailed off and started crying again.

"Baby, what is it?" I was right in front of her, trying to read her expression. "What's happened?"

"Daddy's ring," she said between sniffs. "Someone stole Daddy's ring."

"It's okay, baby. It's okay." It wasn't, of course. That ring loose in the world wasn't okay at all. But I was hardly going to announce that little tidbit to my daughter. Not at the moment, anyway.

Instead, I just held her and told her it would be fine. We had other memories of her dad. Better memories. And certainly better souvenirs.

"Start at the beginning," I said, once she had calmed down. She was dressed now—a feat she undertook after I promised her that she hadn't incurred my wrath until the end of time. Secretly, I was more than a little concerned. But as I hadn't yet explained to Allie why I'd rushed all the way here to protect her, I was trying to keep my expression calm and collected.

Right now, I needed facts. When and where and how.

The part of the program where I freaked out about the fact that we'd lost a tiny ring that just happened to be the key to all of the current demon activity in San Diablo? Well, that could come later.

"I wore the ring to school today," she said. "Because I thought about what you said. About how we'd survived the demon in the park, and so Daddy's ring really was lucky."

I grimaced, remembering the conversation. She'd said the ring brought bad luck. I'd told her that was silly since I'd come to save her.

Considering the ring had brought the demon, she was right all along. So much for a mother's good instincts.

"Did you actually wear the ring?" I asked.

"No. It's too big, you know? And it's really kind of ugly. I kept it on the chain around my neck."

I mentally exhaled a sigh of relief. The demons already knew that the ring had been in my house, and considering the way they'd been hounding me, they must have believed I understood its significance. But if she hadn't put it on her finger, then maybe the demons hadn't come to the school. "Then what?"

"We can't wear jewelry in P.E., so I left it in my locker. But when I came back, it was gone."

"And you don't have any idea who took it? Did you see anyone suspicious going into the locker room?"

She shook her head. "No one."

I clenched my fists, frustrated at the brick wall we'd run up against.

If the thief was a demon, we were in trouble. But if our bandit was a student? Well, that kid would soon become a demon magnet. Worse, the kid would soon be dead.

Fourteen

Laura found us in the dressing room, having sent Mindy back to class. I wanted to talk to David, but the vice-principal (who'd heard about my race through the halls toward the gym) had magically appeared and seemed none too happy about our little visit to the school.

She informed me that Mr. Long had AP classes for the rest of the afternoon, and that she'd be happy to give him a message to call me at the end of the school day. I smiled sweetly and asked her to please do that.

Then I told her that I was taking Allie home for the rest of the day. A family emergency.

I signed a yellow form that would presumably be shoved into Allie's permanent record, and then agreed ever so politely when they made me promise—in the event of future emergencies—to go to the office first rather than racing through the halls and "working the students up into a tizzy."

I'd witnessed nothing close to a tizzy, but I agreed anyway.

I'd learned a long time ago that it was best to simply smile politely. Do what you need to do, of course. But always smile politely when you apologize.

"I thought you said you weren't mad," Allie said as soon as we were in the van.

Since Laura was in the front passenger seat, I looked at my daughter's reflection in the rearview mirror. "I'm not," I confirmed. "I'm relieved."

"Then how come you're dragging me out of school?"

I looked in the mirror again and caught my daughter's expression as she put it all together. "Oh, right," she said. "Demons."

"Smart kid," I said.

"So what happened? Are you going to let me fight? I know you said I'm not ready, and I'm totally on board with that, really, but I want to help. And if you're going, then you really ought to take me, too, because—"

"Allie!" I interrupted with a laugh. "It's not about a battle. It's about the ring."

"The ring? Daddy's ring?"

"Not just Daddy's, apparently. That ring used to belong to King Solomon."

"No way! But it's so ugly."

"Once again proving that royalty and good fashion sense don't necessarily go together," I said. "Now do you want to hear the story or not?"

She did, of course, and so while we were driving, I dove into the full story. We paused once to drop Laura off so that she could start primping for the big date, then finished up around the kitchen table.

By the time I got to the end, my daughter looked a little rough around the edges. "So it wasn't Daddy's ring at all?"

she said. "Then how come he was wearing it when, you know, when he was in San Francisco?"

"I think Daddy did own the ring. I'm pretty sure it was a gift from Wilson."

"Your old *alimentatore*," she said.

"Right."

"And so, what? Wilson decided to mail Daddy a demon magnet? Why?"

"I don't know," I admitted. "We're obviously missing something."

"Hmmm," she said seriously, her chin resting on her fist. "At least we know that it's all related. I mean, yesterday we thought Daddy's murder was totally separate from the Andramelech demons. But they have to be connected, right? Because the demons want to free that Andre dude, and he's trapped in Daddy's ring. I mean, that makes sense, doesn't it?"

"Completely," I said. "So long as Andramelech is really *in* Daddy's ring."

"He's got to be," Allie insisted. "It totally fits." She got up from her chair and started pacing the kitchen. "Daddy was going to meet a Hunter in San Francisco, right? And that's about the time that Andramelech disappeared. Isn't that what you told me?"

I nodded, but my mind was already two steps ahead.

"Your dad didn't go to San Francisco to meet just any Hunter," I said. "He must have gone to meet Nadia Aiken. The Hunter who'd been on the trail of Andramelech."

"Right, right, right," Allie said, bouncing up and down. "Because somehow she knew he had the ring."

"She worked with Wilson," I said. "So that makes sense."

"But something went wrong. The demon must have

found them first, right? Cause we know Nadia disappeared. And we know Daddy's dead." She took a deep breath, then lifted her chin, her jaw set. "But Daddy still won, you know? Somehow Daddy got him. Andra-hoochiemado probably took Daddy on," she said, whacking her arms around in a total parody of a martial arts sequence. "Cause Andre dude wanted the ring, right? So he could free his buddy Ornie."

"Okay," I said, smiling at her excitement despite the underlying subject.

"Well, Daddy got in a good one at least. I mean, something happened to him—we know that—but he still managed to nail Andre. He must have. Because the ring is back here, and all these demons are looking for Andramelech. It *totally* makes sense."

She'd worked herself up, and now she punched the sky, thrilled with her own detective skills. One look at my face though, brought her back down to earth. "Mom? What's the matter? Am I wrong?"

I shook my head slowly, feeling more than a little nauseous as the truth settled in my gut. "No," I said, forcing a smile. "No, I think you're absolutely right."

And I did, too. But there was one thing Allie hadn't figured out. One thing she'd missed, but I'd zeroed in on right away: the question of why the demons had first attacked David.

After all, he'd never been in possession of the ring. So why begin with him?

Being a prize pupil, though, I knew the answer: because until Allie slipped the ring on her finger that day in the attic, the demons had no idea where it had disappeared to. They had only one lead: The body had been long buried. But the soul who'd captured their leader? Find him, and they might find the ring, too.

* * *

I was pacing outside David's door when he got home, my body ready to spring and my mind just as tense.

"Kate," David said, his eyes lighting up when he saw me. "I tried to call your cell and all I got was your voice mail."

"I turned it off."

He looked at me, the smile fading as he stepped from the stairs to the second-floor landing. "Let's go inside."

"Yes," I said. "We can have a nice little chat."

He gave me a curious look but opened the door for me. I entered, still seething, and found myself in a typical bachelor apartment. For a moment, I was taken aback by that simple fact. There were no photos of me or Allie on the walls. No mementoes. Not even the Danish-style furniture that Eric had taken a liking to.

I'm not sure what I'd expected, but I faltered for a minute, wondering if I could be wrong.

"Kate?" He took a step closer, his eyes taking me in. "Katie, are you okay?"

He was right there, right in front of me, and the air between us crackled. The scent of this man was all David, but that electricity, that charge. Dear God in Heaven, *that was Eric.*

I'd been right all along. And now that I was certain, I couldn't believe that I'd ever been unsure. More, I couldn't believe that he'd lied to me. Worse, that I'd believed the lie.

I stood there trembling, my emotions like a live wire sparking with rage, joy, lust. I couldn't move—didn't even want to.

"Katie, what happened?" Concern colored his voice, and I almost answered. Almost fell into a calm and reasonable discussion.

But then he touched my shoulder, and it was like he'd closed a circuit in my soul. All the rage and the betrayal spewed out of me, and I jerked back, slapping his hand off of me.

"You son of a bitch," I cried, tears streaming down my face. "You lied to me. Dammit, Eric, you lied to *me*."

He took a step backward, and I saw the moment when he registered my use of his name. Surprise and shock, but no denial or confusion.

It was true, then, and I wailed with frustration, then hauled back and smacked him hard across the face. His cheek stung my palm, but he didn't make a sound, and I pulled back to do it again.

This time, he caught my wrist. "No," he said. And then he pulled me close, grabbed my other wrist as well, and held me steady. Then pressed his lips to mine and kissed me, his touch so familiar, and at the same time demanding and desperate. This time, however, I didn't kiss him back. Even though I missed him, and even though I wanted, with every breath in my body, to lose myself in him.

Instead I pushed him gently away, then looked deep into his questioning eyes. Eyes still lit with a fire born of need and, this time, with no apology.

"You lied to me," I said.

"I told you I wasn't the man you married. I'm not, Katie."

A bubble of anger rose and my temper flared. "That's bullshit, and you know it. You knew what I meant. You knew what I was asking. And you stood there and deliberately lied to me."

He turned away from me and walked to his patio door, then stood and looked out over the night. I could see his reflection in the glass door and knew that he could see me, too. I didn't move, only stood there, waiting for him to explain himself.

"What was I supposed to do, Kate?" he asked, his voice thick with regret. "I love you. You're married. You have a life. I can't be the guy who messes that up for you."

He turned to face me, and I saw the anger in his eyes. Not at me, but at the world. At the horrible circumstances that had ripped us apart, and then brought us back together with no hope for a future.

"So you tell me, Katie. Did I do wrong by not telling you the truth? Was it such a sin to try and make it easier on you?"

"You kissed me," I said. "You kissed me as David. How the hell was that making it easier on me?"

"I thought I'd lost you again," he said, and I could see the pain etched in his face. Real pain, so thick it seemed to cut me as well.

I shook my head, determined not to cave. I needed to understand, and I needed my head, not my heart. Because no matter how much I didn't want to believe them, Eddie's accusations of black magic lingered.

"You lied, Eric. You said you didn't know anything about the damn stone. How am I supposed to trust you when you lied about that? Allie got attacked. I almost got killed. And you stand there and tell me that you still love me?"

"Dammit, Kate, are you suggesting I would ever do anything to harm you? To harm Allie? I would never—"

"Then why didn't you say something? Why didn't you tell us what was going on from the very beginning?"

"Because I didn't know what was going on. I still don't. Kate," he said earnestly, "you have to believe me. I would never hurt you. I'd die before I'd let anything happen to you or to Allie."

I blinked back tears, the force of his words pulling me in, and yet his past actions keeping me far away. "The ring," I said, as one tear snaked down my cheek. "You should have told us about the ring."

"Wait . . . what?" His brow furrowed, and he took a step closer. "What ring? What the hell are you talking about?"

I blew out a frustrated breath. "Don't play games with me, Eric. I know you better than anyone." Or, I thought, I used to. "Wilson's ring. *Solomon's* ring."

He shook his head slowly. "The ruby ring? With the diamonds?"

I watched his face, trying to see the truth. I saw confusion there, and I saw hurt. Hurt that I would doubt him.

Damn it all, he really didn't know.

I ran my fingers through my hair and dropped onto his couch, then put my elbows on my knees and my head in my hands. After a moment, I felt the cushions shift, and then Eric's arm around me. I leaned against him, my eyes still closed.

"Tell me what happened in San Francisco," I said.

"I went there because another Hunter had contacted me. She said she had a lead. A clue as to why Wilson was murdered."

"Nadia," I said, starting to seethe a bit all over again, since he'd denied knowing her as well.

"No," he said. "I've never heard of Nadia Aiken. I swear, Kate."

"Go on."

"We talked a few times, and she wanted to see the things that Wilson had sent me."

"Things you'd never told me about."

"You were pregnant. He didn't want to disturb you."

"And after I wasn't pregnant anymore?"

He sighed. "Then *I* didn't want to disturb you. Wilson was dead, and I'd set the things aside. I forgot about them, honestly, even after I'd started *alimentatore* training. It wasn't until I heard from Diana that I remembered the packet from Wilson and thought there might be something relevant in there."

"From Diana? She was the Hunter?"

"Right."

"So what happened?"

He got up, started pacing his living room. "I went to see her. But I didn't trust her. I'm not sure why. So I told her I'd given everything of value to a charity, that Wilson would have wanted the stuff sold to support the Church."

He paused, turning back to look at my face, examining my eyes the way he always had, as if he could tell just by looking what I was thinking. I stayed silent, waiting for him to continue, and when he did, he seemed far away, as if talking about it had pulled him back to that dreary night so many years ago.

"She was irritated, I remember that. She said that she'd been counting on me having the things. That she really believed that the key to Wilson's death was in the things he'd sent me."

"So why didn't you give them to her?"

He shook his head slowly. "Honestly? There wasn't anything specific I could point to. But something made me hesitate. So I left. I told her I'd see if I could track them down, but I never really planned to."

"But you did take the stuff with you to San Francisco," I said. "You were wearing the ring when . . ." I swallowed. "When they found your body."

"I took it on the chance I changed my mind. I don't know. I wanted to know what happened to Wilson, so part of me hoped I'd be convinced. But . . ."

"And when you put the ring on, it attracted the demons," I said. "It attracted Andramelech, who'd been looking for that very ring."

"I'm thinking it must have, but I don't remember a thing. I remember leaving Diana and walking back to my hotel. I remember pain," he said, and I winced, hating the thought that he had to go through that. "And then I remember nothing."

"Until?"

He looked at me, his eyes serious. "Until I became David."

"That was years later," I said.

He nodded. "Time meant nothing to me, and once I was . . . well, David, I found you. I saw Stuart, I saw Timmy." He closed his eyes, and I watched the rise and fall of his chest as he drew in a long breath. "I saw the life you now have."

I hugged myself, as if by keeping my arms tight against my body, I could keep the emotions from bursting forth. I wanted to run away, wanted to simply pretend I didn't know any of this, and that Eric was still David and I'd never known the truth. But I did know it. I knew it and, so help me, I couldn't handle it.

"Kate?"

I held up a hand, as if I could ward off all the hurt. "I can't see you," I said, my voice shaking. "It's too hard. You were right not to tell me." Tears spilled down my cheeks, but I didn't bother to wipe them away. "I do have a family, and I can't mess that up. I can't hurt Stuart. He's innocent in all of this. And more, I love him."

"I know. That's what I was trying to do, remember?"

I managed I smile. "I know. Thank you."

"The demons, though," he said, his expression grave. "You do need someone watching your back."

"I've managed alone just fine."

"You have. But for how much longer?"

I turned away, refusing to acknowledge the question. "Maybe it's a moot point. If the demons have the ring, chances are good they've left San Diablo."

"And you're good with that?"

I shook my head. "But I'm not chasing around the globe anymore, Eric. I have a family. They come first."

"All right," he said, nodding slowly. "But what if the demons don't have the ring? What if they're still looking for it?"

I sighed, acknowledging the point. "Then I'll do what I've been doing. And I'll do it alone."

I turned for the door. I needed to get out of there before he saw my heart breaking.

"Allie," he said, his voice a whisper behind me.

I didn't turn around; I couldn't bear to look him in the eye. "You'll see her at school. As for the truth . . . I don't know. I'm . . . I'm going to have to think about it."

He put his hand on my shoulder, and I closed my eyes. "I never stopped loving you, Kate."

"I know," I said, my voice thick. "I never stopped loving you, either."

Fifteen

About the same time that I was confessing to my first husband that I still loved him, my second husband was standing behind a podium announcing his candidacy for county attorney.

Too bad for me, I didn't remember any of that until I was driving home from Eric's. Just one more tickey mark on my ever-growing guilt tally.

To his credit, Stuart took it okay once I told him (more guilt) that I'd had to rush to the high school for an emergency involving Allie, and that the announcement had completely slipped my mind. The emergency, I'd told him, was girl-related, a lie that I correctly assumed would prevent him from probing for more details.

"I've got some campaign functions to go to next week," he'd said after I'd apologized for the nine hundredth time.

"I'm so there," I'd promised, which smoothed the way even more, but not completely. I knew there were still a few bumps because instead of coming home, Stuart informed me that he'd be working late at the office.

I almost begged him to reconsider. At the moment, I really needed to feel my husband's arms around me. But the truth was that his absence was convenient. And that was a truth that made me feel even guiltier.

Wallowing, however, wasn't on the agenda. And so while Eddie dozed in the recliner and Timmy sat far too close to the television, I power-dialed every pawnshop in the Yellow Pages. If it was a student who stole the ring, I couldn't imagine that he or she would want to actually wear the hideous thing. It wasn't much of a lead, but at the moment, it was the only one I had.

Unfortunately, it went nowhere. None of the pawnshops had received a ring matching my description, and by the time the closing credits rolled on Timmy's ninety millionth viewing of *Frosty*, I was trying to decide if I should give up or expand my search to include pawnshops in the adjacent counties.

"What's for dinner?" Allie asked, bounding in from Stuart's study, where she'd been camped out in front of his computer, researching Andramelech and other demon-related things for the last hour or so.

"Whatever you want," I said. "Want to order a pizza?"

"On a Wednesday?" She cocked her head and looked at me. "Why?"

I tapped the phone book and explained what I was doing. "Why don't you make a list of everyone who takes gym at the same time you do. Then circle anyone you think might have it in them to steal jewelry."

"Okay, cool." She shifted from one foot to the other.

"What?"

"You said I could only do the research stuff for an hour, and then I had to do homework."

"So I did."

She rolled her eyes. "Mom, it's been an hour. So, like, if you want me to do this list thing, I have to wait on the algebra. Is that okay?"

I couldn't help my grin. "Yeah," I said, waiving my firm schoolwork-comes-first policy in favor of potentially saving innocent-though-thieving students from the forces of darkness. "That's okay."

"Rock on," she said, then disappeared to order the pizza. She came back in and announced that dinner would arrive within forty-five minutes, and that she'd be in her room.

"Hold up a sec," I shouted. "Did you close Stuart's browser? Did you do that thing . . ." I waved my hand in a circle, trying to remember what Laura had told me. "The history and the cookies," I finally said. "Did you delete them?"

I felt a little ridiculous training my daughter to hide her Internet meanderings from Stuart, but I didn't want to field the questions that might arise if Stuart saw where she'd been browsing. He might think nothing of it. Or, he might think that our girl was getting involved with the wrong kind of crowd.

In a way, I supposed that she was.

She headed off to do that, and when she returned, I thought to ask the most important question. "Did you learn anything?"

She shook her head. "Not really. I think I got a few leads, maybe. Eddie said he'd help me out, though, after I get my homework done this week. And then we're going to the library on the weekend."

"Oh, really?" I'd have to remember that the next time Eddie told me he was out of the game. "And here I thought research wasn't his thing."

She stared at me blankly and I waved her off, watching as she barreled up the stairs before I turned back to my phone calls. Santa Barbara County was next on the agenda, and if that didn't pan out, I just might start with Los Angeles.

Since Timmy was fidgety now that the movie was over, I took the cordless phone and moved to the couch, letting my little boy snuggle in my lap as he oh-so-helpfully flipped through the Yellow Pages for me. I'd managed to call a grand total of three pawnshops when I heard an, "*Ohmigod, Mom,*" from upstairs.

I was on my feet in a second, Timmy tumbling from my lap and squealing with laughter. "Allie!" I called, racing for the stairs and fearing the worst. "*Allie.*"

Her door flew open and she leaped out, the address book in her hand as she did a round of cheerleader-style high kicks. "I got it! I got it! I so, so got it!"

"What you're going to get," I said, "is trouble. You scared me to death."

"But I figured it out," she said.

"Who stole the ring?"

She shook her head as she handed me a list of about thirty names, none of them circled. "I can't believe any of these guys would steal it," she said.

"Then what?"

"Daddy's code!" She grabbed the address book off her bed and tossed it toward me. "And Nadia Aiken's the first person in the book."

"See?" she said, pointing to the entry in the black address book. "That's got to be her."

We were at the kitchen table now, and Allie was a bundle of energy, squirming in her seat and waiting for me to confirm her brilliant deduction.

"It says *Aidan,*" I said. "What am I missing?"

She let her head fall back, then blew out a sigh. "Come *on*, Mom. It's so obvious." She stabbed the book with her finger. "*Aidan A.* That's totally an anagram. N. A. D. I. A. And the *A* stands for Aiken."

"Wow," I said. "You may be right."

"I know I'm right. I'm totally right."

"What if it's just a coincidence?"

"It's not," she said. "Daddy loved anagrams, remember? We used to play them in the car."

I did remember, actually. I'd always been lousy at them, but Eric had been delighted that his eight-year-old daughter was just as tickled by the damn things as he was.

"It might not be her," I said, but now I was speaking only for form. Because "Nadia" was also an anagram for "Diana." And now I had to wonder: Was she lying to Eric about her name? Or was Eric lying to me?

"Just *call* already," Allie said, squirming in her chair. "Either way, we'll know soon enough."

Apparently I was raising a pragmatist. I drew in a breath, a little nervous about what new secrets of Eric's were about to be revealed, but determined to stumble forward anyway.

I was just about to pick up the phone when it rang. I glanced at Allie, who shrugged. I wasn't in the mood for calls, and I didn't recognize the name on the caller ID— Lackland—but I answered anyway. Then soon found myself wishing I hadn't.

"Kate? Is this Katherine Crowe?"

I clutched the kitchen counter, my knees going weak at the sound of my former name. "Who's calling, please?"

"Kate? Is that you? This is Betty Lackland. You know, from the library?"

"Betty. Hi." I let out a sigh of relief. Allie had just talked to her, which means she was probably calling to tell me what my daughter was up to. "Thanks so much for talking to Allie the other day," I said, wanting to nip in the bud any suspicion that Allie was poking around behind my back. "She really appreciated it."

"Oh, I didn't mind at all, dear. She's a lovely girl." She hesitated, then lowered her voice to a stage whisper, "But that's actually why I'm calling."

"Okay," I said. I held up a finger, then signaled to Allie to stay while I went into the other room. I didn't know what Betty was up to, but I could already tell I wasn't going to like it. "What's up?"

"It's just . . . oh, dear. I wasn't going to bring this up," she said. "Not ever. But I'm just so afraid that if your daughter keeps poking around that, well . . ."

"Betty, what?"

"Well, I'm afraid she's going to find out some unpleasant things about her father."

I immediately tensed. "Like what, exactly?"

"Oh, sweetie, I didn't even want to tell *you* this. But, well, Eric was acting quite peculiar before he took that trip to San Francisco."

"Peculiar how?"

"Well, he always kept to himself, but I'd never gotten the feeling that he was hiding something. But that week . . . Well . . . it's just that . . ."

I drew in a breath. "Betty, please, don't worry. It's been almost six years. I'm remarried. Whatever you have to tell me, I'll be fine." That was about as blatant as a lie could be, but it served my purpose.

"It's just that there were so many telephone calls. With that *woman*," she added, as if women by nature carried disease.

"I'm sure it was nothing," I said, trying to sound cheery. In fact, though, it was probably everything. The calls from Nadia—from Diana—were what convinced him to go to San Francisco in the first place, and the secrecy certainly didn't surprise me. Not under the circumstances.

"It's just that, you know, she was such a pretty thing."

That caught my attention. "You met her?"

"She came into the library once. And Eric was very remote after she left. Honestly, he seemed a bit irritated that she'd come at all." She sighed heavily. "Oh, Kate darling, I just hate telling you all this, but—"

"Nonsense," I said, my throat tight. "I appreciate your concern. But she's a family friend. Truly. There was nothing going on. Nothing at all."

"Oh, thank goodness. I'm so relieved."

"Quite a burden to hold on to for all these years," I said, forcing myself to smile so that I sounded cheerful and happy.

"Yes, it was. And I'm so glad to know it was all a misunderstanding. I couldn't believe that Eric would cheat on you. That just didn't seem like him."

I gripped the phone so hard I was afraid it might break. "No," I said, "not like him at all."

An affair. As I hung up, I turned the possibility over in my mind. No way. It simply wasn't feasible. I don't care how much sneaking around he was doing. Eric Crowe would not cheat on his wife. He wouldn't cheat on me. Period. End of story.

But as I tried to push the thought from my head, Betty's words kept coming back to haunt me. And once again, I had to remind myself that I didn't know Eric nearly as well as I'd once believed.

*   *   *

I did finally manage to pull myself together enough to go back into the kitchen, where Allie was waiting impatiently for me.

"Well?"

"Nothing," I said, hoping I was speaking the truth. "Turns out it was nothing at all."

"Then can we call, already?"

"Absolutely," I said. I picked up the phone and dialed the number, only to be rewarded by the telltale clicking of a forwarding service, and then a live voice. "Wayside Answering."

"Ah," I said. "Hi. I'm not sure I called the right place." I read the number in the book back to the operator.

"That's correct," she said. "Would you care to leave a message?"

"Is this the number for Nadia Aiken?"

"No, ma'am."

"Aidan A?"

"I'm sorry, no."

"Diana Kaine?" I tried, figuring the third time's the charm.

"Yes, ma'am."

I grinned at Allie and gave her a thumbs-up sign. In a day gone terribly awry, at least we'd managed one victory.

"Is this service still active? I mean, does she get a lot of calls?"

"I'm sorry, I can't disclose that information."

"Right. Thanks."

"Would you like to leave a message?"

I did, keeping it short and sweet but to the point.

"My name is Kate Connor, but I used to be Katherine Crowe," I began. "We used to work for the same people. And I think I've got information about a buddy of yours. A Mr. Andre." I ended with my telephone number, then turned to Allie with a shrug. "I guess we'll see."

"There was a person on the other end?"

"That's how answering services used to work," I said. "Before voice mail."

"Freaky."

"Mmm." From my daughter's perspective, anything not run with a microchip was freaky indeed.

"So now we wait?"

"You need to be prepared for the fact that she may never call back. Who knows how long ago that service was set up? It might have been paid years in advance. Nadia really could be dead. We just don't know."

Her shoulders slumped. "Okay. So, like, what else can we do? There's got to be a way to find the ring, right?"

I hoped there was, but it was a long shot. "We'll see what Father Ben and Father Corletti come up with," I said. I'd called Father Ben right after we learned the ring was missing, and we put together a conference call to Rome. Father Corletti had immediately dispatched the news to all active watchers and *alimentatores*. *Forza* would keep a close watch on cult activity. If any of the Andramelech cults became active, we'd hear about it. And we'd know that he'd been released from the ring.

"But that only works if a demon stole it," Allie said, after I reminded her of all that.

"True enough," I said. I pulled her student list from my back pocket. "That's why we need to get busy on this."

She sighed. "I don't know most of these kids well enough, and none of the ones I do know are the type who'd steal someone's stuff. But I've been thinking, and I think I can figure it out if I just ask around. I mean, Coronado's a pretty good school, all in all. If someone's bragging about stealing a ring, I bet I can find out about it."

"Allie," I said sharply, "you need to be careful."

She presented me with a major eye roll. "Come *on*, Mom. I'm only going to talk to other kids. I'm not even going to threaten them with a crossbow."

"Allie . . ."

"Honestly," she said, holding up her hands, a mischievous expression on her face. "I'd never manage to smuggle a crossbow into the school. Your stiletto, though . . ."

I couldn't help it; I laughed. "Go," I said. "I'll call you when the pizza gets here."

"Cool." She bounded off through the living room, and I leaned against the kitchen counter, trying to shake the dark mood that was beginning to settle over me once again. *Diana Kaine.*

Who are you? More important, who were you to my husband?

I was balancing on a knife edge, with the man I'd loved so desperately *right there*, close enough to touch. And yet I couldn't have him. Wasn't even sure if I trusted him.

And I told myself I *didn't* want him. I had a new family. A new life. And as sad as that made me, my life with Eric had died when his body did.

I knew that. I knew it a thousand times over. In my head, the answer was so clear. So simple.

My heart though . . . my heart wanted to cry.

"The boy's asleep on the couch," Eddie said, shuffling into the kitchen. He peered at me, then planted himself in my path. "Give it up, girlie. This ain't cramps. What's got your panties in a tangle?"

I couldn't help it. The tears began to flow.

And Eddie—curmudgeonly Eddie, who'd known the truth all along and didn't trust David at all—held me tight and let me sob.

Sixteen

I cried myself to sleep, and was awakened by the press of something soft against my cheek. Immediately, I was on alert, but I managed to rein in my reaction before I impaled my husband with the stiletto I'd slipped under the mattress on my side of the bed.

"Hey," he said from beside me. "I didn't mean to scare you."

"Weird dreams," I said, noticing the rose he held out for me. "Stuart?"

"I'm sorry," he said.

I blinked, wondering if perhaps I wasn't still asleep and having a very odd dream. "What are you sorry for?"

"For being mostly AWOL these last few months getting ready for the campaign. And because I know I'm going to be absent even more, now that it's officially started."

I propped myself up on an elbow. "Stuart, I'm the one who missed the announcement."

"I know," he said. "And that got me thinking. How many

Sunday afternoons have I missed? How many dinners have you kept warm for me?" He shrugged, looking both boyish and sexy. "I wanted you to know I appreciate it. And I love you."

"I love you, too," I said, feeling all warm and tingly inside. "Thank you."

He pulled me close, and I spooned against him. And then I drifted back to sleep, my head filled with both Stuart and Eric, but only one man's arms around me.

To Eddie's credit, he didn't mention Eric the next morning. For that matter, he didn't mention my crying jag. He just squinted at me when he passed by on his way to get coffee. "You doing okay there this morning, girlie?"

I nodded. "Yeah. Thanks. I'm doing okay."

He studied me, and for a second, I thought he might argue. Then he gave a satisfied snort, took his coffee, and left the room.

I collapsed into one of the chairs at the breakfast table and tried to decide if I really was doing okay. Fortunately, I was saved from extreme introspection by a tap at the back door. I heard Eddie's gruff, "It's open," and then Laura's footsteps as she crossed the short distance to the kitchen and the breakfast area.

When she passed through the arch dividing the two rooms, she blew me a kiss and flashed a smile worthy of a Miss America contestant.

"Either you're auditioning for a commercial," I said, "or you had a truly hot date last night."

"I'll leave it to your imagination to guess which one."

"I have a very good imagination, you know."

She rubbed her hands together. "Give it your best shot."

"Laura!" I said with mock shock. "You wild woman."

She waved my comments away. "No, no, no. Not that much imagination. He was much too much the gentleman." She pressed a hand over her heart. "But, Kate, he gave me roses. And he opened the car door for me. And," she added, holding out her hand and patting the air for effect, "the best part? He didn't spend the entire evening talking about himself."

"And he's still single?" I said, trying hard not to smile. "What is his grand flaw?"

"If he has one, I haven't discovered it yet."

"I'm so excited for you," I said as she got up for a cup of coffee. "I'm glad someone's love life is getting back on the rails."

She started to say something then stopped, cocking her head as she looked at me. The she shook her head slowly. "No, no, no. You are not getting off that easy. What happened?"

"Later," I said. "Tell me more about Doctor Love."

"Now," she insisted. "Or you get no more sordid details."

"Okay," I said. "But only because I'm craving sordid details." And then I took a deep breath, and I told her. All of it. The realization that David truly was Eric. Our confrontation. Betty's suggestion that Eric had been having an affair. And, yes, our kiss.

"And then you walked away," she said. "Oh, God, Kate." She reached across the table and took my hand. "This has really been a crappy week for you, hasn't it?"

I laughed. "That's putting it mildly."

"But you're okay now? Really?"

"Better than last night. In case you're wondering, Eddie's shoulders are bony."

"You should have called me."

"And interrupt your date? Not a chance."

She inspected my face, her eyes intense. "For something like that, interrupting a hot date is totally allowed. An old boyfriend living in the body of your daughter's chemistry teacher? No, for that you'd have to wait. But a husband? *Definitely* allowed to call."

I pressed my lips together so I wouldn't laugh. "You're insane, you know that, right?"

"Do you remember when I asked to help you? With all the demon-hunting research, I mean?"

I nodded.

"Sweetie, *that* was your first clue I was insane."

"No, no, no," I countered. "All that research is child's play. I knew you were crazy the first time you offered to watch Timmy. Remember?"

"Oh yeah," she said, nodding. "The weeks of explosive diapers. You're right. I must have been crazy."

"It's good that you are," I said. "Who else would put up with me?"

"I can think of two members of the male species who seem pretty keen on keeping you around," she said. "Although maybe David counts as two people. And one more if we add in Cutter."

"You can't add in Cutter," I said, laughing.

"Trust me, sweetie," she said with a nod. "We can."

"At any rate," I said, turning serious again, "we can cross Eric and David off the list. I told David I couldn't be around him anymore. It's just too hard."

"I know," she said. "Although, actually, I don't. I can't even imagine. But I think you made the right decision."

"Did I?" I asked. "How can I be sure?"

"I think you just have to feel it in your heart."

"And if your heart is numb?"

"Oh, Kate," she said, squeezing my hand. "Do you love Stuart?"

"Of course I do."

She tapped my wedding band. "Have you taken this ring off since you said *I do*?"

I shook my head.

"Does he love you?"

I smiled, remembering last night. About that, there really wasn't a doubt in my mind.

"Then there you go. Eric *died*, Kate. He's back, but like he said, he's not the man you married. It's different. Maybe it doesn't seem like it to you because you're so close, but trust me on this. The whole situation with David and Eric? Very, *very* different."

I had to laugh. Not only at her expression but because she was so very right.

"I just . . . I just miss him, you know?"

"I know, sweetie. And maybe *David* can still be in your life," she said, with emphasis on the name. "I don't know, Kate. I really don't. Are you strong enough?"

I thought of Eric, the man I'd loved for so long. The man who'd been my partner and my lover and my little girl's father. And I thought of him now. The way his hands felt against my skin. The way his lips had pressed to mine. The way my heart had picked up tempo as he pulled me close.

I thought about seeing him at school functions, about patrolling with him along the beach under a blanket of stars. And I thought about never, ever touching him again.

"No," I said. "I'm not that strong." I looked Laura in the eye. "Dear God, Laura. What am I going to do?"

* * *

Hours later, the question still glowed like neon in my mind. I desperately wished I could trust myself—that I could step up to the plate and swear to myself and God that I had enough self-control to work with David and stay faithful to my husband.

Honestly, though, I didn't know if I could.

That kind of self-awareness is sobering, to say the least, and I wasn't sure if I should feel shame for my lack of self-control or pride for my self-awareness.

About all I did know was that I needed to avoid David. Maybe in a few months I'd have my emotions under control. But now? In the wake of that kiss?

Now, I needed to stay far, far away from the man who was no longer my husband.

While my thoughts had been in turmoil, my hands had been busy folding laundry, and now I hefted a stack of jeans and T-shirts and headed for the stairs and Allie's room. I managed to get about two steps from the couch when the phone rang. At one-thirty, I wasn't expecting any calls, and since I wasn't inclined to talk to a telemarketer that afternoon, I let the machine grab it.

"Kate?" David's voice filtered through the tinny speakers. "Kate, if you're there, pick up."

I licked my lips but forced my feet to stay planted to the spot.

I heard him mutter a curse, and then, "Call my cell the second you get home. It's about Allie," he said. "She's not in school today."

I dropped the laundry and sprinted for the phone. "David! David!" But it was too late. He'd already hung up.

I called him back immediately, but naturally I got one of those irritating messages that lie and tell you the subscriber is out of the area even though you know damn well that he's not.

I slammed the phone down, grabbed my keys, and headed into the garage. I was backing into the driveway when a car I didn't recognize pulled up behind me and blocked my path. I laid on the horn, but the car didn't move, so I got out, more than prepared to wail a little bit on the 1970s station wagon.

It was when I got out that I saw who was in the passenger seat—my daughter. And in the backseat, looking guilty and smug all at the same time? Eddie.

I didn't recognize the woman driving the car, but she turned and flashed a denture-white smile at Eddie as he and Allie piled out. I rushed forward, ready to lay in to the both of them, then stopped when I saw Allie's tear-stained face.

"What happened?" I asked, my relief at seeing them turning once again to alarm.

But Allie just shook her head and pushed past me toward the house.

"Al—"

"Let her go," Eddie said. "The girl's got a few things to think about."

"And you have a few things to explain," I said. "Where the hell have you been, for one? And why isn't Allie in school?"

"The library," he said. "And we've been doing research."

Little warning bells clanged in my head. "What kind of research?"

"The girl wanted to know how to use the ring to trap a demon."

"And you figured it out? At the San Diablo library?" Actually, that wouldn't be that remarkable. Eric had been the rare books librarian there, once upon a time. And if he'd been using his budget to fund his *alimentatore* resources, the collection probably had some interesting items. Even without the

Forza influence, I knew that Eric often gravitated toward obscure volumes.

That Eddie had managed to find them, though, surprised me.

"Not the library," he said. "I still got a few connections. Called in some favors, got a few of my old buddies looking in the right places. They emailed a few files. We didn't want to use Stuart's computer. 'Nuff said."

"And what did you learn?"

He glanced back toward the house. "It's Allie's story," he said. "I'm gonna let her tell it."

"Then she can tell it now," I said. "I'm done waiting."

I went inside and found my daughter curled up in a ball on the couch, her knees tucked against her chest and her arms tight around her. My resolve immediately vanished, replaced by a desperate maternal need to comfort.

I squeezed onto the edge of the couch and put my arms around her, pulling her even closer as she turned toward me and buried her face against my thigh.

We sat like that for a while, with me stroking her hair and murmuring soft words. Allie, however, said nothing, merely shook with silent sobs. And the more the silence thickened, the more my nerves frayed.

"Allie, baby, you're scaring me. Tell me what you found."

Nothing.

"Allie, please. At least tell me you're okay."

She rolled over, blinking up at me through eyes rimmed black with smeared mascara. "I know what happened," she said, squeezing the words out between sobs. "To Daddy, I mean."

I stroked her face. "Can you tell me?"

She hiccupped again, but nodded. "I . . . I went with Eddie. And we—"

"I know," I said. "He told me. It's okay. But tell me what you learned."

"It was all in old-fashioned language and stuff, but Eddie and I went through it all, really slow, you know? And we figured it out, Mom. And it's so not good for Daddy."

"Tell me."

She wiped the back of her hand under her nose. "It said that trapping a demon using the stone mounted on the ring forged by Solomon was the greatest sacrifice." Another big snuffle. "That to trap the demon, you had to do the whole eye-stick thing, but with the finger wearing the ring. Instead of being sucked out into the air, the demon would be sucked into the ring."

She paused and I frowned, wondering where the sacrifice came in. I didn't ask, though. There was clearly more to this story, and she'd tell me in her own time.

She didn't, though. Instead, the tears started up again.

"Oh, honey," I said, my heart about to break. "Please tell me. Surely it's not that bad?"

"It sucked out his soul, Mom," she said, her voice a wail. "When Daddy trapped the demon, his soul got sucked out. That's the sacrifice. Not Heaven, not Hell, but just wandering, floating lost in the air, like all around us. *Daddy*, Mom. He's not watching over us. He's just lost. And all because he trapped that stupid demon."

The tears started again, forced out by the sobs that rattled her body.

After a moment, the sobs slowed and she looked up at me, the pain etching lines in her face. "Is that purgatory? Is Daddy in purgatory?"

"I don't know. I guess maybe it is."

"Then we should pray for him? Prayers can get souls out of purgatory, right?"

"Yes, baby, you should pray. Pray very hard." I pulled her close, my own eyes welling as I let her cry it out, her body shaking with grief and loss. I rocked her, wishing I could make it better.

I could, I knew. I could make the hurt go away.

All I had to do was tell her about David. Tell her that somehow—by luck or black magic or pure happenstance—her father's soul had finally found a home.

Somehow, though, the words wouldn't come. Because no matter what I might tell Eddie, I still had doubts. And until I was certain I could trust Eric again, I wasn't going to risk another ache in my daughter's heart.

Except for Timmy's constant singing to himself, dinner was a quiet, melancholy affair. Both Allie and I were lost in our thoughts of Eric. Stuart spent the evening mostly silent, presumably concentrating on his campaign plans. Eddie focused primarily on his mashed potatoes.

Honestly, by the time everyone was done, I was happy to start doing the dishes. And I very rarely use the words *happy* and *dishes* in the same sentence.

I'd just finished loading the dishwasher when the phone rang. I wiped my hands, grabbed it up, then called Allie to the phone for one of her increasingly frequent calls from teenage boys.

She took it and turned her back to me, lowering her voice—yet another teenage vice, but at least she hadn't decided to take the call in her room with the door closed. I couldn't hear her over the running tap water—not that I was trying—but I could tell from her expression when she turned around that the conversation was important.

"Who was it?"

"One of the football players," she said. "He'd heard some buzz about the ring. About how Tyrone Creach is going to try to pass it off to a college student tonight. Some guy who sells stolen jewelry."

"Where? And when?"

"The Dime Box," she said, referring to one of the night-clubs in the warehouse district. "Right at closing. There's an alley behind the club, and apparently a lot of this kind of stuff happens by the Dumpster."

"Tyrone," I repeated. "Who is he again?"

"Lillian's boyfriend," she said. "She has to be the one who took the ring."

"Lillian," I repeated. "That name sounds familiar."

"I beat her out for the freshman spot on the cheerleading team," Allie reminded me. "But I never thought she held that much of a grudge. Man, what a bitch!"

"Allie!"

"Sorry, but she stole Daddy's ring."

"Yes, well, I think she may end up with more than she bargained for." I frowned, considering. "If neither one of them has put it on," I said, "maybe I can get it back before the demons clue in to them."

"And if they have?"

"Then I'll have my job cut out for me."

"I want to help."

"You did. Just now."

"*Mother*. I want to go with you."

"Not on your life," I said, already heading through the living room toward the stairs. It wasn't even nine yet, but if I started slowly, I could transfer some of my better weapons to the Odyssey without Stuart noticing. I figured I had time; after all, a bar's typical closing time is two a.m.

"You have to let me go," Allie said, bouncing a little and actually resorting to whining.

"I'm pretty sure I don't," I said. "As the mom, I have total and complete control. Much like a benevolent dictator."

"Mom . . ."

"I'm serious, Al. This could be dangerous."

She stood staring at me, her hands on her hips, and I knew she was trying to come up with a creative solution to this problem. But there was no way she'd be that creative, because I was determined to keep her out of harm's way.

"I'm the only one who knows what he looks like."

Okay, that was actually a good point. "Where's your yearbook?"

She flashed a smug grin. "This is my first year at Coronado, remember? And he's a senior. I don't *have* a yearbook with his picture."

"Mindy," I said. "Surely she keeps all the back issues of the school paper. Any pics in there?"

She crossed her arms over her chest and stared me down. "Maybe," she said. "But Mindy's staying at her dad's tonight."

I sighed.

"Please, Mom? You'll know him by the demons if it's too late, but what if it's not? I don't like him, but we can't let him get nailed by Andramelech's henchmen."

"I'm hoping he never put the ring on and henchmen aren't an issue."

"But then you *really* won't know what he looks like. There could be tons of kids hanging out in the alley."

Damn it all, she was right. "You stay in the van," I said. "No matter what happens, you do not get out of that car. Do you hear me, young lady?"

She practically vibrated with excitement as she nodded and assured me that she heard me just fine.

"We'll sneak out of the house later. In the meantime," I said, "help me smuggle some weapons down from the attic."

The smuggling part was actually easy since Stuart was tucked away in his study. The waiting, though, was hard. Allie was such a bundle of nervous energy I thought she'd spontaneously combust before we made it out the door. I was on edge, too, especially since I finally decided that this was important enough to break my no-David rule. But when I called him, I got no answer, which left me both worried and irritated.

Finally, the house was quiet. I snuck out of bed and then tapped on Allie's door. She flew out immediately, her face a mix of anticipation and excitement.

"Quiet," I whispered, which was pretty useless, really, since our garage-door opener makes enough noise to wake the house.

We stood in the kitchen as the door opened, listening for any telltale signs of life. Nothing.

"Okay," I said. "Come on."

The drive to the alley was uneventful, and the alley itself was drab and uninteresting. Instead of groups of kids milling around, there was nobody. Not even a homeless person. I shot Allie a questioning look, but she just shrugged. "This is where they said. Honest."

I pulled the van in until we were about twenty yards from the back door to the club, then killed the engine and turned off the lights. As I did, the door to the club opened, and I could see a sliver of blackish-blue light. Two figures stepped out and Allie leaned forward, pressing her hands to the dash as she angled for a better look.

"That's him!" she said, pointing to the burly teenager on

the left. He was talking with a tall, pale skinny guy, and although I peered hard at the fellow, I couldn't tell if he was human or demon. Which, frankly, is one of those little demon quirks that makes my job so hard.

Tyrone pulled something from his pocket and showed it to Skinny.

"That's got to be the ring," I said to Allie, grabbing my stiletto. I had two other knives hidden on my person, but the crossbow I was leaving in the car. If there were no demons, it would be hard to explain a medieval weapon in a dark California alley.

I was about fifteen steps from the car when all hell broke loose. Skinny jumped Tyrone, his body shimmering red as the true demon shone through. Tyrone screamed and I raced forward, determined both to save this kid's life and get the ring back.

Behind me, a huge clatter seemed to shake the alley. A metallic bang was followed by a growl and a scream. I turned, terror filling me at the sight I confronted—a hellhound on top of the van, snarling down and battering the front windshield so hard that the glass shattered.

Inside, my daughter was screaming, but she'd grabbed the crossbow and held it at the ready.

I abandoned the quest for the ring, racing back toward Allie even as the creature broke through the window, then started trying to wriggle inside to get my daughter.

"*Allie,*" I screamed. "Shoot! Shoot now!" She did, but the shot went wild, barely scraping the hellhound, which seemed only to become more aggressive now that she'd injured it.

The canine leaped and then, suddenly, someone jumped from the fire escape above to land on top of my van. It was a woman, tall and thin and dressed all in black leather.

From a scabbard on her back, she pulled out a sword, the

blade glinting in the moonlight, then slammed it down into the hellhound's body.

"Go!" she yelled. "I'll take care of the kid. Get that demon."

I hesitated, but as I did, she reared back with the blade once again, this time crashing it through the hound's skull. An inhuman wail as the creature died, its body sucked into a spinning, hellish vortex, leaving a stain of oil all over the top and sides of the van.

At the other end of the alley, the demon kicked Tyrone in the gut, knocking him to the ground. The demon snatched the ring, then held it high in the sky, his body stock still. I reared back, knife at the ready, my aim on his left eye. I let the knife fly and it spun over and over, landing with a squish in the demon's eye just as a jet-black crow materialized from the night sky, snatching the ring in its beak.

The demon escaped into the ether, its host body collapsing in a heap on the ground. Tyrone grunted something unintelligible, then took off running. And the ring disappeared into the sky.

I drew in a breath and prayed for strength. The ring was with the demons now. Andramelech would be released. And as far as I knew, there wasn't a damn thing I could do about that.

Right now, though, my concern was for my daughter, and as I hurried back to the van I saw her sitting on the pavement, her expression a bit shell-shocked, and the mystery woman standing over her, the sword still tight in her hand.

I squatted beside Allie and pulled her close as she snuggled against me. I kissed her hair, inspected every inch of her to make sure she was safe, then lifted my head up to her defender, who stood right there, impassively staring down at us.

"Nadia Aiken, I presume?"

"Got it in one," she said, then sheathed the blade.

Seventeen

"And you're Katherine Crowe," Nadia said.

"Katherine Connor," I corrected.

"Oh, yeah. Right." She bent down to retrieve a slim cigarette case from the top of her thigh-high boot, then pulled out a hand-rolled cigarette. She offered one to me, and then to Allie. I declined for both of us, thank you very much.

I hugged my daughter closer, stroking her hair and wishing I could make all the bad things go away. "Thank you," I said to Nadia. "If you hadn't come when you did . . ." I trailed off, my mind not even capable of processing the potential horror.

She lifted one shoulder in a shrug, then lit her cigarette. "But I did," she said, as her exhaled smoke drifted lazily around her. She looked from Allie to me. "Come on, Crowe," Nadia said. "Let's get off the street and go someplace where we can talk."

"Give us a minute more," I said, still holding Allie.

From her vantage point above us, Nadia kicked at the toe

of Allie's tennis shoe. "Buck up there, kid. You fall apart every time you get into a scrape, and you'll never make it as a Hunter."

"She *isn't* a Hunter."

"That's what I'm saying," Nadia said.

In my arms, Allie shifted then sat up, pulling out of my embrace. "I'm okay, Mom," she said firmly. She looked up at Nadia. "I'm not falling apart."

"Good for you, kid." She gave Allie her hand and then helped her to her feet. Me, she left to get up by myself.

"So why are you here?" Allie asked, and I had to give my kid points. She'd bounced back, and now she was back on track. In my heart, I knew it was only teenage stubbornness reacting to Nadia's little digs, but that didn't change the fact that she was resilient. And as much as I didn't care for Nadia's less-than-maternal method, I had to admit she was right. Allie might not be a Hunter—not yet, and maybe not ever—but she was in the fray. And falling apart was a luxury left only to the dead.

"I got your message," Nadia said. "I was in L.A., so I thought I'd drive up. See what you needed." She looked at me. "Glad I did."

"Me, too," I said. "But how did you find us here?"

"Drove by your house," she said. "I saw you pulling out so I decided to follow. Scope you out, you know? Make sure you weren't leading me into a trap."

"Why would we do that?" Allie asked.

She took another draw on her cigarette. "No idea, kid. But I've been living off the grid for years now. And everyone I gave that answering service number to is dead."

Allie looked at me, as if I could explain that oddity. I couldn't. I asked, "Why not cancel the service?"

"If I had, I never would have heard from you," she said.

She dropped her cigarette and stubbed it out with her toe. In front of us, two college-age boys came out of the back door of the Dime Box, their laughter drunken and raucous. Nadia watched them, her eyes cool. They saw her and gave a low, appreciative whistle. She smiled sweetly, then flipped them the bird before turning back to Allie and me.

"Let's get out of here."

I debated what to do about the Odyssey, and decided that I couldn't take it home. If Stuart noticed its absence in the morning, I could say I ran out of gas while running to get cold medicine for Timmy at the 7-Eleven. Not the best of stories, but it would work.

If he actually saw the windshield smashed in, though? That would be a bit harder to explain.

I ended up leaving it at the auto body shop we'd used a year ago after a minor fender bender. I locked it up, left a note and the key in the drop box, and then Allie and I headed for Nadia's car. She'd followed us there in a cherry-red Lotus that had Allie's mouth hanging open. She spent the ride turned sideways in the passenger seat, gaping at Nadia, and giving me a running commentary on how hot the Lotus was, and wasn't Nadia cool, and did I have a scabbard like that to keep slung over my back?

There was a twenty-four-hour diner next door to the auto-body place, and so we popped in there, ordering pancakes with strawberries and whipped cream for me and Allie, and plain black coffee for Nadia, who chain-smoked the entire meal despite the No Smoking signs and nasty looks from the staff.

She'd left her weapons in her car—the visible ones, anyway—but I think they could tell she was dangerous, and no one came by to ask her to put out her light.

"So give me the run-down," she said. "Your message was

pretty cryptic, but it sounds like you've clued in to Andramelech?"

"Looks that way," I said, trying to walk a fine line of getting information without revealing too much. I trusted her—she'd saved Allie, after all. But only to a point.

"You can't know much," she said, exhaling toward the ceiling. "Andramelech disappeared five years ago. He must have been bound. That's the only explanation."

"Agreed," I said. "And we have—"

"The ring," Allie put in. "He's trapped in King Solomon's ring."

I kept my expression bland, but gave her knee a quick squeeze. She looked up at me, confused, and I shook my head, just a little. I could see from her face that she still didn't understand.

Across the booth, Nadia laughed. "Your mom wants to take this slowly," she said. "You don't know me and I don't know you, and this is dangerous business."

"But Mom," Allie said, apparently not understanding the finer nuances. I decided that now wasn't the time to explain them to her. Considering she was drowning in leather-clad hero worship, I doubted anything I said would make an impact anyway.

"We found the ring," I said, taking the plunge. "Eric had it. I inherited it."

Her expression didn't waver. Her eyes didn't blink. But after a beat, she did pick up her fork and tap the tines against her thumb. I tried to decide if that meant anything from a grand psychological perspective, realized I had no knack for psychoanalysis at all, and simply waited for her to speak.

"I'm surprised the demons didn't take it after he died. I had no idea the ring had ended up with you."

"Neither did I," I admitted. "We found it only recently."

"It's not something to be toyed with, you know. Once Wilson realized what he had, he sent it to Eric, but told me to track it down. He wanted me to work with Eric to nail the son of a bitch."

"What happened?"

Nadia leaned back against the booth's worn upholstery. "I'm not sure your husband completely trusted me, Kate." The corner of her mouth twitched just slightly, and she focused on me. "Maybe he believed I wanted more from him than just the ring."

My chest tightened, and I wanted to ask why he would believe that. Wanted to ask what had happened between them, what they had discussed during their phone calls, and why she'd come to San Diablo. And, most important, why neither Eric nor David had seen fit to tell me that she'd been here.

Betty's innuendoes skittered through my brain, and I felt my throat clog with tears. I didn't want to believe the worst of my husband, and yet I couldn't help the doubts and fears that were easing in around the cracks.

I thought about what David had said, about how in the end he hadn't trusted Nadia. Why, I wondered. Had he gotten too close to her? Close enough to get burned?

"We should get the ring," she said, her focus wider and encompassing Allie, too. "It needs to be in the Vatican, safe on holy ground." She smiled at Allie. "Have you ever seen Rome? It's fabulous."

"Mom?"

"We can't," I said, realizing that all my mental meanderings added up to nothing. Whatever happened between Eric and Nadia was ancient history, no matter how much that history might hurt me now. And whatever Eric's reasons for not telling her he still had the ring, they didn't matter now. "The ring is gone."

She blinked. "What the hell are you talking about?"

"You were there," I said, my voice calm even though I was screaming inside. I'd lost the damn ring, and I'd almost lost that boy as well. "The ring could be anywhere now."

"The crow," she said. "Are you telling me the goddamn crow took the ring?"

"We'd gone to the alley to try to get it back," Allie said. "It's my fault. I took it to school and then it got stolen." She continued on from there, spilling the story to Nadia even as tears spilled from her cheeks.

"Don't cry," Nadia said. "Never cry about your mistakes. Just fix them."

"That's what we were trying to do," Allie said with a sniff. "That's why we came. To try to get the ring back."

"Didn't much work out, though, did it?" she asked, the question aimed at me.

"Allie's alive," I said. "And so is the boy. Right now, I'm willing to call that a victory."

"That's a crock of shit and you know it. It's only a victory if we stop Andramelech's minions from releasing him and the other imprisoned demons. I've spent my entire life trying to defeat that demon, and because of your fuck-up, now I'm set back for God only knows how long." She took a breath. "He's going to get free, Crowe. Do you realize what that means? Do you realize what kind of demon we're dealing with here?"

I assured her I did.

"God*damn* it," she said, slamming a fist onto the table and making the plates and silverware bang and clatter.

"So what now?" Allie asked. "I mean, now that they have the ring, the demons will leave San Diablo, right?"

"It's a good bet," I said. "Why stay in a town filled with Hunters?"

"Unless they need the town," Nadia said.

Something in her voice gave me pause. "What do you know?"

"There's a ritual," she said. "For releasing the demons."

"And they need something here," I said, seeing where this was leading. "Something in San Diablo."

"The ritual to release or destroy has to take place here," she said.

"Where?"

"I don't know," she admitted. "Not exactly. But I have my notes. Maybe your *alimentatore* can give us a hand reviewing them?"

"We'll go right now," I said, signaling for the check.

"Good." She slid out of the booth and stretched, her breasts straining against the soft leather of her shirt. Every male in the diner strained for a better look.

She ignored them all, her attention focused solely on me. "We have one last chance to get the ring before his followers free Andramelech from the stone," she said, looking at me intently. "And this time, let's not blow it, okay?"

By the time we'd awakened Father Ben, brought him up to speed, and returned home, it was almost four in the morning. Nadia insisted that she could go to a motel, but considering the day was about to begin again in just a few hours, that seemed absurd.

"Stay here," I said. "Sleep on the couch in Stuart's study, and once the house is empty, we can talk some more." Father Ben had promised to go over Nadia's notes in detail. Maybe by the time we were all awake, he'd have found something out.

I taped Stuart a note to the bathroom mirror telling him

that an old friend of mine had called late last night, and that she was sleeping in his study. I also begged him to drive Timmy to day care and let me sleep in.

Thankfully, my husband didn't question the houseguest or the child care. He did, however, notice the Lotus parked in the garage where the Odyssey used to be. The note he left for me—this one taped to the microwave—had an arrow aimed toward the garage and a very large exclamation point.

I grinned. He didn't know the half of it.

I had the house to myself for one blissful hour, and then life began to stir. Eddie returned from his walk, hooked a thumb at the garage, and raised his eyebrows. I started to bring him up to speed, but at that moment, Nadia pranced in, wearing a T-shirt cut so low it was barely decent, and black leggings so tight they left nothing to the imagination.

And, yes, I admit I was impressed. She was probably only four or five years younger than me, but *she* clearly had no problem finding a dress that didn't cling too tight to her thighs.

I looked down at my black yoga pants, ratty PTA T-shirt, and unpainted toenails and vowed to buy new pajamas. And give myself a manicure. Highlights, too, I thought.

"Oh, *man*," she said, stretching so that the already revealing top revealed just a little more. "What a night. Thanks for letting me crash. I think my battery's actually recharged now."

"Looks like there's some current flowing," Eddie said, peering out at her from around the open door of the refrigerator.

She ignored him and looked to me. "Who's Pops?"

"That would be Eddie Lohmann," I said.

"No shit?" She held her hand out to him. "Heard rumors

about you, Pops. Glad to see you're not dead. Although . . ."
She trailed off with a shrug. "Well, this *is* the suburbs."

Eddie made a rude noise and stuck his head back into the
refrigerator, effectively absenting himself from the conversation.

Allie, who hadn't gone to bed until a few hours before she
usually woke up, finally stumbled into the kitchen. She gave
Nadia's outfit the kind of approving glance that makes a
mother nervous, then turned to me. "I'm so late for school."

"I thought you could stay home today," I said, feeling
magnanimous.

"I totally can't," she said, which really wasn't the reaction
I was expecting.

"Why on earth not?"

"Duh, Mom. I've got cheerleader practice."

Nadia rummaged through my cabinets for a coffee cup.
"You'd rather do that than stay home and help us? Benny's
trying to nail down the ritual location. If he finds it . . ."

"I'm not allowed to fight," she said, giving me a sour look
even though we'd already come to peace with that decision.

"Doesn't mean you can't help out," Nadia said. "The best
Hunters have the best backup." She helped herself to a cup
of coffee. "But if it's not your thing . . ."

Allie looked at me, and I nodded. "And we can train this
morning, too," I added, just to sweeten the deal.

"How are you with a knife?" Nadia asked.

"Passable," Allie said, lifting her chin.

Nadia laughed. "That means you're pathetic. What do
you say? Want to go get in a little practice this morning?"

Allie's eyes went wide. "Are you kidding? I'd totally love
that. Can I, Mom?"

"What about cheerleading?"

"Come on, Mom. This is, like, so much more important."
That it was. I nodded and told her to go get dressed.

"She's a good kid," Nadia said. "And you probably have housewife-type things to do, right? I'll take her into the backyard and keep her out of your hair."

"Gee, thanks, Nadia. That'll give me time to scrub the floors and alphabetize the canned goods."

Her brows lifted. "Zing," she said. "Two points to Crowe." She took a step toward the living room. "Although it sounds to me like maybe there's a little chip on your suburban shoulder?"

She left before I could defend the state of my shoulders. As soon as she was out of earshot, Eddie closed the refrigerator door, which had been open so long that the milk had probably soured.

His face was red with unreleased laughter, and he pointed a bony finger at me. "She's got your number," he said. "*That* girl is one you gotta watch."

"Thanks for the tip," I said. I'd pretty much gotten to that assessment on my own. Even so, I wasn't prepared for the dominatrix vision that soon rumbled down the stairs.

"Alison Elizabeth Crowe," I said, taking in the tight black leggings that would have been acceptable for staying around the house, but she'd paired them with a teeny-tiny black vest. The kind that's meant to be worn over a blouse and never buttoned. She had no blouse, and it was buttoned tight, giving my daughter a great deal more cleavage than I gave her credit for. "What the devil are you wearing?"

"Just something to work out in, Mom," she said, but I could tell by the color on her cheeks that she knew damn well that this outfit would not earn the Mom Seal of Approval. Not by a long shot.

"Up," I said, pointing to the stairs. "Right now."

"But Mom!"

"Allie, I swear, if I have to repeat myself . . ."

"Fine. Whatever."

She left, pounding so hard on the stairs that the house shook. Seconds later, she was back. Still wearing the leggings, but this time her top was covered with an oversized pink T-shirt identifying her as a Princess in Training. That, I thought, was true.

"Will this do?"

"Yes," I said. "The attitude won't, though."

She stared me down for a second, then shrugged. "Sorry. Nadia's going to think I'm a complete dork."

"I'm sure you'll survive the deep trauma."

"Whatever," she said again, then went outside to engage in a little teenage idol worship.

"That one's a case," Eddie said from his seat at the breakfast table. I'd thought he'd tuned us out in favor of his crossword puzzle. Apparently not.

"My daughter? Or the other one."

"Which do you think?"

I pulled out a chair and joined him. "She saved Allie last night, Eddie. I owe that woman more than you can imagine."

He snorted. "Fair enough. But do you trust her?"

"No," I said. "And neither did Eric. But I think we need her." Or, at least, we needed her notes about the ceremony to free Andramelech.

"So what exactly do you do?" Stuart asked as he buttered one of the dinner rolls I'd defrosted and baked.

Nadia paused, her meat loaf–tipped fork just inches from her mouth. "I'm a bounty hunter," she said, her eyes never leaving my husband.

"That is so cool," Mindy said. I'd called Laura a few hours before and given her the scoop on our new houseguest. She'd immediately relaxed the parameters of the Mindy-and-Laura bonding time rule and decided that it would be unneighborly not to join us at the dinner table. Which explains how I ended up serving my plain, boring meat loaf with canned green beans at our formal dining room table.

Not that anyone noticed the setting. They were all too intent on studying Nadia, who had actually dressed for dinner. And now her skintight red leather dress, held together by gold-cord lacing, was making quite the splash at our evening meal. My husband, at least, seemed to wholeheartedly approve. How nice.

As dinners went, I supposed this one could have been worse. Nadia played the role of belle of the ball, although she lacked a certain Southern innocence. Mindy and Allie were the enthusiastic groupies, sucking in the stories Nadia told about her efforts to track down and apprehend San Francisco's most diabolical Failure to Appears. Stuart listened with intent fascination. Eddie rolled his eyes and snorted so many times I was afraid someone would suggest calling EMS just to make sure he wasn't having an epileptic seizure. And Laura spent the entire meal hanging on Nadia's every word, turning to me at various moments to send me significant looks that, thankfully, my husband didn't notice.

The only one who seemed oblivious to Nadia's charms was Timmy, and even that ended after the meal when she gave him a large silver bell tied on to a strip of leather. He giggled and clapped and rang the bell over and over and over. So much so that I had to evict him from the kitchen as I worked on the dishes.

Since Nadia didn't offer to help with the dishes (not that I was keeping score), it was just Laura and me in the kitchen after we ran Timmy off, the girls having been relieved of duty once they finished clearing the table.

"Wow," Laura said, a comment she'd clearly been holding in since arriving at the dinner hour. "A bit overwhelming, huh?"

"Allie and Mindy are certainly entranced," I said dryly.

"That dress," Laura said.

I nodded. "But I have to admit, she can pull it off."

Laura peeked into the living room and nodded. "I'm guessing she's pulled it off one or two times in her life."

I grimaced. I'd thought the same thing myself.

"And have you seen the way she's sitting? More important, have you noticed that your husband is in the living room? When was the last time he didn't retreat to his study after dinner?"

"I have the utmost faith in Stuart," I said, which was true. I couldn't say the same for Nadia. But while my Hunter instincts might be telling me to take her out, my suburban mom training was telling me to be the polite hostess. "Besides, he's not allowed to hide in the study when we have company. That's a house rule."

"Doesn't appear to be too difficult to enforce today."

I wiped my hand on a dish towel as I walked to where she was standing. Sure enough, there was my husband on one side of the couch. Nadia was talking animatedly to him and the girls, but managing to lean mostly toward Stuart. A full-body lean, too.

I took a step toward the drawer with the ice picks, then caught myself and said through gritted teeth, "She lacks a few social graces, but she does kick some serious butt in the field."

"So do you think she's the one?"

"What one?"

"The one who visited Eric. The one Betty mentioned."

"Oh." I'd refused to think about it, but now I was forced to acknowledge the point.

"Not that Eric *would* have an affair," she quickly stated. "But if that's what pranced into the library, I can totally see Betty suspecting it."

"And Mr. Hyde having a heart attack," I said, referring to the prim little man who'd been Eric's boss.

Allie bounded into the kitchen then to get a refill on her iced tea, and Laura and I ceased with the gossip, choosing instead to join the rest of the gang in the living room. That was, after all, the polite thing to do. And so what if I sat a little too close to my husband and kept my hand pressed gently against his thigh?

On the whole, though, the evening was pleasant enough. Nadia had clearly spent some time with people who had no clue about her Demon Hunter identity, because her cover story never once faltered. And by the time Allie had gone up to bed and Laura had left with Mindy, I could tell that Stuart and Eddie were fading.

Nadia stood up, her expression businesslike. "Stuart, it's been real. But I'm going to borrow your wife now."

"Excuse me?"

"Come on, Stu. The woman's got to live a little, right? We're going to take the Lotus, tear up the Coast Highway a little bit." She winked at him. "Don't worry. I'll bring her back in one piece."

"You do that," he said, sounding a little befuddled. "Kate? Do you want—"

"Don't wait up," I said, giving him a quick kiss on the cheek. He'd had his fun; now I was going to have a little of my own.

"I drive," I said as soon as we reached the garage.

"Good for you, Crowe," she said, tossing me her keys. "I'd hate to think suburbia broke your spirit."

"Not on your life," I said, then strapped myself in. The car really was magnificent, although after having lived the last few years of my life from the altitude of a van, I felt certain I was going to end up with asphalt burns on my rear. Either that or embarrass myself in front of Nadia with my poor attempt to maneuver a stick after so long.

In the end, though, I did myself proud. I kept to a decent speed in the neighborhood, but by the time we hit Rialto, I opened her up. Since the street is straight as an arrow, I got a nice feel for the machine's speed, but it wasn't until we reached the Pacific Coast Highway that I got to really test out her moves.

"Sweet," I said.

"That she is."

With the engine thrumming beneath me, all of my earlier post-dinner fatigue had drained away, and I was ready to kick a little demon ass. The speed gave me a rush, a bubbling excitement tinged with danger that, scarily, resembled the emotions that coursed through me when I thought of Eric. Or David. Or whoever he was now.

I took a breath, then glanced at Nadia. "So where are we going? Do you have a lead? Someplace where there might be some activity tonight?"

"Not a clue," she said. "I thought we could circle the town a few times, see if anything looks out of the ordinary. Mostly I figured we should talk. You know. Hunter to Hunter."

"Fair enough," I said. "Shoot."

She slipped her shoes off and put one bare foot on the dash. "Oh, hell," she said. "I don't even really know what to say. I guess I should say thanks."

"For what? You're the one who saved my kid. You're the one who brought us the information on the ring ritual. And now you're the one letting me drive this sweet, sweet car."

"All true," she said. "But I'm sleeping in your house, and under the circumstances . . ."

She trailed off, looking out the window at the beach and the Pacific Ocean beyond.

"Circumstances?" I asked. If I'd had antennae, they'd be perking up right about now.

"Nothing," she said. "Just, you know."

Actually, I didn't. But since I also didn't know her that well, I decided not to press. We drove another five minutes in silence, then she leaned over and turned on the stereo, cranking up some band I'd never heard despite the fact that driving Allie's carpool keeps me on the cutting edge of the latest music. Or, if not the cutting edge, then at least the dull butter knife blade.

"Sorry about Eric," she shouted, before the first track had finished.

"What?" I shouted back, since I wasn't sure I'd heard her.

She turned the stereo off. "Eric," she said. "Sorry about what happened. He was . . ." She paused as if looking for the words. "He was a really nice guy." A tiny smile touched her lips. "Yeah. A really nice guy."

A ball of something resembling lead settled in my stomach. "So, how well did you know him?"

"Oh, you know. Well enough."

Right.

"So what's your usual routine? You patrol every night? Go it alone?"

"There's another Hunter in town," I said, my mind still on Eric and the implications, both in her tone and her words.

"David Long, right?" I turned to her, my brows lifted.

She shrugged. "I asked around, and from what I hear, he's rogue."

"I'm aware of that," I said.

"Can't trust a rogue Hunter, can you? Where was he in the alley? You got a partner, he should be watching your back."

"Something came up," I said.

"So he hung you out to dry," she said. "I've got half a mind to go have a little chat with your Mr. Long. I mean, you coulda got killed. You or Allie."

I shivered, her words reminding me of Eddie's theory, his belief that David had a dark plan.

"Anyway," she continued. "Sounds to me like he's excess baggage. I mean, for the most part I'd say you're doing fine on your own."

We'd reached a turnaround, and I veered off the road, downshifting as I spun the steering wheel so that we whipped around until the Lotus was facing north. Then I pulled back into traffic and looked over at Nadia. "What do you mean?"

I noticed that she'd reached up to grab the door frame as we turned, and I took a bit of secret satisfaction in knocking her even slightly off-kilter.

"You're newly back in the game after one hell of a retirement, but I'd say you've done a damn fine job keeping this town in order."

"How do you know that?" I asked.

She did an elaborate neck roll, and I could hear the bones popping as she sighed. "I told you. I asked around."

"With who? You've been underground for years. *Forza* doesn't even know you exist."

"I've got friends," she said cryptically. "And as for my life, I like it this way. There's freedom." She turned toward me, hooking one leg under her as she readjusted herself in the black leather seat. "Come on, Crowe. Don't you miss that? Not being tied down. Seeing the world. Experiencing life."

Her words washed over me, bringing with them a flood of memories of my youth. Days when I could wake up on one continent but go to sleep on another.

I thought of that, and then I thought of my kids.

"Trust me," I said. "I'm experiencing life."

"So you wouldn't trade it? Wouldn't go back?"

"Not in a million," I said. "Although . . ."

I leaned forward and gave the dashboard of the Lotus a familiar pat. "If I could figure out a way to get a car seat in a Lotus, then I'd get me one of these in a heartbeat."

Eighteen

"So where's Nadia?" Allie asked Saturday morning, as she tugged open the refrigerator and inspected the contents. "I was hoping she'd let me practice with her knife again this morning."

"Honestly," I said, "I don't have a clue." I remembered what she'd said about chewing David out, but quickly dismissed that. The girl was ballsy, but that much? Surely not. Still . . .

I looked at the phone. Maybe I should call him. Just to check. A quick phone call would hardly break my own rule, and—

"Mo-*ther*. Hello?"

"Sorry," I said, abandoning my fantasy of calling David. "What?"

"I was talking to you and you were totally zoning out."

"Not enough sleep," I said, which was true enough. Nadia and I had gotten home about two. She'd dropped me off, then turned around and left again, promising to let herself in with the key I left under the aloe vera plant on the front porch. Apparently, though, she'd never showed.

"So?"

I shook my head, once again baffled by my daughter.

She did the major eye roll thing. "*So*, if Nadia isn't here, will you train with me? We can practice knife-throwing in the backyard."

At the moment, the backyard was the only training field we had, since David still hadn't had time to find a loft to lease. I pushed off a wash of sadness as I realized now that maybe he never would.

"Stuart's home," I said. "He took advantage of the fact that Nadia isn't here to work in his study."

"Oh. Wow. That's weird."

I agreed with her that it was weird for Stuart to be home on a Saturday morning. Ever since his campaigning had kicked into high gear, he'd been spending most of his weekends at the office. To myself, I thought about what a sad state of affairs that was. Clearly, the life I loved so much had a few rough edges.

"How about Cutter's? We can't practice with weapons, but . . ."

"Sure!" she said eagerly, and I bit back a smile, pleased to see that she could be just as enthusiastic about training with me as she had been with Nadia. Even if I had no intention of wearing leather.

"Go get dressed, then," I said, hurrying to finish my coffee so that I could, too. I was just putting the mug in the sink when the phone rang. I snatched it up, hoping it was Nadia. She was more than capable of taking care of herself, of course, but my mom instincts kept me worrying.

"Kate," Father Ben said, the second I answered the phone.

"It's today. The ritual with the ring will take place at noon today. Someplace called the mensa of life."

I glanced at the clock. That was hardly any time at all. "Any idea where that is?"

"Not a clue," Father Ben said. "But we need to find out, fast."

To Allie's credit, she handled the fact that our plans to train had been shot to hell pretty well. A bit of whining at first, but when I put her on the phone with Father Ben so that he could go over the details of the ritual with her—and when she realized that while he knew the time, he didn't know the location—her level of enthusiasm ratcheted up a notch.

"The mensa of life," she said, repeating back what Ben had learned about the ritual. "Wow, that's really freaky."

"Hopefully you two can figure it out," I said, having already admitted that I had no idea.

"We've still got a few hours," she said. "We'll totally figure it out."

I hoped they would, because my toes were itching to kick a little demon butt. And to do that, I needed to know where to go.

I also needed help. It was one thing to patrol on my own. It was another thing altogether to walk boldly into a ceremony where a very pissed-off demon was about to be released.

I needed Nadia, but she wasn't answering her phone. I took a deep breath, then another, working through my options. I could go by the library and round up Eddie, but even as I considered that possibility, I knew it was the least attractive option. Eddie still had a spark, but he was getting old. And if he got hurt because I'd dragged him to a battle that he didn't want to fight, I'd never forgive myself.

I needed Eric. Needed him and, yes, I wanted to see him again, too.

This time when I called, he answered immediately, and his calming voice soothed me and promised that everything would be all right.

"I'm coming to get you," I said. "I'll be there in fifteen minutes."

I told Stuart I was going shopping, then raced off in the Infiniti. The drive to David's apartment took about fifteen minutes, and I used that time to buck myself up. My heart was still raw, of course, but I told myself I could handle it. I *had* to handle it if we wanted to prevent the rise of one of the chancellors of Hell.

By the time I arrived at his door, I'd wrangled some measure of control. That control shattered, though, when I saw that his door wasn't completely closed. *Eric.* A desperate fear that he'd been taken or harmed stabbed through my soul and I immediately tensed, my fighting instincts quashing my emotions and forcing me to stay calm and methodical.

I eased my purse off my arm and left it by the door, keeping only the pump bottle of holy water and my stiletto. I used the tip of the knife to push the door open just enough for me to squeeze through. And then I entered, walking on the balls of my feet so that—hopefully—I made no sound to telegraph my arrival.

They never saw me coming.

I, however, was drawn up short, caught by the horror displayed right in front of me—Nadia, perched on the arm of David's couch, her breasts practically falling out of her top and her face so close to his that her hair brushed his shoulders.

David sat on the couch beside her, one hand on her shoulder. From this angle, I couldn't see his face, but I saw hers. More, I saw the possessive, hungry smile.

I heard a little gasp, and realized it came from me.

Immediately, David turned, his eyes going wide as he saw me. He was on his feet in an instant, roughly pushing Nadia back. "Kate. It's not—"

I held up a hand, determined not to cry. "Leave it," I said. "We have bigger issues to deal with right now."

We were in the car racing toward the cathedral when my cell phone rang. I pressed the button to answer in speaker-phone mode, and my daughter's voice blared out. "We got it! We totally got it!"

"Where?" I demanded, my eyes going automatically to the clock. Eleven-thirty. Maybe we could still make it.

"The stone table," she said. "That's got to be it."

"It does?" I asked, slamming on the brakes and making a U-turn to head us back to the mountains and the National Forest. "Why?"

"Everybody says they did sacrifices at the table, right? Huge rituals about life and death. And *mensa* means table in Latin."

"She's right," Nadia said. "Good work, kid."

It wasn't a perfect fit, but I couldn't think of anything else around San Diablo that fit the bill. Somehow, I didn't think that *table of life* referred to a really nice restaurant.

The stone table might be one of San Diablo's famous landmarks, but it's not a commonly visited one. That was good for us. Unfortunately, the reason it was so infrequently visited was that it was near impossible to access. The table had been discovered by some university botanists who'd forged their way through the dense growth of the forest while cataloguing plant life. Now, there was a narrow footpath, but it was still overgrown and rugged. Driving the entire distance was impossible, and running there wasn't much easier.

As we battled our way through the underbrush, I decided that maybe Nadia did have the right idea about wearing leather. Whereas I was being assaulted by branches and stickers, she moved confidently through the brush, her tight leather pants forming a perfect barrier.

Bitch.

I frowned. The thought might be accurate, but at the moment I really needed to keep my head in the game. Whatever she was doing on the couch with my husband—*former* husband—could wait.

"Two minutes," I said. "Where are we?"

"We have to be getting close," Nadia said. "It's been at least a hundred yards since we passed one of the park's markers."

The U.S. Parks & Wildlife Service had taken the trouble to mark various walking paths through the forest. We were following a series of arrows that led to the table. And if the department had accurately labeled the walk, we had to be getting close.

"One minute," I said, my voice tense. "This damn well better be a long ceremony, or we aren't going to make it."

"We'll make it," David said, his voice as tense as his body.

We pressed on, moving as fast as we could, until finally we could see a clearing. The brush thinned and we picked up speed. Still a few seconds until noon. Still time to—

"*Aaaaaaaaaahhhhhhhhhhhhh.*"

The deep bellow split the sky, along with a violent cracking. And as I burst into the clearing, I saw a burly man standing atop the now-splintered stone table, two other demons standing guard at each end. A knife protruded from the risen demon's heart, and I felt a momentary wash of sadness for the innocent human who'd been sacrificed so that the demon might be freed.

"Andramelech!" Nadia yelled and rushed forward, her face a mask of rage.

I looked at David, but there was no time for words. The battle had begun. And if we wanted to keep Andramelech out of this world, the time to cut him down was now.

"You!" the demon howled to Nadia, quelling any uncertainty I might have had that this creature was, in fact, the risen Andramelech. "You who have stalked me, sought to imprison me. You," he said, "must die."

She wasn't the least bit fazed by his words. Instead, she leaped onto the table, her sword at the ready, and thrust it at his eye. He slammed it away, slicing his forearm in the process, but not even hesitating. I swallowed, realizing just how powerful this demon must be. Newly made demons are usually a bit slower, more unsure. And their strength hasn't reached its maximum potential. If this was Andramelech in low gear, then we really were in trouble.

Not that I had time to think about it. David had reached one of the guard demons already, and as I rushed to help Nadia, the third barreled toward me.

"Get back, you son of a bitch," I shouted, pulling the crossbow into ready position. He didn't even slow down. Just raced pell-mell toward me, arms wide out at his sides, his chest exposed.

I fired, nailing him right in the heart. The shot didn't kill him, of course, but it did fell him, and as he tumbled, I leaped on him, then stabbed my stiletto through his eye before he even had time to react.

As the demon was sucked out of the body, I sprang back

up. He might have been an easy kill, but there were two more demons to worry about, and I could see that David and Nadia had their hands full.

Unlike the demon I'd killed, the creature David was fighting was armed with a serious-looking machete. David was holding his own, but as I watched, the demon caught David's saber right at the handle, splitting the metal at the joint and sending the blade flying.

As I screamed and raced toward them, the demon thrust the blade down, aiming for David's heart. David kicked up, his leg intercepting the blade, knocking it off course, but slicing his leg in the process.

He howled in pain, then collapsed as the demon kicked his good leg out from under him. I'd reached them by now, and as the demon lunged again for David, I intercepted, managing to get a good kick of my own in and knock the machete out of his hand.

It went tumbling to the ground, and as the demon scrambled to retrieve it, I leaped to nail him. I caught him off balance and we rolled over and over. My stiletto jerked free in the confusion.

We ended with him on top of me, both of us unarmed. He had his fingers on my throat, and I used one hand to try to force his fingers away and keep my air passage open. With my other hand, I grappled for my lost blade.

I couldn't find it, and as the pressure of his fingers increased, I knew I couldn't afford to scrabble for it for too long. I needed both hands to pry the demon off if I wanted to stay conscious.

"Kate!"

I turned my head and saw David limping toward me. With his bad leg, he couldn't move fast enough to reach me, but he did the next best thing, kicking the machete and sending it spinning over the trampled ground until it stopped just close enough for my fingers to reach it.

As I did, the demon's grip tightened, and the world turned inside out as my body used up the last of the oxygen in my lungs. I fought through the haze, focusing all my effort on my arm and the hand that held the demon's machete. I swung up and over, not aiming so much as trying to make contact. *Anything* to get the bastard to loosen his grip.

I felt a thud as the machete connected, then the tension as I sliced through flesh and cartilage. A single *thump,* and the pressure on my neck loosened. The demon collapsed on top of me. I squirmed sideways, my vision clearing even as I did.

That's when I saw it. The demon's body, but without a head.

I found the head quickly enough, and as it babbled at me in a language surely known only in Hell, I used the machete for one more bit of dirty work—stabbing the damn thing through the eye so that the demon—as well as the body—was dead.

"David!" I called, turning to find him back on the ground. I rushed to his side, terrified by how pale he looked.

"It's not an artery," he said, tightening a tourniquet he'd manufactured from his own belt. "I'll be fine. Nadia needs help."

I gave him a quick kiss on the forehead, then sprang back up. The stone table had cracked down the middle, and now it was merely rubble. They were battling on it, though, and I was once again impressed by the woman's skills.

Even so, she was no match for an angry, resurrected demon, and I got the feeling he was toying with her. I struggled forward, still lightheaded, and scooped up my knife along the way. As I got closer, Andramelech looked straight at me. "Little Hunter," he said. "You will not win."

"I think I will," I said, and as I did, I let my knife fly. It landed square in his eye, and the demon—the great Andramelech, who had caused us all so much worry and trouble—was sucked out of the body and disappeared into the ether.

Honestly, the whole thing was rather anticlimactic.

"Eric!" Nadia yelled as she leaped from the table and sprinted toward him. "Thank God you're safe. Thank God, thank God."

She pulled him to her and pressed a kiss to his lips even as I stood there seething. David looked more than a little uncomfortable, but whether it was because she was kissing him or because I was standing right there, I didn't know.

All I knew was that Andramelech was gone, and with him my last reason to work with David.

Eric, I thought, was truly dead to me now.

"Honestly, Crowe, I didn't mean to hurt you," Nadia said, as she shoved a few more things deep into her duffel bag. "I mean, it's been almost six years, you know? And you're married. So why should you care what happened between Eric and me all that time ago?"

"I guess I'm just a silly suburban mom," I said coldly. "It's so hard for us to rein in our emotions."

"Jesus, Crowe. I thought you'd be a little bit more rational about this."

"About the fact that you're telling me you had an affair with my husband?"

"I never said that," she said with a tiny smile. "Not exactly."

I leaned against Stuart's desk and watched her cram a few more pairs of underwear into her bag, still not sure what to think. I trusted Eric, I did. And yet what possible motive would Nadia have for pretending to have had an affair? I couldn't think of one, and that made me nervous. Very, very nervous.

Finally she finished packing and turned back to me. "Okay, look," she said. "I came here without any idea that Eric was around. Honest. But after you told me about David, I wanted to go have a little talk with him. About leaving you to patrol alone, you know?" She was chewing gum—I'd refused to let her smoke in the house—and she paused to smack it.

"Go on."

"I got there, all ready to rip him a new one, but he seemed so familiar. And he was staring at me like he'd seen a ghost. And that's when he told me who he was. I mean, this is a man I really, deeply cared for." She shrugged, not meeting my eyes. "Anyway, that's when you came in, and—"

"You lying little bitch," I said, the words coming out as a whisper, a defense against her onslaught. As soon as I spoke them, though, I knew they were true. I didn't know Nadia's reason, but I was certain she was lying.

A quick thrust of guilt slammed into my gut. I'd known Eric my whole life, and still I'd doubted. What kind of a fool was I?

She looked up at me, her head angled as she tied the knot at the top of her bag. "It's easier to think that, isn't it?"

"Yes," I said honestly. "It is."

The look she gave me was both cold and pitying, but I held my ground, fighting the urge to slap her as I indicated the door. She hoisted her duffel and headed out of Stuart's office, toward the front door. She paused there, then, and looked back at me.

"In the end, it doesn't matter what you think," she said. "Andramelech's gone, at least for now. It's over. I know the truth, and so does Eric. And now you can go back to folding laundry and making meat loaf. Have a nice life in suburbia, Crowe."

"Thanks," I said sweetly as she stepped out onto the porch. I slammed the door hard, hoping it burst her eardrums, and then I leaned against the closed door. "I will," I said, looking down the hall at the house that I loved, that was my home. "I do."

The phone rang while I was still fuming about Nadia. I had rewound and rerun the conversation in my head so that I had a variety of different endings, ranging from me being incredibly polite but sharp-tongued, to me forgoing chitchat all the way and simply mowing her down with her own Lotus.

Satisfying, and yet . . . not.

I checked the caller ID, saw that it was David, and immediately froze. Part of me desperately wanted to answer. The other part wanted to run away and hide.

Finally, the grown-up part decided to take over, and I pushed the talk button.

"I'm sorry," he said immediately. "She's lying."

"I know," I said. I took a deep breath. "So how's the leg?" I asked brightly.

"Not good," he admitted. "But it will heal. But Kate, about Nadia . . ."

"That will heal, too," I said. "I was . . . Well, it doesn't matter anymore. Because I trust you. I do. I'm sorry I didn't, even for a moment."

"Kate," he said, the edge in his voice scaring me. "I didn't tell you everything. That night in my apartment when you came over. When I told you what happened in San Francisco. I left a few things out."

"What?" I whispered, moving to one of the kitchen chairs because my legs were suddenly weak.

"We hadn't just talked by phone. She'd come to San Diablo, too. She came to the library twice, I think. She hit on me, pretty hard."

"And did you . . . ?"

"*No,*" he said. "I told her I was married. I told her I loved my wife."

"But she didn't leave it alone."

"That's one of the reasons I didn't trust her," he admitted. "Why I didn't tell her I still had the ring."

"She must hate you for lying to her."

"Maybe," he admitted. "If so, she has a funny way of showing it."

"I saw," I said dryly.

He chuckled, the sound teasing my heart and soul and conjuring up so many memories of his laugh. "When she came by this morning," he said, "it was to chew me out for not helping you patrol. Then she looked at me and—"

"Knew who you were. Yes, I've heard the story."

"I had the impression she'd known all along, actually," he said. "Not that it matters. And not that I could prove it."

I frowned at that. If she knew, why the song and dance?

"At any rate, she said that she missed me and that now that time had passed and you were married, the door was open."

"She's right," I said, forcing the words out, and hating the truth of them. And it *was* true. David was single. He could date—even marry—anyone he wanted.

The thought made me more than a little queasy.

"She's not," he said, his voice tender. "The door's not open, Katie. Not to her."

I shivered, hearing the words that he didn't say: It wasn't open to her, but it was open to me.

"Eric, I . . ."

"I know," he said. "We've already been there, haven't we?"

"Eric?"

"After the semester is up," he said. "After that, I'll move away. It will be easier on both of us."

I swear I could feel my heart breaking. "Allie?"

"I'm dead to her," he said, his voice cracking. "This way is probably how it should be."

When Stuart came home, he found me red-eyed and puffy-faced, still at the kitchen table. "Hey," he said, sliding his hands over my shoulders. "What's wrong?"

"It's just . . . Nadia," I said, deciding that half-truth was better than no truth at all.

"She's gone, I take it?"

"And good riddance." I looked up at him and saw him smile. "What?"

"I'm just echoing the sentiment."

"Oh really?" I said, lifting an eyebrow. "I would have thought you'd be sad to see her go. Or, at least, to see her wardrobe go."

"Nonsense," he said. "I can always buy you a red leather bustier."

My mood was lightening by the second. "Yes, but could you make me wear it?"

"Wouldn't matter," he countered. "Since the goal would be to get you out of it anyway."

"Thanks," I said, squeezing his hand.

"What for this time?"

"Just for being there. For making me feel better. I love you, you know."

"I know," he said, and I could see in his eyes that he meant it.

"So where have you been?"

"Took Timmy out for McDonald's, and then Laura offered to babysit. I took her up on it."

My smile broadened. "Good idea."

"Why don't we take a walk?"

"A walk?" I repeated.

"Sure. Like we used to. On the beach. Under the stars." He pressed a kiss to my fingertips. "Could be romantic."

"Yeah," I said, "I suppose it could."

We drove there at a much more relaxed pace than my last trip to the beach, and Stuart parked near my usual space when I come for patrols. We left our shoes in the car, then walked north toward the rocky area and the secluded sandy inlets that you can find at low tide.

We walked hand in hand, talking, but at the same time not saying much of anything. The kids. The night. Plans for the house, for our life.

At one point I shivered, thinking about the ocean and this place and this man. Because the last time I'd walked along the beach, I'd been with Eric, although I hadn't realized it at the time. So I supposed it was fitting that now I walked here again with my husband.

We'd reached a secluded area near the base of the cliffs, and Stuart pulled me close, then kissed me deep. "I love you," he said.

"I know," I said. "I love you, too."

He kissed me again, harder, the kiss wild and possessive as he pulled me down with him.

"We'll get sand in our hair," I said, my voice breathy and my hands never leaving my husband. "In our clothes."

"I don't care," he said. "Do you?"

And you know what? I didn't.

Nineteen

Sunday Mass came and went, followed by brunch at the Coronado Hotel, a nice surprise courtesy of Stuart, who apparently was still in a bit of a romantic mood. Timmy could sense that this wasn't the usual Denny's fare, and was on his best behavior, and Allie spent the morning looking down at the beach from our patio vantage point and commenting about the guys playing volleyball in the sand.

It was chilly for San Diablo—in the low seventies—and we were all wearing sweaters. All except Allie, who sported a black leather jacket.

"Is that Mindy's?" I asked. I'd noticed it earlier, but we'd been in such a rush to get out the door and to the cathedral that I didn't think to ask.

"Nadia gave it to me," she said. "Isn't it cool?"

Since my initial reaction was to toss the thing in the ocean, I chose not to comment on the coolness factor. Stuart, however, came to my rescue. "It's a great jacket," he said. "And you look much better in it than Nadia ever would."

I lifted my mimosa and toasted that, after which we all had to repeat the toast at least twenty times while Timmy demanded "Clink glasses! Clink glasses!" over and over.

By the time the meal was over, I had a nice little mimosa buzz and was in an exceptionally good mood. That lasted until we reached the car, when Stuart's cell phone rang. After a brief conversation with his boss, Stuart's plans for the day changed.

"Forgive me?"

"Absolutely," I said. I was still feeling guilty about missing his candidacy announcement. "Go forth for truth, justice, and all that. Just let me drive you," I added. "I need to make a run to the grocery store."

I'd explained to Stuart that a prankster had thrown a rock through the Odyssey's windshield, which temporarily made us a one-car family unless we decided to break down and get a rental. So far, that hadn't been a priority.

After that, the day progressed more or less normally. We dropped Stuart off, went shopping, then stopped by Payless to buy the shoes I'd meant to buy Timmy more than a week ago.

With the family's basic needs provided for, we continued home, and then everyone went about their ordinary tasks. Me tackling the huge pile of laundry, Allie downloading songs and gossiping with Mindy on the phone, and Timmy constructing vast universes from Duplo blocks and Tinkertoy logs. Eddie was absent, but even that was part of the normal life scheme, as he'd skipped breakfast with us in favor of a cup of coffee and a donut at the coffee shop that abutted the library.

"Mom?" Allie bounded into the laundry room, still wearing the leather jacket, even though our house was a quite comfortable seventy-eight degrees. "Can we keep the ring? Or does it still have all that hoochie-do stuff?"

I'd been bent over, trying to get the lint filter back into our dryer, but now I straightened. "The ring," I repeated. Dear God, we'd never found the ring.

"Yeah. Duh. Daddy's ring." She frowned. "Although I guess it wasn't really Daddy's. But I still want it. I won't even touch it. But I . . . well . . . you know."

"I know what ring you mean, Allie," I said. "And no, you absolutely cannot have it back."

"What's wrong?" she said, apparently noticing my frown.

"I didn't see the ring," I admitted. "Not during or after the fight."

"Oh." It was her turn to frown. "But you weren't there when Andramelech came out, right? You told me you guys were late."

She said the last with a hint of accusation. "Yes," I admitted. "But we got there as fast as we could. And in the end, we *did* stop the creature."

"Maybe they had to smash the ring or something."

"Maybe," I said, but I was dubious, and the lack of a ring bothered me for reasons I couldn't quite put my finger on.

That matter settled, she returned to her room, only to come find me again fifteen minutes later, this time as I was folding sheets. Or trying to, anyway. Sheet-folding is not one of my highly developed gross motor skills.

"Mom?"

"What?" I said, trying to beat the percale into submission.

"I'm bored."

I counted silently to ten. "I don't know what to tell you, Allie. Can't Mindy come over?"

"She's seeing her dad today," Allie said.

"What about your iPod? Everything alphabetized and organized?"

"Yes, Mother," she said, her voice thick with a put-upon sigh.

"Well, I don't know, Al. Is there something you're wanting to do?"

"Couldn't we go train or something? I mean, Stuart's not home, so maybe you and me and Mr. Long could go somewhere and work out? I bet Aunt Laura would watch Timmy. Please? Please, please, please?"

I drew in a breath and decided to be extremely magnanimous. "Well, I can't," I said. "But if Mr. Long wants to pick you up, then you can go train with him." I concentrated on my folding as I spoke, not wanting her to see my face. Because if Eric really was leaving at the end of the semester, I at least wanted to give him the chance to see his daughter as much as possible before he left.

That plan was a hit, and she bounded back to her room to call David. About twenty-seven seconds later, she was back. "He's not answering his phone," she said. "I called both numbers and just got his machine." Her shoulders sagged, and she sighed again. "I'm *soooo* bored."

A little niggle of worry tickled the back of my neck, but I pushed it away. Andramelech was gone. The demon situation—the current one, anyway—had been handled. David was not obligated to answer his phone each and every time it rang. And for all I knew, he was home screening his calls, and didn't want to spend time with Allie for fear it would be too painful.

That didn't sound like the Eric I knew, but as he'd already reminded me, he *wasn't* the Eric I knew.

"So will you train with me?"

"Alison Elizabeth Crowe," I said, reaching my breaking point. "We have been over this. I am catching up on stuff around the house. If you leave me alone so that I can finish—or better yet, help me—then maybe we can train in an hour or two. In the meantime, pick up a dust rag or find something else to do."

She made a face, then sighed again. "I did all that research on Andramelech," she said. "Should I type it all up? I mean, like, is that the kind of thing the Vatican would want?"

"Absolutely," I said. "You would be helping the Vatican in a huge way. That is the perfect project. Go. Do that."

She disappeared, and I bugged out my eyes at my laundry. And to think I'd thought toddlerhood had been the hard years.

Twelve minutes later, she was back. "What about the stuff I'm not sure of?"

"What do you mean?"

"I was poking around last night in some of those books that Eddie got from the library and I found some stuff that mentioned the whole vessel thing." She lifted a shoulder. "I guess it doesn't matter now, but you still want it, right?"

"Absolutely."

She nodded then disappeared, this time with more purpose. By the time she came back, I'd moved on to the kitchen floors, and Timmy had decided to help me. Considering his help involved using a giant sponge to make a wet spot on the floor, and then dragging his bottom through the puddle, I can't say that I was making much progress.

"So here it is," she said, parking herself at the table with a tabbed three-ring binder. It was the kind that had a clear cover so that you could insert your own document, and my daughter hand inserted an enlarged woodcarving of Andramelech.

I had to admit I was impressed. If she would put that much effort into her schoolwork, my kid would be a shoo-in for valedictorian.

"So show me," I said, both because I wanted to be an encouraging and supportive parent, and because I was plain curious.

"This section's all the stuff you already know about old Mr. A," she said. "So you can just read it whenever." She flipped to the next tab, then blew out a breath. "This is the stuff about Daddy and the ring," she said, her voice catching a little. "About how the ring works by, you know, tossing the soul into space, I guess." She paused, then wiped a tear from her eye before flipping to the next section.

I pressed a gentle hand to her shoulder but she shook it off. "I'm okay," she said, sniffling. "Here, this is the new stuff. I can't figure a lot of it out, but I put all my notes together so that maybe someone else can."

"Sounds like a plan. You want to tell me what you did figure out?"

At that point, Timmy decided that cleaning was no longer fun, so he opened the one cabinet I keep without a baby latch, pulled out some pots, and started banging them on the floor. I flashed Allie a *just a second* look, bribed my youngest with a bowlful of Teddy Grahams, then delivered a Diet Coke to my oldest.

"Okay," I said. "Shoot."

"Well, the vessel is all about the ring, at least from what I can tell." She twisted the notebook around so that I could see, and I saw a hideous woodcarving of a demon emerging from an all-too-familiar ring. Beside him, a human was hung on a tree, dripping blood into an ornate cup.

"Nice," I said.

"I know, it's totally disgusting. Anyway, from what I can figure, if the demon comes out of the ring at sunset on the Sabbath—and so long as the vessel is there to be entered—then the demon will be not only human, but invincible forever."

"Dear God," I said. "A demon that can walk the earth forever? Undefeatable?"

"Total creep-out stuff, huh?"

"But he has to have this vessel, right?" I asked, realizing that the stone in the ring wasn't the vessel after all. That, presumably, was the chalice below the body in the picture.

"Exactly. And he has to have it right then. It's like a one-shot deal. Come out of the ring without the vessel around and he's just your ordinary demon dude."

"Do we know where the vessel is?" I asked, hoping she'd tell me that it had been locked up tight in the Vatican for the last twelve centuries.

"That's the weird part," she admitted. She got up and retrieved a bag of Oreos from the pantry, then opened it and offered me one.

I twirled my hand impatiently, way more interested in my daughter's research than her sweet tooth.

"Here's what it says," she said, pointing. "And this is from a translation of a translation, so maybe that's why it's so much nonsense."

"Fair enough. Shoot."

"In the shadow of his enemy's grave, he will fill the vessel and push out his foe," she read. *"Claiming the shell that is both living and dead, so that the captured becomes the captor."*

She looked up at me and shrugged. "That's it," she said. "Does it make sense to you?"

"No," I said. "Although something about it seems . . . I don't know. Familiar, maybe." I shook my head as Timmy started up again with the banging.

As I got up to take care of my budding musician, Allie sighed. "Damn. I know it doesn't matter anymore, but I was hoping to figure it out."

"If you want extra credit, I think there are two or three assignments in your homework."

"Ha-ha," she said. "Maybe I should try to call Mr. Long again. He might have an idea. Or Eddie. I could walk to the library and see if he has a clue."

"That sounds good," I said. "And ask him if he's coming home for dinner, okay?"

That she agreed surprised me, but I chalked it up to the fact that she wanted to show off her research. I couldn't complain. I still had Timmy in the house, but at least I'd be able to finish the cleaning that I'd started.

I grabbed a broom and started to sweep up Teddy Graham crumbs, my mind still on Allie's impressive notebook. I almost wished that David had been home when she'd called, because I would have loved to have shared her work with him. I'd never been much of a bookworm, but he'd loved working with Wilson to poke through all those old records.

David—or, rather, Eric—would have been so proud to see what his daughter accomplished.

I froze, my hand tightening around the handle of the broom.

David. Eric.

Living and dead.

And oh, dear Lord, Eric had been Andramelech's captor.

The broom fell to the ground with a clatter as the truth overwhelmed me. The vessel wasn't a stone or a cup or vase.

The vessel was David.

That's why we never found the ring," I said, speaking so fast that I was stumbling over my words. "Because that demon on the table wasn't Andramelech."

"But then who was he?" Laura asked, still damp from the shower that my frantic phone call had interrupted.

"Just some old demon," I said. "It doesn't really matter. The point is that they were faking it. Pretending so that I'd think that Andramelech was really gone."

"But he's not?"

"He's still in the ring, and when he's released, he's going to move into David's body. And then he's going to be invincible."

"And David?" Laura asked.

A shudder rippled through me. "I don't know. Let's pray we never find out."

With Laura watching Timmy, I made use of her car, tearing as fast as I could to the cemetery. I'd gone by the library first to get Eddie—I needed all the help I could get—but he and Allie weren't there, and I didn't have time to track them down. Allie had said the ceremony would take place at sunset on the Sabbath, and the sun was mere inches away from dipping below the horizon. We'd been late to the fake ceremony; I couldn't afford to be late to this one.

I couldn't remember the details of what Allie told me, but I did recall something about the shadow of the grave of his enemy, and the captured becoming the captor. Since I had no better idea, I had to assume that the enemy was Eric . . . and that the ceremony would take place at his gravesite.

The cemetery gate was unlocked when I got there, and I barreled down the main road following a series of twists and turns until I ended up in the section where Eric was buried. This area was marked by rolling hills, massive shade trees and a two-hundred-year-old mausoleum, which held the remains of one of the town's wealthy forefathers, Alexander Monroe.

I slammed on the brakes just shy of Eric's gravesite,

grabbed my weapons, then got out of the car, armed to the teeth.

I saw nothing, and that terrified me. What if I was wrong? What if they'd taken David away, to the grave of some other enemy? He'd be lost to me forever, and that simply wasn't a conclusion that I could handle.

No. We had to be right. The ceremony had to be here. *In the shadow of his grave . . .*

I turned in a circle, looking around and examining my surroundings. To the west, the setting sun cast long shadows across the grounds. I cocked my head, watching the shadow from Eric's tombstone grow longer and longer until it almost reached out and touched the decorative landscaping that surrounded the mausoleum.

Could it be that simple?

I decided that it absolutely could, then crept quietly in the direction of the mausoleum, my knife and holy water at the ready.

The building was constructed of grayish marble, and now it seemed streaked in orange as the dimming light hit it. I knew from my visits to Eric's grave that the entrance was on the north, marked by an iron gate that was usually locked. Beyond that was a large room, empty except for the stone sarcophagus in the middle, the final resting place of Mr. Monroe. The sides of the tombs provided burial for the patriarch's family.

As far as I knew, the Monroe family still used the tomb, and every time I'd been to the cemetery, the gate had been locked.

Today, the gate was open. Even from my angle off to the side, I could see that the iron bars had swung wide, a silent invitation to enter.

What can I say? I accepted, moving quietly until I was

pressed into an alcove that allowed me a view of the interior—hopefully without being seen.

I peeked out, and what I saw made bile rise in my throat. It took everything I had not to gasp in horror.

David was there, all right. He'd been stripped naked and strung up in a shaft of fading light that trickled through a stained-glass window. Like the picture in Allie's book, his arms were tied above his head to something solid, yet hidden, in the darkness. His feet barely touched the lid of Monroe's sarcophagus, and blood dripped from his feet into a small gold bowl, into which the ring had been carefully placed.

I held on tight to the side of the tomb, afraid that if I didn't, I would rush forward. And while I wanted to rescue David, I couldn't afford to be caught myself.

His eyes fluttered and I watched, holding my breath as he saw me. He didn't move. Didn't do anything that would give me away. But still I could see the fear in his eyes, and what almost brought me to my knees was that it was fear for me, not for himself.

I love you, I thought, hoping he could hear me. *I'm going to get you out of here.*

I carefully examined the rest of the tomb, trying to see if his captor had left him temporarily alone. If the ceremony hadn't started yet . . . if it was only David and the ring . . .

But no, there was a movement at the back of the tomb. A subtle shifting of the velvety blackness. Then a figure cloaked in a black cape stepped forward into the fading shaft of light.

A pause, and then the figure's head snapped up, the light illuminating features I recognized well—Nadia.

I stayed deathly silent, but it didn't matter. She looked right at me and smiled.

"Kate," David croaked. "Run."

But before I could react, my arms were pinned behind me by two hulking demons, one on each side of me, and I was shoved roughly forward. The alcove, it seemed, was really the foyer of a hidden doorway. And I'd walked right in to a trap.

I tried to break free, but the demon held me too tight. I snapped my head back, catching his nose with the back of my skull. Nothing. He didn't even budge. I was being held by the Incredible Hulk of demons, and I could do nothing except stand there and seethe as they overpowered me and bound my legs.

"You raging bitch," I said, as the demons holding me shuffled forward so that our backs were to the gate and I was facing Nadia. "Everything's been a lie with you. Were you ever even working for *Forza*? Or have you been doing Andramelech's dirty work all along?"

"Don't even think of insulting me," she said. "I busted my ass for that organization. And what did I get? Hunted. Persecuted. And not a single damn thing else. I lived like a bum for years carting around the country doing *Forza*'s dirty work and I didn't have a thing to show for it except a beat-up duffel bag and a head full of memories."

"So you decided that was reason enough to join forces with a demon? Why not just retire? Put on a tiny bikini or your itty-bitty red dress and go clubbing. Hang out on a beach in Mexico. Anything but throwing in with the forces of darkness."

" 'Forces of darkness'? A bit melodramatic, don't you think?"

"Actually, no," I said, giving my arms one more jerk in case my captors had quit paying attention. They hadn't. I was still very firmly trapped.

"You want to know? You really want to know? *Power*," she said. "Like you wouldn't believe. Here's the slightest sampling," she said, then disappeared.

I blinked, startled, and then just as quickly realized what had happened. One of the demons loyal to the trapped Andramelech had made promises to Nadia.

"They're backing their promises with parlor tricks, Nadia," I said to empty air. "Do you really believe once Andramelech is released they'll let you live? Your invisibility ring isn't going to work if you're dead."

"Actually, it's a charm," she said, reappearing. "But how clever of you to have recognized the device."

"I've run across one before," I said dryly. "Like I said, it's a parlor trick."

"No, darling, *this* is a parlor trick." She gestured to David, who was going paler by the minute as the blood continued to flow from his veins. His eyes had started to cloud over, but I still saw a hint of cognizance there. Silently, I urged him to hang on. Somehow, I'd get us out of this.

"Once the blood covers the ring, the transformation will take place. *Poof*, just like that. And Andramelech will be free once again."

"You're sick," I said, eyeing the cup and the blood that kept rising in it, so high now that only the tiniest bit of gold from the ring still peeked out above the liquid.

"I'm smart," she said, her voice tight. "And I'm a realist."

"Why not come after me sooner?" I asked, hoping to keep her talking so that I could think. "I've had the ring for years."

"Truthfully? We didn't know where it was. *You* didn't even know where it was. Not until you put on the ring."

"You knew about Eric, though. You attacked him on the beach."

"Actually, we weren't certain. Not at first. I'm not entirely sure how the demons feel each other in their disembodied state, but they explained that they could tell that he was gone, he who was supposed to be trapped for all eternity." She smiled. "It was a fabulous opportunity, of course, because by landing in a body, Eric handed us the ceremony to free Andramelech. Ironic, don't you think?"

"What do you mean?"

"Oh, Kate, darling. Surely you know that to jump into a body requires a certain . . . je ne sais quoi. We were quite surprised that Eric had it in him. Makes me think that perhaps he's more amenable to our little plan tonight than he'd like you to think."

She ran a finger up his leg, and David jerked away, the hatred in his eyes far surpassing the exhaustion.

"I don't think so," I said.

"No?" She waved my comment away. "Too bad you'll never have the chance to ask him."

"What about me?" I asked. "Why not kill me?"

"At first, we tried," she said. "You're not an easy person to kill. And then we realized you were more useful to us alive."

"How so?"   •

"Well, right now for one thing. I think it's safe to say that Eric knows that if he does something foolish—not that he has the strength to manage that—Laurence and Arnold there would break your pretty little neck."

"Ah," I said, not much liking the sound of that.

"Now, we don't much care if you die. Before, though . . . Well, we realized that the death of a Hunter might get *Forza* snooping around where they didn't belong. But keeping you alive, driving a little wedge between you and snooky-wookums, hopefully ensured an interruption-free ceremony." She made a face. "*That* didn't work out quite as well as we planned."

"That's because you didn't make it plausible. Eric would never sleep with you. *Never*. And I know him well enough to realize that."

"Oh, Kate, darling, that's such a heartwarming story of trust and reunion. But before you get your hopes up, I should probably warn you that you won't be seeing your beloved again after this death. The spell is going to bind his soul to this body. Trapped without a voice, but inside with Andramelech, so it's sure to be a good time."

She smiled and traced a finger down David's bare side. "Considering the . . . *relationship* . . . I have with Andramelech, I guess David and I will be a lot closer soon, too." She reached down and drew her finger through the blood in the cup, then lifted it to her lips. "Delicious," she said. "And now, I'm afraid your time is up."

The tomb began to shake, razor-thin cracks appeared in the walls, and a deep groaning sound came from the ground, as if Hell was opening up all around us.

As I struggled against my two captors, Nadia climbed onto the coffin. She took the cup with the ring and poured the blood over David's head. At first, nothing happened. And then he started to glow, his skin illuminated a deep red, pulsating with the beat of his heart.

"Good-bye, Eric," she said. "Hello, my darling Andramelech." And then she kissed him, hard, as he struggled against her.

"Eric," I screamed.

"Kate." His voice was low and weak, and I had to strain to hear it. "Don't hesitate. Don't let him in. Kill me before he's locked inside me. If you don't," he said, sucking breath in for strength, "it will be too late."

I shivered, suddenly understanding what we were up

against. Andramelech would be truly invincible. Even a sword through the eye wouldn't kill him.

"Too late, Eric darling," Nadia said as the red poured out of Eric and turned into a misty demonic haze, which spun around him like a cyclone.

I raged against my captors, but it was no use. The demons behind me each had an arm, and they'd bound my legs as well. I screamed out, desperate but impotent.

A loud wail sounded from behind me, and the demon holding my right arm collapsed, the steel point of a crossbow arrow protruding from his eye from where it had been shot through the back of his skull.

I didn't waste any time wondering about that gift. I used my now free hand to whip around and slam a fist into the other demon's eye. While he recoiled, I saw who had shot the arrow—Eddie. I took the knife he tossed me and then slammed it home, taking immense satisfaction in the feel of the blade sliding into his eye.

"Your timing is perfect," I said to Eddie, with a nod to the crossbow slung across his back. He didn't say anything, just sliced the bonds that held my ankles together. As soon as I was free, I raced to David, scrambling up to the top of the stone sarcophagus.

"I don't think so," Nadia said, landing a quick kick to my gut. I fell back, then stayed down, thrusting both my legs out to catch her in the knees.

She howled in pain, and then rolled off the coffin.

"I'll nail the bitch," Eddie said. "Cut the boy down."

I didn't hesitate. I pressed against David, feeling the life draining from him as I cut him down, then pulled him off the coffin onto the cold, stone floor.

"You're too late, Crowe," Nadia said as Eddie came at

her. And then, rather than try to defend herself, she simply disappeared.

David collapsed into my arms and I held him close, my vision blurred by the tears I couldn't stop from flowing.

"Do it now, Kate," he said as the mist descended on him, turning the whites of his eyes a deep bloodred. "Kill me now while you still can."

"Eric . . ." I could barely force the word out.

"I love you, Kate. Don't let me suffer in here with this bastard. Don't let him have life."

"I love you too," I said, unable to stop my tears.

And then I took my knife and drove it through his heart.

"Nooooo!"

I turned to find Allie rushing toward me, and I knew in that moment that she'd heard and seen almost everything. Including the fact that I'd just killed her father.

She tumbled to the ground next to me, her anguished cries ripping my heart in two.

"I figured it out," Eddie said softly. "What the book meant. Borrowed a car from my lady," he added, hooking his thumb back over his shoulder, presumably toward where the librarian's car was parked. "Swung by the house to grab a few weapons, and then we burned some rubber getting here." He sighed, his shoulders dropping as whatever disdain he'd once held for David melted away. "Sorry we didn't make it in time. And sorry that bitch from hell got away."

"You did great," I said, rocking David's body in my arms. "Andramelech would have killed me first thing. As for Nadia . . ." I trailed off, then gave Eddie a hard look. "Someday, she'll pay."

Eddie nodded, his expression acknowledging the truth of

my words. "That one was supposed to wait in the car," he said, with a scowl toward Allie.

She looked up, her eyes glazed, her expression shell-shocked. Slowly, she reached out to touch the face of the man who, in his soul, at least, had been her father.

"Mom . . ."

"I know, baby." I pulled her close and held her tight, expecting her sobs. They never came, though. Instead, she pulled away, looking up at me with determined eyes.

"Allie?"

Without saying a word, she took off Nadia's leather jacket, then pulled out a small velvet bag. She tossed the jacket across the tomb with a single whispered word. "Bitch."

I barely even heard her. I was too focused on the bag, too focused on what I knew it could do.

She handed it to me, not speaking a word, but still communicating volumes.

I knew I should say no. I knew I shouldn't do it. Cross the line into magic—mess with nature—and I was opening a door. A door that could never be shut and, worse, could taint Eric's soul forever. And my own.

I loved him, though. And so help me, with the key to his salvation right there in my hand, I couldn't bear to lose him again.

I crossed myself, wishing I were stronger, but knowing that I wasn't.

And then I opened the bag.

I looked once at Eddie, who crossed himself, too, but didn't make a move to stop me.

With one hand, I held tight to my daughter, and with the other I sprinkled the dust of the Lazarus Bones on David's lifeless body. I'd heard the incantation only once, and I hoped that the intricate Latin preface had only been for show. I didn't remember that part. I remembered only the end. And after taking a deep breath, I spoke the words: *"Resurge, mortue!"*

At first, nothing happened. And then David's body began to glow with an eerie yellow light. Allie's hand was tight in mine, and together we watched his face as David seemed to burn from within.

After what seemed an eternity, his eyelids fluttered. I looked down, my eyes seeking the wound. As I watched, the skin knitted together, the wound healed, and David's body became whole.

Whether Eric's soul had returned though . . . that, I didn't yet know.

He stirred, just the slightest of movements. Behind us, I heard Eddie shuffle to the side of the tomb, then come over with a crumpled shirt. He spread it modestly over Eric's hips, then put a supportive hand on my shoulder.

In front of us, David's eyes opened. For a moment, he looked confused, and then his expression cleared. "Katie," he said, his voice as raspy as a man lost in the desert.

"I'm here," I said taking his hand.

"What happened? Why aren't I—"

I pressed a finger to his lips. "Later," I said.

Beside me, Allie squirmed, her gaze darting between the two of us, and hope flooding her bloodshot eyes. "Daddy?" she asked, her voice small and tentative.

David looked at me. I froze, wishing we'd never reached this moment, but knowing that it was impossible to go back. And then, ever so gently, I gave one tiny nod of my head.

"Yeah, baby," he said, holding his arms out for her as the tears spilled from his own eyes. "It's me."

Stay tuned for
Kate Connor's
next demon-hunting adventure

Deja Demon

Now available from Berkley Books

NEW IN TRADE PAPERBACK

Saving the suburbs from evil—
one fiend at a time…

Deja Demon

The Days and Nights of a
Demon-Hunting Soccer Mom

**By *USA Today* bestselling author
JULIE KENNER**

Keeping the local kids in line at a neighborhood Easter
party will take all of Kate's skills as a mother and Demon Hunter, just when she'll need them the most. An
old, very powerful enemy has returned to San Diablo,
this time with a full-blown army of the undead and a
powerful demonic ally. Once again, it's up to Kate to
save the world. Good thing she can multitask…

penguin.com